THE HOWL OF THE
WOLF

RONALD B. HALL

Printed in the United States of America
First Printed 2022

Cover Art by Victoria L. Hawkins

Published by:
Southern Willow Publishing, LLC
1114 Highway 96,
Suite C-1, #340
Kathleen, Georgia 31047

ISBN: 978-1-956544-25-1

This book is the second in a series, the first being _The Russian_. The third and final book in the trilogy will be _Natasha_.

INTRODUCTION

How often do people search and pursue the right words in life, heard at the right moment, that allow themselves or others to move forward, sometimes just for another day, or in some cases to completely impact their direction or outlook in life? Danny Thomas, with a wife and baby on the way, moved by the words of a Detroit priest, placed his last seven dollars in a collection plate. When realizing what he had done, he asked for God's help with his medical debt. The following day, he found a small acting part that paid ten times the amount he'd given to the church. Danny had experienced the power of prayer!

Returning to the church in times of struggle during his career, and praying to St. Jude Thaddeus, the patron saint of hopeless causes, Danny asked the saint to "help me find my way in life, and I will build you a shrine." His prayers were answered, and St. Jude is a monument to the good works people can do if the right words are given or received in a timely manner.

The inspiration for finishing this book was provided by a window repairman. I knew immediately that the story being told to me was going to be my inspiration in finishing this book. I had prayed for something, anything, that would move me beyond the creative nothingness of past months. His story of the life of a wolf that he and his family had raised bounced off the inside of my skull as he spoke. It changed my perspective, my understanding, and my knowledge. It compelled me to write about my characters with the sense of their inner animal needs and the howls heard bouncing off the inside of their skulls.

The repairman was on a hiking trip in Canada several years back with two of his friends and stumbled on the howls of three young wolves crying for their mother who had been killed by a hunter. He and his friends took the littermates and smuggled the wolves into the United States. This man raised one of them on his farm in Georgia.

I was fascinated as I listened to this man's story. He was in my home to fix the wooden window blinds in my office, and he saw that I was a writer from one of the published books on the table. He asked what I was writing about, and I told him my newest book was titled "The Howl of the Wolf." He said, "You know, a wolf doesn't really howl; it is s more of a guttural response." He pulled out his wallet and showed me a picture of his wolf standing on two feet and towering above this man's six feet four-inch, two-hundred-and-forty-pound frame. He said, "He was one-hundred-and-ninety-pounds and stretched out to twelve feet. He was as gentle as a puppy, even with my two young children. He died last year."

The man told me that the wolf was peaceful and functioned mostly as one might expect from a pet dog. "He never once bit or attacked my children no matter how rough the young ones were with him. But, as the wolf grew older, his nature to dominate and become the alpha of the pack led him to once a year challenge me to a fight." This answered my immediate curiosity of where the man's scars had come from.

He said, "It would start with some growling about two months in advance and gradually escalate until I had to clear the living room of my house and take the wolf on in a full-scale brawl for dominance of the family. I won every time, and it was no easy task. The last time we fought, I had to sit on him for over an hour after the fight was over until he finally gave up. Once he did, I got up and let the children into the room, and we all played together, and we were friends as if nothing had transpired between us."

Hearing this story, I knew exactly how I wanted to present the stories of Anton Lupu, the Wolf, his soul mate Nikolai Baskov, the

Russian, and Ivan Ivanovitch, the President of Russia. Their souls howl with primal discontent, a continuous noise that allows them a normal life, until it didn't. When their darkest thoughts dominated and banged their demands against their skulls without regard to the more peaceful souls around them, the consequences of their actions are ignored and only the result is relevant.

Please enjoy *The Howl of the Wolf*.

PROLOGUE

Anton Lupu, known internationally as the Wolf, and Lustin Ardelean, alias Nikolai Baskov, and known internationally as the Russian, survived the miserable conditions of a Romanian orphanage to become billionaires by selling stolen oil siphoned from Nigerian-owned oil pipelines at the bottom of the Atlantic Ocean off the coast of Africa, by bunkering in Hong Kong to sell to the North Koreans.

When seventeen, their ages forced them to leave their home since birth, an orphanage in Budapest, Romania. Russian President Ivan Ivanovitch brought Lustin to Moscow with false papers as a birth citizen of Russia. He was renamed Nikolai Baskov and trained in the Russian language and its ways. Nikolai became known as the Russian in a further public relations attempt by the President to emphasize that Nikolai was indeed Russian, and that any rumors that he was Romanian, were simply

1

that, rumors, and would not be favorably looked upon by the President.

As the years passed, Nikolai became Ivanovitch's personal assassin. Anton Lupu, the Wolf, survived on the streets of Romania until he was pulled off those streets by Nikolai to develop and manage the oil investments purchased by Nikolai with money provided from the assassinations.

Due to Nikolai's demonstrated loyalty and efficiency, President Ivanovitch appointed him General of the Armed Forces. He wanted Nikolai to implement his plan with China to solidify Russian and Chinese influence, at the expense of the United States, in controlling the use of shipping lanes within the Asian Pacific Rim and the newly opened shipping lane along Russia's northern border that resulted from melting ice. After a year of training, Nikolai led the specially trained Spetsnaz troops in the initial phase of the war in the invasion of the Kuril Islands, located north of Japan in the Asian Pacific Rim and in dispute with Japan for ownership.

Natasha Ivanov, a Spetsnaz major and personal bodyguard of the Russian President, was assigned duties to oversee Nikolai's year-long military training for the war. The President asked Major Ivanov to become close to Nikolai as there were still trust issues with Nikolai being Romanian and not Russian. During the training, they became lovers, and Nikolai was told by Natasha that President Ivanovitch intended to betray him after the completion of his initial mission in the Kuril Islands. She had quickly fallen in love with Nikolai, furious with the President for wanting to betray him, and joined Nikolai and Anton in a plot to assassinate the President.

Separately, and without Natasha's knowledge, Nikolai and Anton initiated a plan to engulf the world in a nuclear war when they were informed of the President's pending betrayal. It was a suicide pact based on all the betrayals in their lives. With world destruction in mind, Nikolai, as General of the Armed Forces, diverted four Russian nuclear missiles to be used to start the war. The plan would have worked, except the President found out about the four missing warheads and confronted Natasha. Natasha confessed to the plan to assassinate him when informed of Nikolai's betrayal of her. She agreed to help the President kill Nikolai when he returned from his now successful invasion of the Kuril Islands.

The 2013-14 Asian Pacific Rim War, as it came to be known, abruptly and prematurely ended with a single transatlantic telephone call from the President of the United States to President Ivanovitch of Russia to stop the war. He threatened public exposure of Nikolai Baskov as a Romanian. President Ivanovitch considered for a moment that his plan was working but knew the truth would be unacceptable to the Russian people that a Romanian was leading Russian troops in the war. He knew that he was compromised and made the decision to end Russia's participation in the war. He made a telephone call to the President of t the People's Republic of China, President Ho Li Chung, of his intentions to withdraw. He could only hope that none of the other participants in their plan, i.e., North Korea, Iran, Hezbollah, and the Egyptian Brotherhood, went rogue and started a conflict that only nuclear weapons could settle.

As a result of his order to withdraw Russian troops from the war, no independent actions were taken by the other countries involved or the immediately opposing forces of Japan and the Philippine Air Force. The war was over and unprepared and confused leaders questioned as to why the war started in the first place and prepared to put their best face on their reasons for participation.

Meanwhile, Anton Lupu, the Wolf, had taken the four nuclear warheads to China and retrofitted an old oil tanker as a launch platform for the weapons. He was now in the Indian Ocean with his two product ships preparing the launch, unaware of Natasha's confession to the President of her role in planning the president's assassination, unaware that the war was over,

4

and ignorant that a Russian submarine had found him after a frantic search.

CHAPTER ONE

ANTON LUPU, THE WOLF, MALDIVES (2013-2014)

Anton Lupu, now well known as the Wolf in the international world of smuggled oil, looked back over his right shoulder at the ship he had just abandoned. He watched as the four Russian nuclear-tipped cruise missiles on the deck rapidly disappeared below the ocean surface. The radiant colors of the raging inferno resembled the Henri Matisse painting 'le bonheur de Vivre,' but inaptly named for Wolf's situation 'The Joy of Life.'

Anton knew that he was fortunate to be alive, and only because he chose to view the launch of the missiles from his helicopter above his ship. He had escaped the primary blast that sank his ship, but now found himself riding a wave of heat and air displacement that surged his helicopter towards heaven as if he was the Silver Surfer and the helicopter the surfboard. Some twenty miles behind the explosion was the other oil product ship he owned that was destroyed in a similar fashion only minutes before. The remnants of both ships were left in the form of trash on the ocean surface.

The oil product ships were retrofitted in Hong Kong to accommodate the launch of four stolen Russian cruise missiles intended to start World War III. It was the idea of the Russian to take revenge on a world for the continued betrayals, particularly the brutal treatment received while growing up in the Budapest orphanage. Anton now reiterated to himself Nikolai's thought that "the world never came to save him from the nightly brutal beatings and sexual abuse, so why do I owe the world anything?"

Anton thought to himself that Nikolai was right to want to take his revenge on the world, but it likely meant nothing now that Nikolai was either dead or wasting away in a Russian gulag in Siberia. Anton knew that if it was the latter, there was no amount of money that would free him, even though money was not an issue. He and Nikolai had made billions in selling stolen oil. As a result, there were hidden accounts and safe houses all over the world, including in the United States.

It appeared to him that Natasha had chosen her loyalty to Russia over her pact with Nikolai and Anton after discovering their plan to destroy the world. She must have informed President Ivanovitch of the intended missile launch and was the reason President Ivanovitch destroyed the product ships with their four nuclear cruise missiles and why he now found himself in this situation. The Wolf had little doubt that he was now a fugitive, and President Ivanovitch would use every means to see him dead, if he didn't already believe that Anton was indeed already dead. He would have to reach out somehow to obtain clearer information.

Anton's mind retreated to the orphanage in Bucharest, Romania as it always did when he was distressed. The beatings and depravities and starvation he and Lustin and all the others endured in that orphanage were unspeakable. He cried out for Lustin Ardelean as the person who made it possible for him to survive that torture chamber and gave him reason to continue to live. An emotional bond with Lustin had been formed by the horrors they experienced together. The only solace he had found in the years suffered there were the singular words of a visiting Romanian priest.

The priest had spoken to them about God and the Bible but had provided them none of the sustenance of food, health, and safety the orphans had all so badly required, but that day the words of the priest had spoken to him, nonetheless. The priest had referenced Exodus 40:18: "So the cloud of the Lord was over the tabernacle by day, and the fire was in the cloud at night, in the sight of all Israelites during all their travels."

Those words had calmed him. He thought, "How comforting that would have been for me and the other orphans if we could have been looked after by the Lord twenty-four hours a day. Surely then we would have been fed, loved, and protected, and the Lord would be with me now in my travels." He smiled for the first time and felt some of the immense tension leave his body.

But the reality he could never escape was that the orphanage showed him that there was no God, for when night befell, and the lights were turned off, the security guards and staff preyed on all of them for whatever they craved, and surely no God would have allowed evil such as that to happen. It was in that instance that he recognized fully that he was now all alone in the world. He cried without restraint for the first time in nearly a year since that February 2013 night in Moscow with Natasha and Lustin.

In short, while insanity slowly turned to reality and Anton ordered his mind to logically assess his situation. "President Ivanovitch would eliminate anyone who participated in or knew about our plan to start World War III. The only way President Ivanovitch knew about Nikolai's plan was that Natasha all along worked for the President, or she was captured in her failure to kill the President, and the information was tortured from her." Anton was sick to his stomach with such a thought.

In the latter case, assuredly, she was dead. If the former, she was and always would be working for the President. Anton had warned Lustin that he did not trust her and told him it was not good to be involved with her, but Lustin had not listened. However, Anton remembered how convincing Natasha could be. He had to smile to himself with the memory of her beneath him in Moscow and the pure perfection of her body. She had promised to be one with Lustin and Anton as both were one with each other. He knew he would have died for Lustin, but he couldn't hate Natasha if she had betrayed them to the President. They had, after all, lied to her about their true plan to destroy the world.

His thoughts continued to swirl. Nikolai was the President's appointed General of the Armed Forces, and the idea that a 'mad man' could dupe the President to come so close to destruction of the world, especially using the President's own nuclear missiles, would be unacceptable to the Russian people and the world. The President could not and would not let the Russian people knew what happened. He would have to kill them both if he found out that either of them was alive. The rumors that Lustin was secretly Romanian would haunt the

President night and day. That would surely increase the President's eagerness to clean up this threat to his power.

Anton slowly shook his head as if disbelieving all that was happening. The submarine commander who sank the two product ships would probably die quietly in his sleep and the Chinese that retrofitted Anton's product ships to launch the Russian missiles would be of no threat to the President, as China was a co-conspirator with Russia in the war.

Anton watched as the ship below him disappeared into the vast expanse of the Indian Ocean. He shook his head again and frowned. "The President must think I went down with the ship and no one else knew I am alive. I must keep it that way," he said aloud to himself. For the first time, a satisfied smile came upon his face.

Still, his mind couldn't completely focus. He tried to imagine life without Lustin, but he couldn't. Natasha was the only other person he had ever had any feelings for and look what had happened with that! He looked down at his gages and figured it would be close, but he had just enough petrol to make the Maldives. He reiterated his previous thought but with less confidence this time. "At least the President should think that I died in the explosion of the oil product ship and that would give me some time to sort things out which I so desperately need."

He looked down at the Indian Ocean traveling fast beneath him and felt something he has never felt before, joy at being alive. It was time to make some phone calls. His first call using his satellite service was to his London banker, one of his several bankers where hidden assets allowed him flexibility and travel to all parts of the world, to alert him that large funds may soon be needed to be moved. The Republic of The Maldives was chosen to have a safe house as it was centrally located in the Indian Ocean between Nigeria, where Lustin and Anton made billions in stolen oil, and Hong Kong where he lived and sold the stolen oil.

His next call was to his manager of the Maldives safe house to advise him that he would be landing shortly for an extended stay. He paid yearly for a private hanger for his helicopter and a seaplane at Male Ibrahim Nasir International Airport, simply called Maldives Male Airport. After landing, he would fly his seaplane to the safe house located on one of the more isolated and remote islands of the eleven hundred and ninety-two islands that encompassed the over thirty-four thousand square miles that composed the Republic of the Maldives. Here he would enjoy the privacy of an elaborate ocean setting with room and board, private spa, and pool facilities, and more importantly to him, his prized speed boat to practice his racing skills to once again, when things become settled, join the worldwide racing circuit with no one made wiser that he was alive.

Safe Houses

From the start of building their oil empire, all safe house arrangements were handled by Anton at Nikolai's insistence. President Ivanovitch was not told of these arrangements, as Nikolai knew that he needed safe houses available to him and Anton in case that relationship should change. The safe houses also meshed with Nikolai's growing illegal theft of oil from Nigeria and the possibility of complications with law enforcement in that line of work.

Personnel selected to guard and maintain the safe houses were carefully vetted: chosen for their intelligence and discreetness. They were all single and extremely well paid. Anton emphasized to each manager their need to stay quiet about their work and not brought anyone near their safe house, however tempting it may be.

Anton reiterated time and again that exposure would bring death to them all. "Understand that this is not a job, but a life choice," he told them. "If I die, you die, so embrace it. If Nikolai or I am exposed, you would always be considered a loose end that must be silenced. If you see something as a problem or a potential to be a problem, I had better know about it right away. I would have people observing you and you should do the same for your contacts. There is always a possibility that bribes and extortions in conducting the affairs of our business could compromise you, so develop your contacts carefully and pay well. Otherwise, lead a normal life of no extremes, nor breaking of the law." Anton always said as a last reminder, "Things can change quickly, so be ready with contingency plans for all possibilities."

NSA Headquarters

At the National Security Agency headquarters in Fort Meade, Maryland, a cell phone call made by Anton Lupu appeared on the big screen as a call from a helicopter without a flight plan. NSA was an agency within the Department of Defense responsible for cryptographic and communication intelligence and security. They had been monitoring all air and ship communication within five hundred miles of the explosion of the two product ships in hopes of picking up any related chatter from the Russians. The information obtained was quickly forwarded from NSA Director Adam Shaffer's people to CIA Director Elizabeth Downing at CIA headquarters in Langley,

Virginia, and then quickly passed on to Harry Snead, Director of CIA Operations.

Upon being briefed of the two messages and their contents, Harry realized that this could be Anton Lupu, the Wolf. Would he have made such an obvious a mistake of using an open cell phone line to make personal calls from his helicopter? How could he have lived through all that inferno?

Harry quickly issued orders to his staff to "notify CIA operative Sam Mountain to stay in place awaiting orders and find out who and where that banker is that the Wolf called and freeze the bank's assets if within United States jurisdiction." Harry knew that it was time to put this ghost to rest. So far, Anton had been extremely fortunate and one step ahead of the CIA at every turn. "I need to stomp down on that lucky rabbit's foot he is wearing," Harry sighed to himself.

He turned to his lead staffer, James Dean, and said, "Contact the Ambassador of the Republic of the Maldives and arrange the necessary clearances and permits to allow entry to Sam Mountain to conduct a hunt for a known terrorist that we think is taking refuge within their country. And make a note that if this operation didn't go as planned, to add Anton Lupu's name to Interpol's Red Notice list."

As an afterthought, Harry added, "Make sure that Sam has the necessary money, clothing, and other items he would need for his stay." With a sly smile to James Dean in front of the entire staff, Harry finished, "I knew you have been doing this job as long as I have and you don't need to hear me bark out details like this, but sometimes I have to sound loud and in charge to convince myself that you actually need me, If I had your job and was receiving the orders, I couldn't do it."

James laughed as he got up and left the room. He was used to the Director being overprotective with his friend, Sam Mountain.

Maldives

The Wolf set his helicopter down in the Maldives and debarked and greeted his safe house manager, Philippe Adnan. The manager informed him that all the necessary arrangements for his stay had been made, including the readiness of his seaplane that would fly him to his island. He further informed him that there were three ex-army green berets guarding the safe house and a speed boat manned by two ex-army females with special forces training located a half-mile offshore ready to assist in his protection.

"The two women are equipped with the precision shoulder-fired rocket launcher that is ninety percent accurate at a half-mile," Adnan smiled. "It is s an unlicensed modified American clone of a Soviet/Russian RPG-7. The rate of fire is three to four rounds per minute. All mercenaries are carrying the short version of the m4-cqbr, a close-quarter assault weapon. Additionally, I have government officials on the payroll in customs and on the president's staff that would alert me if anyone were looking for you."

He waited for Anton to speak, but he didn't, so Adnan continued, "I feel confident we can protect you, but not if the Americans knew where you are hiding."

The Wolf turned to him, and with some anger said, "What are you saying? And why would they know where I am hiding? Speak up!"

"You said that everything must be told to you as it was a matter of life and death, did I do something wrong?" Adnan asked.

"No, but I did, and now we are going to have to correct it," Anton frowned. He knew that by calling from the helicopter so close to the sinking ships, they were on to him. "If the Americans intercepted my cellphone calls from the helicopter, they would come quickly. If they do not come within a month, I can assume they did not intercept them, nor do they know where to look for me. We would wait and see about the latter before we make any final plans, but in the meantime, we would anticipate the former by assuming they are coming. We would prepare ourselves and show the Americans that chasing me has consequences."

Adnan nodded and waited for his employer to continue. Wolf said, "We have the advantage of surprise, and we would use it. But firstly, I need a place to stay out of sight for a couple of months, preferably in a crowded downtown area of Male City to see what the Americans are going to do. I need a place where I can prepare and make my plans for them. And, by the way, do not let those guards at the safe house walk around parading their weapons. Some passing ship or boat with a person onboard checking out the scenery may report them to the police and the Americans might be using their eyes in the sky to find me."

Anton walked away for a moment to return a call to his Middle East banker in London, England. He told him to immediately initiate emergency procedures to close all his accounts and follow the procedures in protecting and further hiding his assets and disappear as instructed until otherwise notified. He smashed the one-time use cell phone just to be safe that it couldn't be traced. "Maybe money truly is the root of all evil," he smiled to himself. But one thought of his orphanage overtook him, and the smile vanished.

The Ford, United States of America Supercarrier

RONALD B. HALL

On the Ford CVN-78 supercarrier in the middle of the Indian Ocean, the Admiral was informed of the end of the war. As such, he turned towards the former army sniper and the man now batting clean-up for the CIA, Sam Mountain. With a thumbs up and a smile, he passed the good news that the Asian Pacific Rim War is now over to the twenty-five hundred-plus personnel of the city on the ship. The resounding cheers were loud as celebrations with the slapping of high fives combined with jumping around and body slapping hugs and slaps on the backs quickly permeated the air. It was as if a balloon full of helium had been released and the pent-up energy alone was now powering the ship forward. Everybody was smiling at the end of the war.

That night, a separate classified message was delivered to both the Admiral and Mountain, as he was commonly addressed, in honor of his twin brother, Joe, that died when a car running from a convenience store robbery left the road at one hundred miles an hour hit his vehicle parked in a shopping center parking lot. The message told him to stay onboard the ship and await further orders.

A separately classified folder provided Mountain pertinent information on the Republic of the Maldives, their current political unrest with the upcoming end-of-year presidential election, and their military capability. Mountain was extremely impressed to find out that their special forces were one of the best trained and equipped in the world. He had heard the rumors in his traveled but had no idea of that level of competency.

The information brochure said in part that "the Coast Guard is divided into four squadrons and deployed in the southern, central, and northern regions of the Maldives, and a Reserve has been established at the capital, Male. The Coast Guard is experienced as it saw action daily in dealing with maritime terrorism, transnational crime, drug trafficking through maritime routes, smuggling, piracy, and other crimes on the water. The youth serve in key positions immediately and learn quickly." Mountain understood that this organization was best understood in the context of the archipelagic nature of the country.

He read on, "The Maldives, a nation of islands, lies in the Indian Ocean four hundred and thirty-five miles southwest of Sri Lanka and India. Almost ninety-nine percent of the country is covered by the Arabian Sea of the Indian Ocean. It was one of five archipelagos in the world recognized under the Law of the Sea. As a water-bound nation, much of its security concerns lie at sea. It was the lowest country in the world, with maximum and average natural ground levels of only seven feet ten inches and four feet eleven inches above sea level, respectively. When the two thousand and four tsunamis hit, the islands were submerged for several minutes. More than eighty percent of the country's land is composed of coral islands. Only near the southern end of this natural coral barricade do two open passages permit safe ship navigation from one side of the Indian Ocean to the other through the territorial waters of the Maldives. The President heads the executive branch of the government and leads the National Defense Force. There is no separation of powers."

After four days of waiting, Mountain was called by the Admiral to the bridge at first light and handed a classified message. The Admiral had already received his marching orders. Mountain's message read, "You have been cleared by the Maldivian authority for entry into their country. You would be met upon landing by Embassy personnel and provided all personal items needed. We have good reason to believe the person you are seeking is Anton Lupu, the Wolf, and he may have a safe house somewhere in the country. Good luck and good hunting." It was signed by his friend, Harry.

Mountain wondered why it had taken so long to get clearance. That passing of time allowed the Wolf to settle in, and it wasn't like Harry to dally.

"Your helicopter awaits," the Admiral said. "Breakfast and coffee would be provided for you on board. Your military gear and weapons were stowed for you." They shook hands and the Admiral slipped him a separately classified folder, and said, "Good luck. It was a pleasure to have you onboard, Mountain, if that is your real name."

"It was, and good luck to you, too, Admiral," Sam replied.

The helicopter flight from the John Fitzgerald Kennedy Aircraft Carrier touched down mid-morning in a back area of Maldives Male International Airport in front of a hanger made available to the Americans. Male International Airport was one of two international airports and twenty-two other regional airlines in the Republic of the Maldives. The helicopter was promptly towed into the hangar and Mountain and the crew were finally allowed to debark. The crew was instructed to stay in the hangar and remain on alert until further notice. A refrigerator with food and a variety of non-alcoholic drinks were provided. Pizza and other meals would be delivered at mealtimes if an extended stay was necessary.

An Embassy staffer from Sri Lanka, Mr. Rohan Silva, greeted Sam Mountain as he debarked from the helicopter and pulled him aside separately from the crew. Mountain quickly learned from Mr. Silva that the United States did not have a consulate or embassy in the Maldives. The U.S. Ambassador and Embassy staff in Sri Lanka, four hundred and thirty-five miles away, were accredited to the Republic of the Maldives. Mr. Silva said, "The Ambassador asked for your forgiveness for not being here to welcome you, but he thought a formal visit by him at this time might create an unnecessary fuss over the purpose of your presence here and the government's approval of your investigation."

Sam nodded and the man continued, "Frankly, to have your investigation approved at all is a major diplomatic achievement that required approval of all eighty-seven members of the Maldivian Authority Board that includes eight different political parties, and most of them Muslim. This country is listed as a democratic republic but was originally established by a Turkish sultan and still operates under standard Islamic laws. The Ambassador also thought that on this occasion I am the better choice as your host as I speak a number of the languages spoken here, including Dhivehi, the national language."

Mountain was beginning to slowly understand that four days to get his investigation approved was really a world record. He walked with Silva to the awaiting car to drive to another building to facilitate his clearance through customs. After customs, Mountain was led to a private room set up for his briefing. Mr. Silva sat across from him at the end of a standard twelve-seat boardroom table and asked him if he needed anything before he began, but Sam shook his head and said, "No thank you, please begin."

"The man you call the "Wolf" is not here according to official records and the President. If he is here, he has protection based upon bribing the right people. And if this is true, the Wolf already knew you are here and why. I feel reasonably sure the President is not involved in any corruption, but it was a turbulent and uncertain time in the politics of the nation, and he is running for election at year's end. He wants to fully cooperate, but for political reasons, he needs your investigation to be expedited," Silva explained. "You should know that the approval for you to be here came about because of a talk between the Ambassador and your CIA Director of Operations, a Mr. Harry Snead. Director Snead asked that his conversation with the Ambassador be passed on to the President and the Maldives Authority Board. Director Snead told the Ambassador that if the investigation is not approved and the criminal is not found, Anton Lupus' name would be added to Interpol's Red Notice list with a high probability of his present location being in the Republic of the Maldives. The Ambassador, after passing on the message as directed, added that if the Wolf commits a terrorist act while in the Maldives and it was pointed out that the Maldivian government was warned of that possibility by the American government and took no action, it might ruin an economy based solely upon tourism and catering to the rich."

"I am glad the Ambassador is on our side," Sam Mountain nodded. "Do you have any leads as to where the Wolf might be?"

"The President was kind enough to assign to me three of his best police from their National Defense Force. They all speak English. We did the best we could in the time afforded to us before your arrival and found five properties, all on the ocean, that show promise. These were identified using several criteria based upon several assumptions," Silva revealed. "We knew the fugitive is rich, which means that the property we are looking for is probably very high end with lots of amenities and is isolated for him to move freely about and to be able to see his enemies coming. This automatically eliminates a majority of the two hundred inhabited islands. The property likely is deserted most of the year, except for an on or off-site manager. It was probably purchased through some type of dummy corporation that would be hard to trace, and when the property was originally purchased, the buyer must have visited our country and at the same time hired a local manager to look after it. Somewhere there are paper trails, maybe a passport or maintenance bills on the property with the caretaker's signature. I would send the officers back over to the administrative building if none of the properties we came up with pans out."

Mountain pursed his lips and gently rubbed his chin between his thumb, index, and middle finger, and said, "Pans out? Wow, you do know your English!"

"I was told you are a suspicious man, Mr. Mountain, and that you trust no one," Silva smirked. "To answer the question, you really want to ask, I am a Harvard-educated man, the first person from Seychelles to graduate from an American university. I was a nerdy kid with glasses and no personality that did nothing but study, study, and study some more. Sometimes I even took time to take a two-or-three-hour nap and maybe have a slice or two of three-day-old pizza with bottled water from my mostly empty refrigerator. At the conclusion of mid-terms my senior year, I'm guessing my roommate had enough and said pack your bags for a week, we are going to Daytona Beach for spring break, and I won't take no for an answer. I had no idea where this beach was and had never even been downtown at my school. I had always left the school at the end of the year and taken a taxi to the airport and flew directly home. Seychelles has the most beautiful beaches in the world, and I hadn't even noticed them in growing up."

He shook his head slightly from side to side as if remembering those very sad times and continued, "Anyway, after much arguing and me throwing a number of tantrums, we got to the beach. It was the first time I truly realized how beautiful the beaches are in my country. I had no idea how to have fun. I didn't even swim. The first day I just sat on a towel under an umbrella all day long trying not to get my ivory skin any darker. I didn't even understand the subtleties of America's racism that I was absorbing at my school. The second day it happened, she walked right up and plopped down beside me and said, "You are about the most miserable boy I have ever witnessed." I'll spare you the details, Mountain, except for what she said, "We're going to have fun and if it didn't pan out by the end of the week, then you just won't ever know what fun is." She said that to me, a stranger!" Silva paused and swallowed hard. "We've been married for twenty years and have three kids and they knew what fun is. The Sri Lanka Embassy hired me immediately after graduation, primarily because I had grown up on an archipelago of one hundred and fifteen islands in the Indian Ocean," he laughed. "May I continue my briefing?"

Mountain said, "Please do and thank you."

"Late last night the President agreed to send a patrol boat to each of the five properties for an initial assessment. They all left at daybreak from the regional Coast Guard ports nearest the properties. Four of the boats are either in the process of completing their inspections or have finished their inspections and none reported anything suspicious or out of the ordinary. We have lost contact with the fifth boat from the Northern Area that stopped to check out what the police patrol boat called a party boat that is locally owned. We are waiting for them to report back."

Mountain pointedly asked, "What do you mean a party boat'?"

"Two women were reported sunbathing on the deck," Silva explained.

Mountain said, "Please tell the assigned police to have my crew and helicopter out of the hangar and ready to fly immediately."

They were suddenly interrupted by one of the assigned police officers who was monitoring the VHF marine-band radios on the police patrol boats who said with obvious excitement, "We have a report from the captain of a fishing trawler that he is seeing ahead of him an explosion on the water, and he is on his way to assist any survivors. The boat is in the area of our fifth boat!"

Mountain stood and calmly gave instructions to the police officer. "Make sure that the trawler captain knew that it may be a police boat that exploded, and his boat may be in danger as well. Also, get somebody over to check out the registered owner of that party boat, and find out who is on that boat, and how they may be involved. Make sure my helicopter has my weapons pack on board and keep me posted on any further developments through Mr. Silva. Let him know if you hear anything, and I do mean anything, now go."

Sam turned back to Silva and said, "Mr. Silva, please notify the president of what is happening here and be his point of contact for updates. If his military cutter boat is in the area, get a medical team and special forces unit on board to help in response if needed. This all could be nothing, but I suspect it was going to be nasty. As a courtesy, remind the president to tell the cutter captain that if the patrol boat did explode that we may be dealing with weaponized drones, short-range rockets or missiles, or even underwater explosives. The Wolf is also a top professional boat racer who owns some of the fastest boats in the world, so do not hesitate to stop anyone that fits this description and identify them. Let the President knew about the two women on the party boat and keep radio traffic to a minimum. Emphasize safety, safety, safety as there is nowhere for them to run, and please find me a driver and get me to my helicopter."

At that instance, a second police officer rushed into the room and said, "Sir, we have suddenly lost all contact with the fishing trawler after receiving a Mayday signal."

"Damn," Mountain said as he rushed out of the building.

Earlier

The fifth police patrol boat spotted what appeared to be a nonmoving boat on radar about three miles in front of them in the direction of the island property they were to inspect. The boat continued to be unresponsive to radio calls to identify itself. This information was relayed to headquarters and the officers were told to "approach with caution." As they closed in on the boat, the bow officer used high-powered binoculars and announced that "the boat appeared to be a party boat." The officer could see two women sunbathing on the front bow on reclining deck chairs in what appeared to be only bikini bottoms and showing no awareness of the approaching patrol boat.

The deck chairs were facing towards the stern to greet the afternoon sun, which was bright, but not directly in the officer's eyes as they were heading northeast. The driver pulled the police patrol boat within fifty yards of the other boat and started to rapidly power down. In doing so, the officers became instantly aware that the music coming from the boat was extraordinarily loud. The bow officer wrongly surmised that it was probably the reason why the women did not answer their radio calls in that they were alone and expecting no visitors. Headquarters was advised that the circumstances suggested a party boat with two women sunbathing on the deck. When headquarters was provided the boat's registration numbers, it was confirmed that the boat was registered in the Maldives and owned by a local citizen and homeowner.

What the officers did not knew was that the ladies were hired professional mercenaries paid one hundred thousand dollars each for doing what they were trained to do best: kill. As an extra incentive to ensure they would be the terrorists needed for Wolf's plan to succeed, they were promised the boat if successful.

The used boat was identified the previous day by the Wolf as the one needed for the ruse and the owner was given one million dollars on a numbered account in India that immediately transferred the money to the owner's account provided. The owner was ready and willing to sell his quarter-million-dollar Lagoon Power Catamaran 2005 with twin 315s and four staterooms for the offer as stated as "needed by the buyer for a family emergency" just in case the owner needed a reason to rationalize his decision. The owner did not.

When the ladies were offered the boat as an incentive prize for this suicide mission, they had turned to face each other, smiled, and one pointed her finger at the other and said, "I'm Thelma, you're Louise." The other information not known by the officers was that the informers within customs and the President's staff have fully briefed the Wolf of the President's plan to send out the five boats that following morning.

The driver of the patrol boat let out a blast from the air horn to get the women's attention. One of the ladies responded by turning around and waved. There was no attempt at modesty. This made the officers grin in anticipation. The other woman jumped up and scrambled to find a towel to cover her bare breasts. What the officers did not knew was that under the large towel laying on the deck that she was now reaching for was one of the rocket launchers.

The officers had clearly let their guard down since the boat registration belonged to a long-time male resident of the Maldives and was purchased five years ago. They were convinced that these women were either the owner's wives, friends, or mistresses. They had even lowered their weapons. The driver had started to slowly power the boat forward to enjoy the view.

He saw the woman that was searching franticly for a towel in mocked horror that they might have seen her half-naked calmly rise to her feet. She had thrown aside the large beach towel, and with her breasts now fully exposed and all eyes on her, she held the rocket launcher to her right shoulder. The officers stared in disbelief as the rocket launcher fired at point-blank range. Their boat and lives disintegrated as if they never existed. Thelma thought at the time, "the boys deserve at least one more look at what they would soon be missing."

The two women held on tightly to the boat's bow bars as the heat and waves created by the blast rocked their boat. They looked upwards, not for prayer, but to avoid any debris in the air. Louise screamed at Thelma, "ride-um cowgirl," and laughed with glee as Thelma had somehow straddled across one of the bow bars trying not to fall overboard. When the waves dissipated, the women moved briskly to turn off the music and cleared the deck.

Below deck, they quickly donned scuba diving suits and prepared to deal with any ships in the vicinity that may have seen the explosion or patrol boats responding to reports of an explosion. Thelma said to Louise, "If no one saw the explosion, we have a good chance of getting the boat to the pre-arranged storage location and out of sight. The authorities can only assume what caused the explosion."

At that moment, the radio crackled, and the women heard, "This is the wet fishing trawler Lazy Susan. We see the smoke on the water and are three miles out. We are responding to provide any assistance as needed, do you copy?" This was repeated several times over with no response.

The women knew that the horizon was three miles out and the trawler was within range of viewing their boat with a good pair of binoculars. They knew that an ocean wet fishing trawler was probably local, as they must operate in areas close to their landing place as the time spent fishing was minimal due to the fish being thrown into the hold in a fresh condition.

They couldn't spare the time to wait for the trawler to arrive, as the next phase of their mission needed preparation time. This was confirmed when their contact in the President's office let them know that the President had notified the Northern Area to send the cutter boat to check the explosion out and placed his helicopter on hold, pending determination that it was not a missile. The women knew their spies did not have an arrival time on the scene yet for the cutter boat.

The women did know that the trawler traveled at about four and a half miles an hour, so they must wait patiently for at least thirty minutes plus for the trawler to be in the range of their rocket launchers. The women knew this was unacceptable and made the move to go topside. They couldn't wait for the approaching cutter boat.

Louise took the wheel and Thelma grabbed a rocket launcher. Thelma braced herself as Louise pushed the boat forward at full throttle. Within minutes they were within a quarter mile of the trawler and brought the boat to a quick stop. It was best to be in a sure-fire kill range for the rocket launchers. Louise grabbed her rocket launcher and settled in next to Thelma on the boat's deck and both pulled their triggers at the same time. Both grenade rockets found their mark, and the fishing trawler was destroyed. As there was nothing further reported by the trawler captain, it could only be assumed by the women that the trawler captain assumed their cabin cruiser was also responding to their call.

The women now knew they couldn't keep their boat, but $100,000 each was a good payday. The happenings so far had met their expectations of keeping things fun and interesting. Most people in combat couldn't function in chaos, but this was the opposite for both women. For them, it produced clarity as it matched their need for adrenaline and living on the edge. They were both clearly psychopaths.

They knew they had very little time before their boat became a target for every eager cop to make a name for himself. The trawler alone had wasted time they didn't have with the approaching police cutter boat. They knew, too, that the police were not sure of what they were up against. They would approach with caution.

Louise took the wheel and returned the boat to its original position a half-mile from the island. This was a precautionary position in case they were surprised by a faster police response than expected.

When the boat was securely anchored, Thelma grabbed the two rocket launchers and carried them below deck. She carefully packed them in a specially designed buoyant and waterproof carrying case and carried it from below deck up to the boat's stern. She then returned below deck and grabbed the twenty-three-pound Lian Innovative Diver Propulsion Vehicle carry case by its handles and carried the Divehead 1500 contained within from below deck to join the rocket launchers at the rear of the boat. There she unloaded the two-person water propulsion system that would easily tow both women and the two attached rocket launchers the half-mile distance to the island.

While Thelma was busy preparing the gear for their swim, Louise was donning her scuba gear. When Louise finished dressing, she took over for Thelma in getting the gear into the water and ready to go while Thelma put on her scuba gear. When Thelma was done dressing, she set the timer for the explosives on the boat for one hour. She unloaded the two boxes of Dual Vent Rapid Release Black Smoke Grenades and threw them around the floor of the boat. She then joined Louise in the water to begin their half-mile journey to the island's safe house. There they would join the other three mercenaries for a final event.

～～～～～

The Sikorsky SH-60/MH-60 Seahawk helicopter blades were already turning as Mountain arrived and hurried to board. He gave a quick nod and right hand in the air and wrist snap wave to the pilot and co-pilot as he was welcomed aboard by the enlisted crew chief. A standard crew would have two-door gunners or a rescue swimmer to complement the other three crew members, but it was not uncommon to have a crew of three for what was originally considered a taxi ride mission for Sam Mountain.

Unlike the Army, the Navy SH-60 did away with the left side sliding access door for cabin entry and exit. The right-side sliding door held a standard door mounted M60 7.62mm machine gun firing 7.62 x 51mm at 51 rounds per minute. Seeing the gun, Mountain made a mental note that the life expectancy of a Vietnam War door gunner was two weeks. The sick joke to newbies was that they were told a five-minute life expectancy as if two weeks was not sick enough to think about.

Sam dismissed these thoughts as he strapped in and felt the helicopter seeking air to lift and rise. The pilot announced an ETA of one and a half hours to the Northern Area safe house and island.

Sam then brought the crew up to date on what they may be facing and told the crew chief he was on the door gun upon arrival. The crew chief looked pleased that he was going to possibly see some real action again.

After forty minutes over water, Mr. Silva was on the radio to provide Sam with a much-needed update. "The President reports his Coast Guard cutter is four miles out from the party boat and is responding to the threat." Mountain knew these men were professionals and wanted to be the first responders in protecting their country, especially since close friends and fellow officers were already presumed dead, but Mountain knew that the Wolf was not a normal terrorist and had the resources to win at any cost.

Mr. Silva continued, "The party boat was a quick sale the previous night. They knew that the sale would not show up on records for several weeks. The description of the buyer of the boat fits that of the Wolf, and the seller said there were two women with him."

Mountain's back stiffened. "The police described the fifth boat as a party boat, so it fits. The Wolf set a trap using the two women to help lure them in for the kill, I bet!" Mountain sighed. "These are professional policemen who would check the registration and find it to be locally owned. Two women drinking on the deck of a locally owned boat! No wonder the trap worked so well."

Mountain thought for a moment before continuing. "The boat was destroyed, so it had to be an explosive device big enough to take out the boat and officers at the same time, but why would they need them in close? Would not the blast jeopardize their own boat? Was the Wolf or a hire waiting below deck with a rocket device, or underwater with some type of attachable bomb, or was a missile or a drone launched from the island that got there later than expected? These are questions that we need to be answered."

He turned back to the phone and said, "Separately, I want you to inform the President to break radio silence and inform the cutter boat captain that the two women were used to lure the patrol boat to the party boat. If he would not break radio silence at this point, be sure he passed on to the cutter captain your earlier comments about two women being somehow involved. If the President chose to not pass on that information earlier to the captain, insist that he break radio silence and do so immediately. If not, you do it, but let the cutter captain know. Is there anything else?"

Mr. Siva replied, "The President has a special forces team on standby in the Coast

Guard Northern Area, ready to parachute onto the island day or night if needed. The airplane and a medical helicopter are loaded and ready for departure if needed." "Thanks," Mountain replied. Then he hung up. discontinued the call.

∿∿∿∿∿∿

There were twenty-nine enlisted men and four officers on board the Trinkat class CGS Hideaway fast track cutter boat. It was received from the Indian Navy via the Seychelles Coast Guard in 2006. The ship was approximately fifty yards long and armed with a 30mm/40mm Mk44 Bushmaster Automatic Cannon effective up to two-and-a-half miles. It was made for a night or day use, gyro-stabilized, and was directed by an electro-optic fire control system that made it fully automatic search, detection, and acquisition of target with a video feed about target distance, bearing, speed, and course. This vessel was meant for counterinsurgency operations and was capable of detection and destruction of fast-moving small surface craft.

The cutter boat captain stopped three miles from the reported position of the anchored party boat. The cutter captain had added nine Maldivian special forces personnel to crew three amphibious rigid inflatable fast boats now being unloaded from the cutter boat. The fast boat was an even-meter-long, high-speed, high-buoyancy, extreme-weather craft with a primary mission of special forces insertion and extraction and a secondary mission of marine interdiction operations. It was constructed of composites with an inflatable tube gunwale made of reinforced fabric. It had a crew of three, a speed of forty knots, a range of two hundred miles, and a propulsion system of Dual Caterpillar 3126 DITA, 6 in-line cylinder diesel engines.

The inflatable boats hosted a mounted M60 7.62mm machine gun effective up to 6.8 tenths of a mile, with a rate of fire of 550-659 rounds per minute. The captain radioed that his boat was in place and requested that both the airplane carrying special forces and the medical helicopter be launched in support of their impending advance on the party boat and island.

The captain's plan was for one fast boat to attack from the port side of the cutter boat, one from in front, and the third one from the starboard side. Two officers on deck would monitor the island as they approached, looking for any sign of movement, including drones or missiles. Posted officers on deck would keep watch on the water for incoming torpedoes, mines, bubbles from divers, or anything that appeared as out of place. All boats would approach the party boat at half speed until within a mile. At that point, the captain would command the fast boats to attack at full power while the cutter boat provided overall coverage and response in any direction.

If there was a terrorist response at any point, the order was for the fast boats to immediately move to full speed and attack and destroy the party boat and proceed onward towards the island and eliminate any further resistance encountered. The cutter boat would continue to provide overall cover. The special forces would be called in to parachute onto the island providing boots on the ground to mop up any resistance not subject to the guns from the four boats.

When the fast boats were unloaded and everyone was in place, the captain gave the attack order and the boats moved forward. One of the spotters immediately reported a cabin cruiser leaving the cutter boat's starboard side of the island heading southwest and adjusting itself to parallel the arrival path of the cutter boat while maintaining a two-mile distance. The boat was easily in range of the cutter boat's gun, but the cutter boat captain couldn't yet consider it as a hostile since it wasn't showing signs of aggression. He engaged the gun's electro-optic fire control system to track the speed boat in case of attack.

Earlier

Thelma and Louise pulled themselves from the water after the vigorous half-mile swim to the island and gave each other a high five to celebrate the destruction of the fishing trawler and the first police patrol boat. The other three mercenaries greeted them and congratulated them on their success. They pulled the carry-bags ashore and carried the grenade launchers, the diving gear, and the underwater propulsion system to the back dock to the two awaiting cabin cruisers.

They placed one of the grenade launchers in each boat and the diving gear and the underwater propulsion system in the women's boat, a twenty-four-foot fiberglass half-cabin-boat. Anton had purchased the two boats for cash the same day as the party boat. Grenades and other gear for the next phase of the plan had already been prepacked as needed in each boat. The grenade launcher carry bag was discarded next to the house as the grenade launchers would be discarded overboard at the end of this phase of the plan. Timing was critical to their escape. The cabin cruisers were covered again in their camouflaged tarp.

The women were handed a cold beer and they all clinked their bottles together to toast their continued success. They felt relatively safe to take a moment as the paid informants of the President's staff and within the government now kept them abreast of every movement within the Maldives Defense Force. As such, they were quickly informed that the police cutter boat would be arriving within the hour, which didn't give the women much time to get ready. Air cover was not a concern as the President was reluctant to approve it without some knowledge of what kind of missiles they would be dealing with.

The two women quickly left the group for the safe house bathroom to prepare Thelma for her role in the next phase of the plan. All necessary paints and accessories were laid out for her. She quickly stripped off the diving suit and stepped naked into the shower area. There she put on the ruby red diving cap and Louise promptly began to paint her face. Using a sponge applicator, she applied the Paradise, a Mehron brand of ruby red glycerin-based face paint that would not crack or flake off with movement. While that was drying, she grabbed the airbrush and completed the coverage of Thelma's entire body in a matching ruby red. She then went back to the face to apply a warrior's face in light blue, yellow, and black over the red paint. She finished off the body in yellow and blue stripes.

Thelma stepped out of the shower area and pulled on a tribal bikini bottom and a multi-colored headdress over the diving cap and grabbed her spear that was adorned at the top in flowers, a form of Japanese flower arranging called Ikebana or Kado, a tradition that dated to the Heian period when floral offerings were made at alters. She was ready for her role as a living figurehead on the bow of the cruiser boat. She hoped that the distraction of her warrior-like appearance and being a half-naked crazy woman would cause enough hesitation in the officers firing their guns to allow Louise to rise from her cover position on the deck and use the rocket launcher at point-blank distance.

When the Wolf explained his plan to the women, he said that the last mercenary on the island would drive the women's cruiser boat but would have to sacrifice his life for Thelma and Louise for their plan of escape to work. Thelma squealed with delight and expressed her love for him for doing that just for her. She would be the one putting a bullet in the back of his head. The women would then use the explosion of the party boat and the additional black smoke added by the grenade canisters placed on the boat as cover to escape. The island would be found deserted after the battle was over, and the women would have earned their money in showing the Americans that there was a price to pay in pursuing the Wolf.

Cutter Boat

At the one-mile point, the fast boats assumed the offense and moved forward at full speed with the cutter boat stopping in place as planned. At that moment, four events happened simultaneously. A cutter boat spotter reported another cabin cruiser departing from the cutter boat's port side of the island and attacking the fast boat on the cutter boat's portside flank. The spotter monitoring the paralleling cabin cruiser reported the starboard side boat was now turning and beginning what appeared to be an attack on the cutter boat. The cutter boat's captain received a radio transmission from the President that was interrupted by the fourth happening: a monstrous explosion on the water ahead. The party boat had disappeared, leaving nothing but fire, lots of smoke, and flying debris. The incoming fast boats were now dealing with the added danger of hitting large pieces of debris on the water from the explosion.

The explosion was large, but all fast boats were too far away to be affected. As the cutter boat captain quickly processed all that was happening around him, a rocket fired from the cabin cruiser on his starboard side and fell harmlessly into the sea. It was fired too quickly by one of the two island mercenaries manning the boat, a mistake that would cost them their lives as the cutter captain returned fire and dismantled their boat.

The 30mm machine gun cannon quickly neutralized the cabin cruiser and turned to lock onto the second cabin cruiser on the port side, but it couldn't track it through the fire and excessive smoke of the exploded party boat. He silently wondered in those brief seconds why his starboard fast boat had not opened fire. He heard his officer yelling "What the hell? What is that a spear? Is that war paint?" But all was silenced as the fast boat blew up in front of him with more officers lost.

The cutter boat held fire in fear of hitting one or both fast boats as the excessive smoke obscured any view of the cabin cruiser. The fast boat in the middle lane swerved to starboard to avoid running directly into the explosion, and after a short delay, attacked from the right to replace the other lost patrol boat. The fast boat attacking from the port side passed through the fire and thick smoke only to be met with another rocket from the waiting cabin cruiser hiding behind the smoke. Sixty seconds later, the cabin cruiser appeared racing back towards the island. It blew up as the guns of the last fast boat and the cutter boat destroyed it.

Earlier

Louise threw the rocket launcher overboard after her rocket exploded the second police patrol fast boat. The women knew they had only seconds to make the plan work as she helped Thelma loosen herself from the makeshift apparatus holding her to the bow bars. Thelma stripped her warrior bikini bottoms off and donned her wet suit, fins, scuba tank, regulator, and scuba gloves. She attached the console to the regulator by a high-pressure hose that carried the various gauges that display information such as remaining cylinder pressure, current depth, elapsed dive time, and direction of travel. Thelma got into the water and was handed the underwater propulsion system by Louise.

While Thelma was dressing, Louise was busy anchoring the driver's wheel in place to head the boat in the direction of the island. She set the explosive charge for four minutes just in case the police boat did not sink her boat as planned. She donned her diving gear, placed the gear shift in neutral and attached the noose of the strap around the gear shift knob, and joined Thelma in the water. She then pulled on the strap to place the boat in gear, and it rushed forward towards the island. Seconds later it was destroyed by the police cutter boat.

The underwater propulsion system would take them back to the island. There they would wait underwater for nightfall and an opportunity to use Wolf's speed boat to make their final escape. The women were tired and ready to bid farewell to their island home and look forward to their great escape tonight. If there was a security team left on the island, they would be eliminated.

They would live until their escape of a weeks' worth of rations and drinking water stored in canisters stashed in the water offshore along with oxygen tanks. They were moored far enough out to not be seen and where police could not see the air bubbles during an inspection if the women were there. At night, the women would enter the boathouse underwater and sleep on the boat dock beside Wolf's speed boat, being careful to avoid angles to be seen with night vision binoculars. At first light, they would re-enter the water and moor themselves with the extra oxygen bottles during daylight hours if necessary.

Night vision recognition was something that did not really worry either woman as the best military equipment available was only good up to and around two hundred yards. In the 2011 assault on Osama bin Laden's compound in Abbottabad, Pakistan each elite Navy Seal Six Team member on the raid was issued a pair of $65,000 four-tube night-vision goggles that allowed unprecedented ability to see in complete darkness while navigating through the heart of the enemy territory. But Thelma knew that kind of equipment was not going to be found in the Maldives, so generally their sleep would go unimpeded.

She knew also that if they could successfully get Wolf's speed boat into the Indian Ocean that the worry of living offshore in the water would be unnecessary and that the Maldivian Defense Force had nothing in their inventory that could match their ninety-mile-an-hour speed except a medical helicopter and a seaplane, and they weren't practical for night use or for a fight. Also, they would have to find them and knew where they were heading. The women still had their m4-cqbr, close-quarter assault weapons, if needed.

~~~~~~~

Mountain and the helicopter crew viewed the battle scene result from the helicopter upon arrival. Mountain arrived too late to participate in the battle which greatly disappointed his crew chief. The Maldivian special forces had parachuted onto the island only to find it deserted; the mercenaries all had seemingly died on the water. The balance of the day was spent by all searching for any survivors and the bodies of the dead. One mercenary was found floating on the water where the party boat had exploded. There was a bullet hole to the back of his head that could not be explained.

The search for bodies continued into the night, as did the police who blocked off boat traffic, the notification of families of their loss, and looking for and documenting evidence on the island. The following morning was more taking of crime scenes pictures, documentation of evidence found, and a further search of the island, particularly the safe house and dock area in the rear of the house to include a boathouse, for anything helpful in finding the Wolf.

~~~~~~

The boathouse was built directly on the water with perfectly cut and treated imported mahogany with a waterway entrance for Anton Lupe's beloved racing boat. It was tied down inside the docking slip and additionally protected from the elements by a boat cover. A completed search of the boat and boathouse showed no recent activity or use. Photographs were taken and documented as part of the investigation.

The bathroom area of the safe house showed lots of activity that appeared to be abnormal, and photographs were extensively taken and documented. The rest of the safe house appeared to have been used by the terrorists as living quarters, but nothing was found that was out of the ordinary. All items found in all the searches, other than boat debris, were properly documented and placed in plastic bags and sent as evidence to a designated building in the Coast Guard Northern Area. Debris was loaded onto two barges and offloaded in a designated outside area for inspection and disposal in the Coast Guard Northern Area.

All this was proceeding in great haste to accommodate the following day's gathering of family and friends for a memorial service and boat parade on the water. This was the result of a morning media briefing whereby the President assured the world that all the terrorists were accounted for as dead, and the Maldivian people would remain strong and united in getting through this act of terrorism. Nothing was mentioned about the Wolf. He concluded his briefing by inviting everyone to a candlelight memorial service and parade of boats the following evening without any thought of the timing or logistics of such an event.

On the third day, Mountain accompanied the captain of the cutter boat as a guest and watched the preparation for the nighttime candlelight boat parade in honor of the fallen. The police were starting to line up boats hours in advance of the parade. The process and available information frustrated participants, but by the end of the evening, it had somehow all worked out. At the conclusion of the service and the parade, the water was marked by hundreds of flowers floating on top where once the party boat and 'Lazy Susan' trawler had floated.

The Wolf had disappeared and was still at large. He was not mentioned as being involved or responsible for the carnage, such as the death of fifteen people, including nine National Defense Force police officers and six local commercial fishermen now viewed as heroes.

As rumors were beginning to circulate that the CIA had been allowed into the country to search for this terrorist called the Wolf, the President consistently argued that there was no evidence that the Wolf was involved or had ever been in the Maldives, and that the terrorists that were responsible for the deaths were now dead.

On the morning of the fourth day, the President announced to the world that the waterways were once again open for boat traffic and police were returning to normal duties. He reminded everyone "that the island was private property, and anybody, including reporters, caught on the island without authorized permission would be fined and jailed." He concluded by saying, "The facts of this terrorist attack as we knew them and the conclusions of our investigation would be documented, published, and made available to everyone in the shortest possible time. I can report at this time as fact that two of the five terrorists killed were women. This is confirmed by the first patrol boat reporting two women sunbathing before the first patrol boat was lost and evidence found in the bathroom of the house on the island rented by the terrorists. "

He continued, "One of the women in the latest attack painted herself in all red with other colors as a war paint to make herself look like a maidenhead warrior. She wore only a tribal bikini bottom, a warrior's headdress, and carried a spear. She tied herself to the bow of her boat as a distraction to the policemen. The distraction caused the policemen to hesitate in firing their weapons and provided the time needed for the second woman hiding on the boat to fire a grenade rocket launcher at point-blank range to kill the officers. When the second patrol boat responded to help, the thick black smoke from the party boat explosion hid the terrorist boat until it was too late for the patrol boat to save itself. Black smoke canisters found in the party boat's debris showed how carefully the attack was planned. The assassins were then eliminated while trying to escape to the island by the brave policemen of our patrol boat and the crew of our cutter boat."

Same Day
CIA Director Harry Snead issued the Interpol Red Notice List as promised on Anton Lupu, alias the Wolf, but did not say he was in the Maldives, not because of anything the Maldivian President had done or not done, but because the Figurehead Massacre, as it was now being called in the media worldwide, made it necessary. Mountain knew the Wolf did not participate in the battle and merely used it as a

distraction to cover his escape and to make the point that pursuing him would come at a cost.

Northern Coast Guard Station

Sam Mountain's fourth day started early with hot coffee, eggs, and toast. He would enjoy it much more if he could just grab that nagging thought that something wasn't right. The three previous days had flown by with him being basically ignored while the President and police claimed the narrative for what had happened. Mountain somewhat understood them going it alone into battle as it was their country's pride at stake, and their men were trained professionals. Still, he knew most of it had to do with the politics of the President being practically blackmailed to obtain Sam's entry into the country, being American and not being Muslim. He thought, "I would spend the rest of the day alone looking through the bagged evidence and maybe my mind would clear."

By mid-morning, Mountain was sweaty and tired of digging through trash bags when he found a bag containing the carrying case for the grenade rocket launchers left next to the safe house. Mountain knew the weapon used by the women was a missile launcher of some sort, but he had never seen a homemade carrying case for such. He examined it closely and brushed off any thought that it was relative to the investigation other than the women being truly professional and taking special care of the weapons in their possession.

In the late afternoon, Mountain opened a bag containing a scorched, half-burned carrying case for an underwater two-person propulsion system and suddenly the nagging thought became clear. He realized that the carrying case for the rocket launchers was not to protect the equipment, but to transport the rocket launchers underwater. The case was waterproof, and he grabbed the case and confirmed his find.

He thought, "The two women were underwater and traveling with their weapons in a specially designed waterproof carrying case. The body found floating with the bullet hole in the back of his head was the driver of the women's boat and he was the odd man out as there was no room on the two-person underwater propulsion system for him. These two women were a team. A driver was needed because one woman was on the bow of the boat and one woman was the shooter. There was no time for double duty by the shooter to drive." He said the obvious out loud and to himself, "They were alive and somewhere on the island, they have to be." He rushed back to his living quarters while calling his helicopter crew to meet him there.

Mountain telephoned the cutter boat captain. "Do you want to get back at these terrorists? The captain replied, "I thought they were all dead, were there more of them? Mountain replied, "Find me a Linxup GPS tracking device with a wired harness adapter. They were primarily used by commercial car/truck fleet owners to track their vehicles by tapping into the onboard diagnostic port (obd2p). As boats do not come with an obd2p as do cars and trucks, I need the wired adapter conversion harness for installation and tracking of a boat; I need it now. If one cannot be found meet me anyway at my helicopter and I'll explain everything, and we'll find another way to resolve the problem. Bring a key to the safe house, two of your best special force's men, and your weapons."

Mountain's primary problem was how best to approach the task of eliminating the terrorists and he had no time left as it was about an hour before dark. He knew that the problem was that everybody was under the impression that the terrorists were dead. The President had staked his reputation on it and for people to find out otherwise could cause a lack of trust in him and his ability to be reelected. There was no telling how the president would react if told. Also, there was no hard evidence of the women being alive and the paid informers would alert the terrorists; it was unknown what kind of capability they still had left.

Mountain thought, "It was an indefensible situation. If I successfully deal with the terrorists, it looks like the Maldivian government is incompetent and it took an American to go behind them to resolve the problem. It also hurts their national pride. If I am unsuccessful, and especially if there were further deaths, I would not be able to count the ways America and the president would be criticized."

He thought, "There were only two places left on the island that they can sleep, the safe house or the boathouse. The cabin cruisers were no more. Surely, they could not be living and sleeping underwater twenty-four hours a day for the last four days, but he cannot dismiss the possibility as money can provide things that a normal person simply dismissed because it was not a reality fathomable for them. If politics wasn't involved, he would simply destroy the boathouse and surround the safe house until the terrorists were found, surrender, or were killed. But he knew it was going to take a lot more creative answer as governments had fallen on lesser trust and perception issues."

Mountain gathered his crew and informed them that the women terrorists were still alive and how he had come to that conclusion. He then explained the politics and the possible fallout to the governments involved in going after the terrorists and presented his plan and why he felt it must be handled in this manner. He jokingly added, "If you were Navy Seals, I would just tell you my plan and go, but you were not. I cannot ask you to jeopardize your career and family and possibly face court-martial if in good conscience you cannot do this." He paused and said, "If you say no, I will not think any less of you. No matter your answer no one can ever knew of this plan, not even family or friends." When the vote was taken, all agreed to participate. This left only the Maldivians, and it was a big ask.

It was after dark when the cutter captain and two soldiers finally showed. They had an impossible task in locating a tracker with a wired harness but found one from a commercial fisherman who was using the conversion kits to track his three commercial fishing boats. The cutter captain said, "He promptly informed me that if I break it, I pay for it," and laughed. Mountain thought, "These guys are all professionals, and look the part and I knew I can count on them. I am late in getting to the island, but this conversation has to be done." He informed them of everything he knew about the two women terrorists, gave them the same option as given his men, and amazingly, all agreed to the plan.

Now they understood why they must get to the island as quickly as possible. Mountain wondered where men like these were made that understood the importance of their role in history and needed no fanfare. Somehow, Mountain now believed that he just might be able to pull this off. He glanced at his crew chief who was grinning from ear to ear. He knew he had one last opportunity at blowing something away.

Mountain had no intention of hiding their approach to the island and had the helicopter land directly in front of the safe house. Mountain put on his pair of night-vision goggles and he and the two Maldivian special forces men debarked quickly, covered by the door gunner. Mountain went around the left side of the house to cover the back and water approached. The two special forces men used a forced entry to enter the house. He wanted the women to think this was a routine inspection of the property to ensure there were no thieves in the house or on the property to steal the two million-plus dollars speedboat, a real possibility with the press and media providing a daily account of the tragedy with family members and government officials fueling the fire.

He saw no one on land or on the water, but sensed they were watching. He hoped that they would not make a suicide stand at this point when they were so close to making an escape. He knew when first coming around the left side of the house that he had given the women ample time to observe him, and his night vision goggles. He did this purposely so that when he approached the boat dock to cover the water, the women would be forced to stay submerged and could not watch them install the wired tracking device on the speed boat. He also knew that he could be wrong and that this could be a nightmare in the making. That is why he sent the cutter boat captain to the right side of the house to cover the water behind the helicopter and the grounds to the right of them. It allowed the door gunner to remain focused on the house.

The special forces men came out the back door of the house in a low crouch peeling to the middle and right of Mountain at the same time giving him an 'all clear' for the house. They carefully approached the boat storage facility and entered the back with Mountain entering the front. It was again an 'all clear,' but Mountain saw what he suspected all along, which was the wetness of the wood on both sides of the boat. The women had climbed up for a few hours' sleep before leaving when they heard and then saw the approaching helicopter and returned to the water.

The men worked quickly to remove the boat cover, installed the wired tracker system, replaced the boat cover, and returned to the helicopter with Mountain right behind them. The cutter captain joined them, and Mountain knew they were at risk now if the women had moved in behind them. He asked the pilot to take off over the house, staying low before heading out past the horizon where they would stay until they were assured the assassins were in for the night. They needed to be assured their tracker was working perfectly at all distances and direction if the women tried to escape using the speed boat. Mountain thought, "This system is sort of like the GPS tracking system one would put inside their dog to find him anywhere, except this system is much more capable. In this instance, my dogs are wondering how much we knew and how vulnerable they are." Mountain did not underestimate their capabilities both for planning and violence.

Earlier

Thelma and Louise decided to catch at least four hours sleep to be rested for their trip. The first three nights were too busy around the island for a safe escape, but this night was perfect in terms of weather and opportunity. They climbed up from the water and discarded their diving gear, leaving on their diving suits as per usual. This practice was making them feel more like a prune and was extremely tiring, but the time to put on the diving suit plus the diving gear took too long. As such, when they heard and then saw the helicopter's lights, they rapidly put on their gear and re-entered the water and headed back to their mooring spot.

When the helicopter landed and the police debarked and headed towards the house, the women felt confident that this was more of a follow-up to the police surveillance team leaving the island than the knowledge that the women were alive. After all, the police knew that the only way off the island was by Wolf's boat, a seaplane, or submarine that would have taken more advance planning time than given the Wolf. It did startle the women to see CIA operative Sam Mountain.

Anton had warned them about him. Anton had said, "He is their best operative, a former Army sniper, extremely smart and competent and at home anywhere in the world." He had on night-vision goggles and the women knew he would be wearing the best equipment available, so they decided to retreat and swim around to the front of the island. They were not armed but saw no reason to expose their weapons to open ocean water by taking them out of their waterproof carrying case. Their informants did not advise them of this raid which begged the question of why they were not informed. The women did not feel it to be a double-cross by them, or the Wolf or the police would have come directly to the boathouse, and they felt assured that the Wolf did not betray them as he really wanted his precious boat back in one piece.

Thelma asked, "Could this be some rouge operation hoping to catch a few people sneaking onto the island that they could take some revenge out on for their losses?" Louise replied, "No, Sam Mountain would not have participated in any such actions." They knew that something was not right and concluded that they had either made a mistake and he had reason to think were alive, or Sam Mountain was given carte blanche approval to work on his own in seeing if the Wolf left a trail of where he might be heading. In any case, the women now felt the need to get away from the island.

They patiently watched from the water in front of the house the efficiency of the police team as they returned to the helicopter to depart. They noted the coverage of the water and their position from the right corner of the house and the abnormal flyout low and over the house and to the right to possibly give the grenade launchers a hard target or to avoid water areas most suitable for more conventional weapons. They concluded that Sam Mountain knew his stuff and that he also thought they may be somewhere in the water alive.

Later, in conversation at the boathouse and reviewing their situation, Louise stated that "Sam Mountain cannot seek the open support of the President for a continued investigation, and I think I knew why? Since our informers told us that the President has told the world that we are dead, Sam Mountain knew the president wanted to keep us dead to maintain his precious tourist trade and chances for reelection. If he had notified the president, our informants would have contacted us. That is why I think this CIA agent Sam Mountain is working independently with no backup except for a few rogue soldiers."

Thelma said, "Wouldn't that be highly unlikely that both the CIA and the Maldivian police would both go rogue?" Louise said, "You have a point, but something isn't right, and it all revolves around politics I am betting."

Reflectively, Louise said, "So, the president has a political problem. We could cause him a lot of problems with one final effort in the airport area, but it was of no benefit to us.

Thelma said, "He is lucky we are not terrorists, but thrill-seekers in search of only money. We could really put an end to this president's career." She laughed and added, "His Islamic brethren would turn on him with a vengeance having knowledge of a second terrorist attack."

Louise said, "With no one on the island, we can leave now and be in open water with nothing that can find us in this darkness. With us gone the President can deny any report that said we are alive and therefore would not pursue us in the morning. He would continue to blame everything on the dead terrorists and blame Sam Mountain and the CIA for being incompetent if it comes to more than that. At least that gave us a reasonable chance. Only the American helicopter is capable of coming after us in the morning and they don't know where we are going."

Thelma said, "We'll watch the stars together, let's do it."

An hour later they were in open water and running at half power with lights on to get a good feel for the boat. As it was early in the evening, Louise acted as a spotter to avoid any traffic on the water that might arouse suspicion of their boat running drugs.

~~~~~~

The cutter boat captain said to Mountain, "The tracker is working great. They are on the move and heading for open water. What do you want to do?"

Mountain replied, "We'll trail them from over the horizon until we are as sure as we can be that no one is around to see any fireworks. Let the others rest until we decide to attack." He thought, "I must somehow verify that the women are on the boat. They haven't lived this long by making too many mistakes."

One hour later, Mountain said, "It was time. See anything, captain?"

The captain replied, "Nothing but ocean, but who knew in this darkness."

Mountain turned his mic to open position. "Everybody up and to battle stations. Pilot, can you get me safely behind their boat using their lights only? I need to confirm that the women are actually on that boat."

"Yes sir," the pilot replied.

Mountain said, "Crew chief, are you ready?"

"Yes sir," he said.

"Pilot, if you see any other lights on the ocean, back off. Now, take us in," Mountain commanded.

The pilot took the helicopter down to five hundred feet and went black. He brought it in over the horizon at one hundred and twenty miles an hour and started his gain on the lights ahead doing a comfortable seventy miles an hour on a relatively calm ocean surface. There were no other boat lights on the ocean. At approximately one hundred yards, the pilot dropped his speed to that of the boat and swung out to the left at Mountain's request. Mountain took off his night-vision goggles and peered out the open-gun-door with his binoculars and saw the backs of two women, one driving and one standing up beside the driver as a lookout ahead. Mountain thought, "These are two remarkably disciplined assassins." He asked the pilot to pull the helicopter back in place behind the speed boat and said, "Pilot, get your door gunner in a shooting position. Crew chief, fire when ready."

~~~~~~~

Thelma and Louise were starting to feel better about their chances of escape. They knew that they were free of the Maldivian Defense Force, but the Americans were a worry. Louise shouted at Thelma, "He is CIA, they can use a satellite to track us if they consider us important enough. They can even send in a drone strike, a submarine, or a fighter jet from a base or aircraft carrier in the area, why don't they?"

Thelma reflected on Louise's comment and said, "Yes, why don't they? If they really wanted us found, they could. I think we were right, to begin with. This Sam Mountain is working alone with a few renegade soldiers that agree with whatever he is trying to do."

Thelma answered, "If that is true and he knew we are alive, then the raid on the island was meant to scare us into running and we chose to run to open water where he wants us. He must have us on satellite, or the purpose of the visit earlier was to put a tracking device on our boat."

Thelma reached down and frantically searched for and found the tracking device. She showed it to Louise and promptly threw it overboard. Louise said, "Stop the boat and turn off your lights."

When they came to a stop, they heard the fast-closing helicopter and reached for their m4-cqbrs guns and fired randomly at the noise as the helicopter quickly passed over them veering sharply to the left and seeking altitude. The crew chief had not had time to return fire. Thelma slammed the gear knob forward seeking distance and the darkness to lose the helicopter.

～～～～～

Mountain thought, "I walked us right into that one and we are alive only through the skill of our pilot and the women not having a missile launcher handy."

The cutter boat captain said, "I'm guessing they found the tracker and threw it overboard as they have disappeared off the screen. We are now flying blind."

Mountain was thankful to discover that everyone on board was fine.

Mountain said, "Pilot, maintain one thousand feet of altitude keeping your lights off and bring the helicopter into a slow and tight circle movement. Crew chief, let me in your seat." Mountain took out his sniper rifle and attached his Precision Acquisition Rifle Thermal Night Sight–Elevator (SPARTN-E) onto the front of his daylight vision scope. He searched the water as the helicopter slowly circled and found the boat at about five hundred yards out. He gave the pilot verbal directions to bring him in closer.

The shots would be extremely difficult in constantly changing conditions, not to mention from a helicopter at a boat rising and falling with the ocean waves. At two hundred yards, he placed the crosshairs of the scope on the driver of the boat. He had the pilot hold the helicopter in place and squeezed the trigger. The driver slumped forward resting her chest and head over the wheel.

He brought the scope onto the other woman who was screaming at him and giving him both middle fingers while alternating hands to try to keep from falling overboard. Mountain helped her fall overboard with the next shot. Mountain said, "Crew chief, take your seat. Pilot, put on your lights and bring us into the boat." When the lights found the boat, Mountain said to the crew chief, "Light her up Chief, she is all yours."

The Chief smiled and he did just that.

The following morning there was no fanfare, but only a quiet moment with the President and a shaking of hands goodbye for when Sam Mountain and his helicopter crew left the Maldives. But this was not true for the captain of the cutter boat, his crew, and anyone else the President could find worthy of pinning a medal on, as in his mind this was the biggest break in his forthcoming election for President that he could have hoped for, never mind that he was as proud of them as they were of themselves. It was 'Honor our Heroes Day' in the Maldives and the President was making the most of it in attaching himself to their achievements.

The President thought, "the worldwide press would have a field day with this, and the resultant tourist trade would contribute millions to our economy. They would all want to visit the new park and 'Figurehead Massacre' statue being created of the painted half-nude woman and hear the story as told by taped voices played into the headphones provided at a five dollar a play, and especially the women." The President thought that the Figurehead woman and story would be used by women as an incentive to get their men to give them some additional attention.

But to the women visitors, it was but another current monument to their gender of all the legions of women throughout history that have used their bodies whether forced or unforced to make history and would never be recognized for their true contributions. They knew that it was women who make history, but it was men who wrote it. And because of that, women were depicted for their sexual exploits and not their accomplishments. Peggy Guggenheim of the various Guggenheim Museums around the world was once asked how many husbands she'd had, she replied "Do you mean mine or other peoples?" No one cared about her accomplishments. Women like Cleopatra, Helen of Troy, the women who fought valiantly in every war or were sex slaves to their conquerors all have important histories mostly unrecognized except for the sex.

The park and statue would be another symbol of the constant struggle of women to define their identity. It was the same struggle that Malcolm X wrote about as being invisible in a white-dominated world as one of the biggest challenges for African Americans living in a racist society. Yes, women tourists would visit the site as wished by the men in their lives, but not for the President's reasons, but to place another sharp pin in the invisible voodoo doll of their choice and location for the implied inequities in life.

Mountain observed the Maldives below from his helicopter and thought, "The President may wonder where his soldiers and boat captain were all night, but in this business, there are always these kinds of problems, and I don't think the President would really want to know or care. The fact that women were killed with no attempt to arrest them would be a secret hard to keep, especially for a helicopter crew trying to explain to their Admiral the bullet holes. I may have to get Harry involved with the Admiral to help them out there."

Overall, he felt comfortable with the men that he had asked to take on this responsibility and proud that he had served with the men and women of the Maldives' Military Defense Force. They proudly earned the reputation they valued, and he would further contribute to that value in his report. He would ask for special recognition by the CIA for the boat captain and his two Special Forces men of some kind and the Ambassador and Mr. Rohan Silva to receive proper medals for their efforts. Separately, Mountain looked forward to seeing the Wolf soon.

CHAPTER TWO

NIKOLI BASKOV,

THE RUSSIAN-KURIL ISLANDS (2013-2014)

The Russian was on the Pacific Ocean side of Iturup, the largest island of the South Kuril Islands that connected the territories of Russia and Japan. The Russian President's plan to secure the Northern Sea Route and Asian Pacific Rim was underway for the takeover and control of the South Kuril Islands. Japan claimed the two most southern islands of Iturup and Kunashir as well as Shikotan and the Habotai Islet and Russia the remaining fifty-four islands. Ownership of these islands was challenged with the discovery of oil and rare precious metals needed in the advancement of technology, particularly in computer software. Fishing rights added to the conflict as developing economies after World War II saw this area of their economy as vital to their economic growth.

The intent of Russian President Ivanovitch in invading these islands was to settle all disputes in favor of Russia. Since the approximately twenty thousand inhabitants of Iturup favored Russian rule and had requested help to secure their rights, he chose these islands for the initial invasion. He thought, "After all, this type of reasoning worked successfully for Hitler in his early justification for the invasion of nearby lands belonging to other countries."

Nikolai was worried as he had not heard from Natasha or Anton. There was nothing on the news about the President of Russia being assassinated, and Natasha should have killed him by now, according to plan. Further, there was no news about any nuclear explosions, so he knew that Anton had somehow failed in his mission to launch the stolen Russian missiles against intended targets. He thought, "No news is not good news."

The Russian sensed he was in trouble, and there was no scenario he could foresee that projected a safe way out of the situation. He thought, "If Natasha killed the President as instructed, the Russian would have known as would have every soldier on these miserable nothing islands; the same would have been true of an assassination attempt." His mind raced, "She is certainly cut out to kill another person as she did so without regret that time in Mali. Maybe the President slept in the Kremlin that night and was not in his helicopter, and there was no opportunity presented to use the

American-made stinger missile provided to Natasha for the kill, or maybe she is in jail or dead, and the President is awaiting my return to Russia to have me killed. It would certainly be an embarrassment to have me killed or arrested here in front of my men."

"The President could just summon me back to Russia on the pretext of a needed meeting or emergency and simply make me disappear or have me killed here as a casualty of war. Maybe I think too much of myself and she has always worked for the President, and I have always been the fly in her spider trap. Maybe, maybe, maybe," he said with some frustration. "I must assume the worse and that Natasha has informed the President of our plan either by choice, actions, torture, or even by her death. I must think and be ready."

Nikolai knew he was vulnerable to open arrest and was pushed for time before they came for him. He silently kicked himself for not having made a contingency plan for his escape, but he did not expect both Natasha and Anton to fail him. He wanted desperately to contact Natasha, but he could not trust that his military communication system was not compromised. He could abandon his troops and return to Russia, but if nothing was wrong and Natasha had delayed killing the President due to unforeseen circumstances, he would be considered a traitor who deserted his post and left them vulnerable to Japanese air attack. He thought, "Deserting his post and returning to Russia during wartime would certainly give President Ivanovitch a legitimate reason to make me disappear."

At the end of the week, he would have to return to Russia as the second phase of the President's plan called for his presence to lead troops into the Arctic. He must be patient, and by then, he should know something one way or another and could make a better decision. Nikolai quickly looked up and about and noted that the Japanese had certainly taken exception to the Russian invasion as the sky above was well lit with air battles, but for whatever reason, ground action was delayed. The Russian felt "it was only a matter of time."

At that moment, General Baskov received a communication from the Russian Minister of Defense. It said, "Withdraw your troops immediately. You may take all precautionary actions to protect your troops during the withdrawal. Report directly to the President upon your return." The Russian was confused. Something was very wrong, and he needed to figure it out. He thought, "The President would not order the withdrawal of all the troops just to get at me, so this cannot be about me." Reports from the field were now starting to show withdrawal of Russian and Chinese planes to their own air space. Japanese planes were not following the withdrawing aircraft.

General Baskov thought, "I need information and need it now." He ordered a secure communication line with the President and made the call. Ivan Ivanovitch answered immediately and said, "I cannot chance that this line is not secure. The Americans' latest technology has compromised much of our communications. I'll have Natasha meet you at the airport. We need to talk; come home." The President hung up before Nikolai could respond.

"So, Natasha is alive," Nikolai thought as he placed down his receiver. "Or maybe this is a trap." The question remained, was he safe to return to Russia, or was he walking into a trap? There was only one way to find out. He used Nobel Com, a long-distance international cell service available to the public.

Natasha saw that it was him calling and answered the phone on the second ring. She said, "I can't talk right now, but I am fine, and we can still complete our vacation if you can come home right now while it is safe. Your brother will not be joining us." She hung up quickly.

Natasha reluctantly hit the end button on her cell phone. She wanted desperately to tell Nikolai that she loved him and to run, run as fast as he could and as far as he could. She wanted to throw up. Here she was betraying the only man she had ever loved, and her heart ached. She knew Nikolai lied to her about the intentions of his plan to destroy the world and used her, and that he would have willingly killed her with the rest of the world if his plan had worked, but it still hurt her so badly, and she knew he did love her as best as he could love anyone with the pain he carried from his youth in the orphanage.

She knew that his wounds festered over the years to the point that it absorbed his thoughts and love, and life was dismantled in the process. Now he would have to be put down like some wounded animal and she was the one ordered by the President to do it for her beloved Russia. Natasha thought about what the President said after she was told to have General Baskov arrested and quietly executed. "We would blame him for our failure in the Kuril Islands and the aggressive behavior of our military."

The Russian slowly paced back and forth after ending his call with Natasha. He thought, "So Anton is dead?" It both saddened and maddened him at once. "And why are you not dead, Natasha?" he asked sarcastically. Was it because she confessed under torture where the missiles were, which led to their destruction and the death of Anton? He took out a cigarette, the first since departing Russia, and lit it up before taking a long drag.

He continued his thoughts, "The plan was perfect, but Natasha chose Russia over me." He took another long drag, and he tossed it. "Natasha didn't sound stressed enough to have been tortured, so I must assume she is working with the President and has been all along." Nikolai knew that if he was wrong, nothing else mattered, as he would have twice given up his chances of love with Natasha and life itself. If he was right, everything mattered as he had another chance for revenge. He knew now what he must do.

General Baskov immediately issued the order for the evacuation of the Kuril Islands. With preparation completed, the troops that were mostly welcomed with open arms wondered silently what this was all been about, but they were the best of the best and orders were enough for them. As quickly as the Spetsnaz troops had appeared on the island, just as quickly they had disappeared on their return trip to mother Russia. General Nikolai Baskov considered his situation one more time before he approached his helicopter that would take him back to Moscow. He and his pilot were the only remaining Russian troops on the island. "Is Moscow really a trap and do I have another choice?" he wondered. He knew he did not.

He thought back to his time with Natasha in Moscow when she had held him when he had tried to disappear into his own mind. He loved her as best as he knew how and he knew she loved him, but he had also betrayed her, and he knew she was aware of it. The pilot gave the signal that the helicopter was ready for takeoff and Nikolai considered again his plan and made his final decision. The helicopter lifted into the air for the return trip to Moscow and Nikolai gave one last salute to the pilot from the ground below.

In the time before Nikolai and his pilot were to leave the island, Nikolai prepared his plan. He informed his pilot of his conversation with the President and informed him that he had received orders to stay on the island, "Moscow has further demand of me," he said. The pilot did not question the orders, nor the package Nikolai handed him to deliver to the President. He instructed the pilot that ten minutes after takeoff and over water to report to Moscow that all troops have left the island and that Yeti was on board. Yeti was Nikolai's code name. "This will be the only message you would send, and no other discussion should take place with anyone until you have landed and given your package to the President. Do you understand? The Americans will be listening."

"I understand," the pilot replied.

To help the pilot absorb the many questions he must have and to further accept that Nikolai was now on a secret mission for the state,

Nikolai said, "The Americans must think I am on board."

The pilot answered, "Yes General. Be safe my friend."

Ten minutes later and over water, the pilot reported in as ordered the bomb in the package exploded. The South China Sea absorbed another aircraft and pilot. The Russian SU-35 fighter, sent to establish contact and provide escort, provided a report of the loss of contact, and soon thereafter verified wreckage on the water.

Nikolai, now feeling much better about his situation, put on civilian clothes and headed away from the encampment towards the coast. Upon arrival, he located a trawler captain who for the right price took him to a container ship at sea where the captain, again for the right price, took him on board as a deck officer for the remaining and relatively short trip to Kobe, Japan.

Arriving at Kobe on the larger container ship allowed him less chance of discovery by the Americans that he was in Japan unannounced. Japanese associates had already cleared him through customs under a new name and passport and the safe house contained everything else he would need for his new life.

CIA Headquarters

Harry Snead, Director of Clandestine Operations, followed the conflict in the Pacific Rim and the now retreating armies. He noted particularly the last aircraft leaving Iturup Island and the last message sent from the plane, "Yeti is on board." Did this mean General Nikolai Baskov was on board and was now dead, or was it just another ploy to provide misinformation? "I am betting the latter as the Russians are too smart to communicate over an open line. The war and the subsequent retreat of their troops may have shaken them up a bit, but these are hard and well-trained men and do not typically make this type of an amateur mistake," he mused. "But why inform us about the possible whereabouts of Nikolai? They knew we have the capability to intercept this communication and that we could use it to go after his plane. And, why no rebuke of the Russian pilot for his indiscretion?"

Harry Snead paused for a moment in his thoughts before saying out loud. "There is no reported firing of a land-based missile in the area and the Russian escort plane was not in range to fire his missiles? It appeared it was a plan to destroy the plane for a purpose, but what? Are the Russians possibly offering up General Baskov as a scapegoat for the war, sacrificing their own pilot to convince us and the world he is now dead? Or do they suspect General Baskov was not on the plane when it was destroyed, and that Nicolai has instructed the pilot to provide the message because of fear of returning to Russia and being blamed for the war and is now on the run?"

Harry continued his thoughts, "The Russian would certainly recognize that he is a liability to the Russians alive and he has the asset, connections, and knowledge to make himself disappear. It would certainly explain the lack of Russian response for the pilot to stay off the air if the pilot is told by Nikolai or the Russians to deliver a set communication and is then betrayed and killed by an in-plane bomb. I guess time would tell me the real story." He placed the American Embassy in Japan on alert as Japan would be General Baskov's nearest point of retreat if was alive and he did not intend to try to return in one trip to Russia.

CHAPTER THREE

IVAN IVANOVITCH,

PRESIDENT OF RUSSIA (2013-2014)

On December 25th, 1991, the Soviet hammer and sickle flag lowered for the last time over the Kremlin, thereafter, replaced by the Russian tricolor. The eighteen newly independent republics of the former Soviet Union were recognized by the United States over the following three years. The 1993 constitution declared Russia a democratic, federative, law-based state with a republican form of government. State power was divided among the legislative, executive, and judicial branches. In 1993, Ivan Ivanovitch was elected President and he was determined to restore the former Soviet Union as a world power with him as Tzar Ivanovitch. He called "the breakup of the Soviet Union as the greatest geopolitical tragedy of the 20th century."

President's Office-Russia

Ivan Ivanovitch, the President of Russia, was quickly informed of General Baskov's downed helicopter and the last radio contact and that some type of bomb, probably a missile, not an engine failure, had brought the helicopter down. The President reacted quickly in demanding answers but smiled to himself that the tragedy seemed to resolve his immediate problem with General Baskov and that was a good thing. He was aware too that engine failure could be induced, or an onboard bomb planted. He had killed too many people in his rise to power not to know that seemingly facts were sometimes created and that General Baskov was wise in the ways of creating his own facts. Whether he was dead or alive would only be provided in time, for time was always the fortune teller of fate.

President Ivanovitch ended his conversation with Chairman Li, as the President of China preferred to be addressed. He had withdrawn Russia from the war and now sat back in his cherished old leather chair. He understood that Chairman Li had to be concerned with him as a partner after making an independent decision to withdraw Russian troops from the war without consulting him in advance. President Ivanovitch thought, "I had no choice this time, but I cannot make a misstep like this with him in the future."

He reflected on what he might have done differently, and it didn't take long to answer his question. He thought, "Obviously, placing a Romanian in charge of the Russian military knew too that he assassinated my best friend, probably ranks number one." He added sarcastically, "and that's not even considering having Natasha, my personal bodyguard, a beautiful woman though she is, in a plot to assassinate me and coming close to starting World War III using my own nuclear-tipped missiles against me. Outside of that, we were winning the war." He slowly shook his head back and forth as if only now recognizing how foolish he had been.

These moments alone were becoming somewhat of an obsession with him, but necessary in eliminating mistakes in the regeneration of his expansion plans. He knew the time for action was now and that the war was behind him, and any rumors leaked at this point about Nikolai Baskov being Romanian or why the war was started or stopped could be answered with a plausible explanation or a firm denial. The United States had lost its window of opportunity to blackmail him.

President Ivanovitch knew he must first deal with the people who could bring down his regime. He thought, "It seems that Natasha can still be of value, and her loyalty to Russia was proven. She may disagree with me at times, but she recognizes that I am Russia and would do as I ask. Certainly, the submarine commander that launched the missiles must disappear. The crew did not have access to all the information, and that would not prove a problem. My Chinese comrades would see that there would be no information forthcoming about the retrofit of the product ships, and there appear to be no survivors among the crews. The other participants in the war, North Korea, Iran, Hezbollah, and the Egyptian Brotherhood, offered no threat to my presidency, and only North Korea actively got a bloody nose from their participation."

President Ivanovitch thought, "The Wolf is not a threat to my presidency if he lives, as he has no leverage. Also, Wolf's future would be with China, and I can work with President Li if there is a problem. General Baskov has nowhere to hide in this world if he is alive, and there is no one to tell his story to even if he chooses to do so. The United States already knew most, if not all, the facts. Only the United States can harm me, but my agreement with their President to keep my secret to stop this war should hold. How strange that I trust my enemy to do what is right." He then made the obvious observation, "What a world!"

CHAPTER FOUR

HO LI CHUNG,

PRESIDENT OF THE PEOPLES REPUBLIC OF CHINA

(2013-2014)

President Li Chung of the People's Republic of China (PRC) reflected on the events of the war and felt betrayed by Russia. The telephone call from President Ivanovitch about his military force's withdrawal offered nothing but excuses and platitudes. "Why did President Ivanovitch back down to the Americans and force me to reveal my intentions in the Asian Pacific Rim? Is there a hidden agenda of which I am unaware? I risked everything on a Russian plan that was working and then abandoned. Why? I must be careful in dealing with this man," he mused.

With further thought, he did realize that China seemingly lost little in the attempt to implement Russia's plan. Most of the world seemed to accept that China's non-response to the Russian and Japanese aggression in the South China Sea was appropriate and properly ended since no missiles were fired at the Japanese airplanes or ground armies used to invade territories claimed by others. Some now viewed a mature China as deserving to lead a new world order for their calming and reasonable approach to what could have easily developed into World War III.

He had to admit that China was now viewed openly as more of a world power both economically and militarily. He thought, "Taiwan would look to the Americans to boost their defenses and the Americans would beat their chests more about China's aggressiveness, but realistically China has the advantage of location. There would be some trust lost with neighboring countries in the negotiation of land ownership, oil, fishing, and mineral rights but as the power in the Region, they would have to come to us in the long view."

He decided overall he was glad that his intentions in the Asian Pacific Rim were now out in the open and that he could actively pursue an aggressive PRC expansion of lands and acquisition of the holdings in the disputed territories. For decades, Chinese diplomacy had largely heeded the words of Deng Xiaoping, the reformist leader, who exhorted his countrymen to "hide our light and bide our time, keeping a low profile while accumulating China's strengths." President Li banged his fist on the desk while rising halfway out of his chair and screamed, "I am no Deng Xiaoping. It was time to let the world knew who I am. China will be respected. I will be respected."

Letting out the years of frustration in coming to terms with the past sufferings of China inflicted by the West calmed him and he slowly slumped back down into his seat even more resolved to rectify China's past. He thought "We would no longer build our history on failures but on wins. Firstly, I must eradicate any notion that China is still some released colony of the West yapping at its master for past unfairness, and now seen as a beggar on the world stage for inclusion as a world power. Hong Kong must be my first prize to demonstrate that even the idea of a weak China deserving of colonization is forever dead in the eyes of the world. China must clearly convey to England that Hong Kong was never theirs, to begin with much less to give back."

Chairman Li continued, "The only reason Hong Kong would be sacrificed to us is that the West thinks we will not change Hong Kong's financial market as we need access to the international banking that Hong Kong provides to grow our economy and military as a player on the world stage. It was typical, in that the West's leadership only thought in terms of money or the power that money brought. We will take Hong Kong not for the money but because it makes a statement to the world that Asia is our playground, and you must play by our rules. I am tired of hearing the arrogant whispers of the Western elite: Look at what we gave them and look at how they wasted it. They must come to know the truth that they gave us nothing and took away everything. They plundered, pillaged, and drained all of China's resources except time and opportunity. Will, our time is now, and every resource will be available shortly to take our opportunity."

He continued, "When Hong Kong is secured, the world will accept that Taiwan is lost as a free country. After all, if the West would not stand up to us when we have openly broken our written agreement with Great Britain that the city could retain the rule of law for fifty years after Britain returned the territory in 1997 and meant to keep Hong Kong free and self-governed, and more importantly never belonging to China, then why should we think they would they fight for Taiwan that we can justifiably argue belongs to China."

Taiwan sat in the middle of the First Island Chain, which ran through the Japanese archipelago, Luzon in the Philippines, and Borneo, terminating with the Vietnamese coastline, and was the key chokepoint to limit China's maritime exit points into the Philippine

Sea and the Indian Ocean. The taking of Taiwan was key to China's control of the shipping lanes of the Far East.

He continued, "China must be made whole by reuniting with Hong Kong and Taiwan to further dismantle the illusion of white supremacy. It was an illusion that only the West has the leadership and ideas and subsequently the answers to a better life, particularly the illusion that is democracy. The Americans must be openly humiliated by making them look impotent in responding to China's military takeover of Taiwan. I will know when the timing is right. Further, if the United Nations readily accepts the Law of the Sea and ownership of lands two hundred miles out from a country's shoreline, then I would extend China's shorelines if I must dig up half the ocean's bottom for the sand to do it. I would make the world acknowledge the legal rights of China to the islands in dispute in the Asian Pacific Rim, by force, if necessary. It was time for China to step out of its comfort zone and see if the world is ready for a new and aggressive China, one that is centered on the Han Chinese majority and loyalty to the Communist Party? The party would control the education and the industries of the people and rein in private sectors to include shutting down of dissenting voices. We would target minorities for assimilation using surveillance and restrictions;

minorities such as the Turkic Uyghur people living in an autonomous territory in Northwest China along the ancient silk road trade route to the Middle East and Tibetans spinning their prayer wheels in Lari, a small Buddhist monastery in the Qinghai province.

We would become technologically superior and strengthen the connections of the civilian and military sectors. We would upgrade our military and extend their influence and reach by establishing out-of-country ports and military bases. China would not take a second seat in this new world order."

CHAPTER FIVE

NIKOLAI BASKOV,

The Russian, Japan (2014)

After leaving the Kuril Islands, the Russian settled in a safe house in Kobe, Japan, and felt comfortable he had succeeded in his escape. It had been six months and there was nothing to make him think otherwise. He had two new and separate identifications to include passports and money to support both identities. The fighting part of the war ended without any noticeable outcry from the Americans about him being alive. Russia listed him as a war casualty and the Russian President openly blamed him as a rogue general who aggressively overstepped his authority in the Kuril Islands and wrongly involved Russia in the war.

As Japan's sixth-largest Japanese city, Kobe was Nikolai's first choice for a safe house when he and Anton originally made such choices. The city always brought a smile to his face when he thought about it being a designated nuclear-free zone. His thoughts turned inward, "Money can't bring back the loss of humanity I suffered in that snake pit of an orphanage or my inability now to control the resultant anger, but it did allow me a chance to remain sane. Now I have another chance at revenge." He missed Anton and the anger swelled within him. He was proud of his discipline for remaining out of sight, but now bored from the months of hiding and limited human contact.

He was extremely fit from the excessive exercise in trying to fill the many boring hours alone in the safe house, but proud of his discipline and ability to tire himself out to sleep naturally. Daily swimming in the pool provided was especially helpful, but he missed his time at the Arima Onsen, the famous volcanically furnished hot springs he frequently used while visiting Kobe at another time in his life and eating the world-famous Kobe beef at the fabulous restaurants he had enjoyed over the years. Kobe was a cosmopolitan city with lots to do and see. He needed a drink and craved human contact and a good time. "I'll be especially cautious," he told himself.

As night felt, he left the house to find a bar, a drink, and the human contact he now felt he deserved. Nikolai headed down toward the docks where activity always abounded in his past visits, as Kobe was the fourth-largest container port in the world. He found a bar he thought was suitable and entered. He chose a table near the rear and took a seat facing the front door and away from most of the crowd that seemed to prefer the front window locations and bar stools.

A noisy group of three Japanese dockworkers were three tables over bemoaning their union and work conditions and seemed far ahead of the other patrons in their consumption of alcohol. A small group of Japanese bikers occupied the dart game and bar chairs towards the right front. The remainder of the crowd was scattered sparsely throughout the front bar area.

With a few drinks and growing memories of Anton, the tears came unexpectantly. The bar atmosphere, the loud conversations, and the barking of orders to the barmaids added to the return of his thoughts of Anton and the orphanage in Budapest, Romania. From that moment, their lives and thoughts were as one, and their loyalty to one another was unbreakable. They had endured and lived through the worst depravities of the guards and administrators with no food, comfort, or the niceties of life most people take for granted. Many of the children who died before the collapse of the Nicolae Ceausescu government had brought attention to their plight.

As a result, the Palace of the Parliament in Bucharest provided no memories of pride and beauty for most of the Romanian people. It was built by communist leader Nicolae Ceausescu on the backs of his people as a monument to those who had little to eat and were denied basic needs such as hot water and heat. The second-largest building in the world by surface area, second only to the Pentagon, its gold and marble pale in comparison to the joys, hopes, and freedoms Romanian citizens are again discovering after Ceausescu's reign of brutality and repression ended in 1989.

Nikolai could never contain the tears once started; it was a part of him. It wasn't a sobbing type of cry he made, but merely a saddened face with water dropping in a constant stream from his eyes. Unfortunately, there were those who thought these tears a weakness. The three dockworkers had now approached Nikolai's table, the closest man carrying what looked like a bourbon on ice in a cheap standard plastic drinking glass with a straw.

The first man stopped in front of Nikolai watching as if in wonder and took another slow draw from his straw. Nikolai knew men like this, a man who likes to watch but not participate, who lives vicariously through others and is in two words, a coward. He was not a threat. Nikolai could see the bartender now moving rapidly to his cell phone to seek help.

The second man, clutching the neck of a beer bottle firmly in his right-hand grip and getting madder by the moment, stepped around the first man and banged his beer bottle down loudly onto the table while looking Nikolai straight in the eyes. Some of the beer splashed out of the bottle and onto the table and somehow the bottle did not break or spill onto Nikolai. The man did not release the neck of the bottle but leaned into it and further into Nikolai's face. He was obviously drunk and no longer in control of himself.

He slurred in English, "Look at what we have here boys, a crybaby!" he slowly turned his head away from Nikolai to the third man approaching on the other side of the Russian. He nodded slowly to him through pursed lips to acknowledge his intent and expected support. He then leaned in close again, looking Nikolai straight in the eyes, and repeated in English, "a crybaby." At the same time, he raised his left index finger towards Nikolai 's face to physically remove a tear from his cheek while leaning forward on the bottle in his right hand, demonstrating to his buddies what a coward he had in front of him. It was a move he immediately regretted.

Before the second man's finger left Nikolai's cheek, the beer bottle he was holding smashed against his forehead and his head was pulled forward violently into the table. Blood spurted instantly from the pieces of glass now sticking out of the man's throat. His mouth openly gasped for air and his eyes showed disbelief that he was dying as he grasped at a shard of glass from the neck of the beer bottle embedded in the center of his throat. Several cell phones around him started to snap pictures and record the event.

The third man tripped backward grasping for a gun tucked in the back of his pants and fought the leather jacket that kept him from reaching the handle, but it was too late. A stiletto pierced his chest, and he reeled backwards to the floor dropping hard and took his last breath choking on his own blood trying to flow from his mouth. The first man still stood frozen in place with the drink still at his lips with the straw now dangling from an open mouth into his drink. It was an unmistakable look of fear; he did not move. Nikolai knew that killing him offered no benefit as there were others in the bar that could identify him if it came down to that. Nikolai stared at the first man for a moment and sensed no threat from him or the others around the bar.

Nikolai thought again about killing everyone in the bar for a split second, but there were too many. He had made a mistake. "Damn," he thought, "I cannot afford to have this kind of trouble, especially in a public place with witnesses." He recognized too that the memories of the orphanage came and went at their own times and controlling them was not possible for him. Nikolai tried to dismiss his worries, but they would not go away.

He nodded to the bartender and dropped five hundred dollars on the table, carefully wiping the table down along with his glass. After lifting his glass and taking the last swig, he slowly rose and walked around the table placing his left knee on the top portion of the dead man's chest and forcefully removing his stiletto. He wiped it clean on the man's shirt. He looked around and noted the stunned looks on the bystanders' faces. The bartender had already made his call for help and did not move. Blood was now pouring from the removed stiletto onto the floor. He looked around one last time and carefully walked around the gathering pool of blood and left the bar. The bikers recognized his skill and willingness to kill when none was warranted and gave him plenty of room with no trouble.

Back at the safe house, Nikolai knew he must leave Japan immediately. It was only a matter of time before the safe house was found. He could not believe that what should have been a simple night out turned into two deaths. This was not like him, but he felt there was no choice after the broken glass became embedded in the first man's throat ensuring his death. Then again, he was not used to being in the shadows, and maybe that was affecting his judgment. He knew he must rethink his strategy, but for the moment, he needed to find safety in another country and another safe house.

Three weeks later, the ongoing police investigation of the bar murders identified the Russian from a cell phone photo taken by a customer at the time of the murders. The American Embassy confirmed the identification. The CIA confirmed him as a wanted man and received from Interpol a Red Notice List for Nikolai Baskov, the Russian. An all-out manhunt was conducted by law enforcement within Japan with no success. Nikolai Baskov, the Russian, was positively identified as the killer with his present location listed as unknown.

CIA Headquarters

At CIA headquarters, Harry Snead blew out a sigh of "the world is getting complicated" and reached for a glass and openly poured himself a shot of Maker's Mark bourbon-whisky private selection. This was now his favorite drink since the pure bourbon he once enjoyed and exclusively produced by Maker's Mark from the spring waters of Marion County in Loretto, Kentucky, was no longer available. He made the obvious observation, "What a world!"

CHAPTER SIX

IVAN IVANOVITCH,

PRESIDENT OF RUSSIA (2014-2015)

Sitting at his desk, President Ivanovitch cupped his hands behind the back of his head and rocked slightly forward and backward with his lips pulled together in deep thought picturing the future Soviet Union with Tzar Ivanovitch in charge, the first occupant of the House of Ivanovitch in his vision of a new Russia ruled only by tzars. Clouding his vision was his research on the heirs of the old tzars and finding no one to marry or with enough credentials on the male side to use in eliminating the Russian democracy. The 1917 revolution was quite thorough in killing almost everyone. He thought, "I would find a way or the House of Ivanovitch would have to be a new bloodline and acceptance would be harder."

With his dream of being a tzar given due diligence, President Ivanovitch turned his thoughts to the present and Ukraine. He thought, "Ukraine needs my immediate attention as the vulnerable underbelly of Russia and is the key to unlocking the doors to the other thirteen countries that originally composed the former Soviet empire, like Armenia, Azerbaijan, Belarus, Estonia, Georgia, Kazakhstan, Kyrgyzstan, Latvia, Lithuania, Moldova, Tajikistan, Turkmenistan, and Uzbekistan. The old USSR must be made whole again and the time for action is now."

His thoughts were interrupted when one of his administrative assistants knocked and entered the room handing him a standard yellow envelope containing two Red Notice Lists and the accompanying staff notes. The first Red Notice List he extracted from the folder was on Anton Lupu, the Wolf, and the accompanying staff noted on his adventures in the Maldives with the CIA. President Ivanovitch was shocked that the Wolf was alive, but he was not shocked when looking at Interpol's second Red Notice List on General Baskov and the staff notes on his killing spree in Japan. He marveled at both of their survival skills and thought, "a new breed of cats with more than nine lives," and smiled to himself. He instantly chastised himself for using such an overused proverb as a commoner would do.

He summoned his aide, Major Natasha Ivanov, and handed her Interpol's Red Notice Lists on the Wolf and General Baskov. She could not contain her excitement and apologized for such to the President. He said, "I want you to find General Baskov." She was excited and quickly got up to leave. He said purposely, "I'm not finished." She gathered herself tucking her military skirt beneath her legs and sat down again. He now knew she was most vulnerable, as the carrot, in the form of her lover Nikolai Baskov, had been provided as an incentive for her to accept the rest of his plan.

He proceeded to outline his need for her to take responsibility for a plan of action in Crimea as the first step in returning Ukraine to Russia. Without saying this to her, he saw this as a first step in confirming her allegiance to him and demonstrating what other abilities she may bring to the table. He then outlined his broad plan for a new tzar-led Soviet Union, with him as the first tzar of the House of Ivanovitch.

Natasha listened in shock, but was somehow not surprised, as it seemed to her that all the men in her life were demented. She thought, "At least this time she would not be trying to destroy her beloved Russia," and she agreed to assist and help where she was needed. She thought, "This may be the only way I can walk out of this room alive, but there is a lot of the plan I can readily support." Major Natasha Ivanov expressed to the President "I am excited with the opportunity to prove my value to you and to serve my beloved country." President Ivanovitch said, "We'll see," and dismissed her.

Russian Imperialist Movement

Major Ivanov reached out and secretly found and negotiated the help of a little-known extreme-right white supremacy group based in St. Petersburg, Russia, called the Russian Imperialist Movement. Her plan was for RIM to work within the borders of Crimea as an insurgency group that supported pro-Russian Ukrainian citizens. President Ivanovitch would then use this as an excuse to insert Russian troops back into Crimea as a need for the protection of its citizens when the Ukrainians responded.

RIM promoted ethnic Russian nationalism, advocated the restoration of Russia's tzarist regime, and sought to fuel white supremacy extremism in the West. The group agreed to readily give their support to President Ivanovitch as the next tzar but needed money and proper papers for infiltrating an agent into the United States in return for their service. They had plans to expand their influence worldwide and use the Ukraine as a training ground to consolidate, organize, and breed the growing right-wing malcontents. They would willingly act as the 'tip-of-the-spear' for President Ivanovitch to grow their membership and were serious about supporting the return of tzar rule, just not President Ivanovitch as he had no tzar blood in him.

When briefed of her plan, President Ivanovitch was pleased and considered RIM a group that presented no threat to him but could clearly pander to the Ukrainian pro-Russian population, so he agreed. William J. Sparks, not his real name, was picked as the RIM representative and was sent to America.

Over the following year-and-a-half, RIM quickly grew in membership and became a fixture in eastern Ukraine and a hub for networking, training, and fighting on both sides of the conflict, cultivating skills and connections that strengthened white-supremacy extremist networks worldwide which were becoming more violent, more organized, and more capable. With RIM's success, President Ivanovitch, ostensibly under its military partnership with Ukraine to protect its citizens from extremists, sent Russian troops into the Crimean Peninsula.

President Ivanovitch's military action was successful as there was no opposition, and in July 2015, President Ivanovitch declared Crimea as fully integrated back into Russia. For President Ivanovitch, the announcement was the second step in Russia's take back of Ukraine after the agreement with RIM. He was pleased with Major Ivanov's demonstrated abilities and told her so. In retaliation for the invasion,

Ukraine cut off all water to Crimea. To emphasize Russia's intent to keep Crimea, President Ivanovitch built a twelve-plus mile railway bridge from Russia to Crimea to ensure delivery of needed supplies, including water, necessary to sustain the Russian troops now stationed there.

CIA Headquarters

At Langley, Harry noted Russia's successful invasion of Crimea and said out loud to his lead staffer James Dean, "Russia was feeling their oats, and rightly so. They have taken back the Crimea and they knew we could not justify a military response. And I'm not sure of what a military response would have gained us if anything. I was shocked when they were successfully able to jam our GPS during their occupation in Ukraine. That is a big step for them. They also came out of the war smelling like a rose and have successfully started a five-year military capability upgrade. Yes sir," he said out loud, but mainly to himself, "they must be feeling pretty good about themselves."

The Arctic

In the Arctic, the Russian icebreaker easily split the thin ice in advance of the product ships as it cleared all obstacles as it did an eight-knot speed hugging the Siberian coastline. Only the indigenous people remembered the real cold as the ever-increasing heating of the earth has melted the Siberian coastline and made each passing year an ever-widening waterway for bigger and faster ships to service the needs of the West. Polar bears and other animals of the Arctic found themselves riding break-away melting icebergs to ever warmer areas and running through the middle of settlements, too disoriented to understand that their house was on fire.

The Arctic Ocean, one of five oceans worldwide, the smallest, shallowest, and coldest, was heating up rapidly as the world's carbon dioxide count rapidly multiplied. The oceans absorbed approximately ninety percent of all extra carbon pollution in the air, as well as much of the carbon dioxide itself. Irreversible climate change could only be slowed if the world would stop the excesses. However, for people like President Ivanovitch, the melting of the ice presented opportunities for more power and wealth. He estimated the value of Arctic mineral resources alone at thirty trillion dollars.

President Ivanovitch shook his head and thought, "If swimming at the beaches in Siberia in May would soon be the norm, then there would be no ice left and only water." President Ivanovitch was thinking of all the buildings and pipelines that were constructed on permafrost solidly frozen for hundreds of thousands of years and the large oil storage tank near the

Arctic city of Norilsk that just toppled over due to melting permafrost. He thought, "The end result of a melting ice and permafrost would be quite a mess, but Russia would be best prepared for the future it holds." Russia needed the rich resources of oil and minerals and control of fishing, tourism, and shipping with the expanding opportunities there because of the melting ice.

President Ivanovitch was proud of his scientists for foreseeing the melting of the ice and the opening of a northern commercial shipping route to the West. Following the annexation of Crimea, President Ivanovitch submitted a bid to the United Nations for vast territories in the Arctic, claiming over 463,000 square miles of Arctic Sea shelf, extending more than three hundred and fifty nautical miles from shore.

He thought, "The concept of 'Global Warming' was real, but not correctly interpreted by Western scientists who seem to have a more political agenda. Russian scientists had forecast that the earth was merely returning to its normal temperature as it was when the dinosaurs roamed the earth. Their interpretation allowed advance planning to dominate in the Artic in expecting the ice to melt."

Sixty-six million years ago, an asteroid hit the Gulf of Mexico. This asteroid was the size of a small country; the resultant effect of debris in the atmosphere deflected sunlight from reaching the earth and brought on the ICE AGE which wiped out most of mankind and animals, including the dinosaurs. The debris dissipated over time, and as a result, the world waters have risen over four hundred feet and are still rising, as is the heat.

There were bumps for Russian scientists along the way like the asteroid that exploded in Tunguska Siberian-Russia in 1908, and the nuclear accident at Chernobyl. The Siberian asteroid was about one hundred and eighty-five times more powerful than the Hiroshima atomic bomb that the Americans dropped at the end of World War II. The five-hundred-mile fireball and explosion destroyed over two thousand square miles of remote forest. The knowledge gained from the explosions in Siberia and the nuclear accident at Chernobyl provided the Russian Academy of Scientists much needed additional information in properly defining this new term 'Global Warming.' This allowed Russian scientists to be far ahead of the United States and other Western countries in recognizing the Arctic's potential as the ice melted.

The Arctic Council members included Canada, Denmark, Finland, Iceland, Norway, the United States, Russia, and Sweden. China participated in events as a self-appointed observer. Although China's most northern point was nine hundred miles away from the Arctic Circle, it declared itself as a near-Arctic state and sought and obtained membership. The Council's purpose was to focus on climate change, rules for sustainable economic development, and the welfare of indigenous communities. This focus has shifted more to security matters for most of the participants as Russia pushed hard to claim territorial dominance.

President Ivanovitch foresaw the Northern Sea Route as requiring Moscow's authorization for foreign vessels to navigate along with it. He would justify the new fees by proclaiming that "the complex ice conditions make it necessary to organize safe shipping." Russia's stated position was that "this is our territory, our land. We oversee keeping the Arctic coast safe."

In 2014, President Ivanovitch started and completed the rebuilding of Nagurskoye Air Base, Russia's northernmost military base, and a similar base on Kotelny Island on the eastern end of the 3,470-mile Northern Sea Route, both with missiles and radar and a runway that can handle all types of aircraft, including nuclear-capable strategic bombers. His plan included the building of new ports along the route to handle the increase in traffic, and the newest ones being armed to include missiles. President Ivanovitch knew that only a polar icebreaker could provide year-round access to the Arctic even with melting ice and the United States was far behind in ships and capability. Russian icebreakers like the Russian 50 Let Pobedy were capable of plowing through ice sheets as thick as 16.4 feet.

But, unlike Antarctica, the United States had sovereign territory to protect in the Arctic and security needs were paramount as the ice melts. There was also the question of Greenland's strategic location for port facilities to the eastern United States and rare earth and other minerals. Russia assumed the leadership of the Arctic Council in May 2021 for two years and President Ivanovitch knew that this would be the time to strengthen Russia's grip there.

CHAPTER SEVEN

ANTON LUPU,

THE WOLF, DELHI, INDIA, (2013-2015)

With the Maldives behind him, the Wolf moved northeast to his safe house in New Delhi, city and national capital territory, north-central India. The city of Delhi consisted of two components: Old Delhi, in the north, the historic city; and New Delhi, in the south, since 1947 the capital of India, built in the first part of the 20th century as the capital of British India. He left Philippe Adnan, his Maldives safe house manager behind in a rented establishment in downtown Male City to wait for further instruction. He would be safe there as no one should be looking for him.

The safe house in Delhi, with approximately two acres was originally purchased for a little over a million dollars and considered a moderately high-end property at the time. Since the purchase, the property had increased in price tenfold; the house contained four bedrooms and a two-car garage. The garage housed two cars that were purchased on the black market at the same time the house was purchased, one a Mercedes-Benz second-generation passenger van, and the second a luxury sports car. The Middle East banker now on the run was responsible for the house and grounds and contracted with an agency caretaker staff for upkeep. He had flown in once a year for oversight and needed property and maintenance requirements.

The Wolf knew that the American CIA agent Sam Mountain had somehow made his favorite race boat and lady assassins go missing in the Maldives. His spy in the President's office assured him that he nor the President had any knowledge or information concerning a race boat or two missing terrorists and that the President would have had to approve any operation of that magnitude and an official report filed. Anton knew that CIA operative Sam Mountain was responsible, and it bothered him that he just didn't knew how he did it. The Wolf thought, "I'll give Sam Mountain credit, he's smart. Somewhere along life's journey, we are due to meet, and may the best man win."

Shortly after his arrival in Delhi, the Wolf realized that he needed to buy another property to use as a research laboratory to explore a new idea in the sale of petroleum or crude oil. He wanted to pitch an idea to Chairman Li of China as a partnership to avoid United States oil sanctions. As time was short, he requested that the Far East banker, Mr. Fredrick Wilcox III, presently located in Singapore, China took on the responsibility of finding him another Middle Eastern banker to administer his asset and holdings.

Within days, Mr. Wilcox had worked his connections and found who he considered the perfect candidate, a Ms. Charlotte Hallstrom, an MBA Finance Honor Graduate of the University of Pennsylvania (Wharton), recently divorced, no children, and after ten years of nine to five corporate workings in New York and getting nowhere, had decided to cut all ties and look outside the United States to broaden her perspective and hopefully find something exciting.

In a virtual interview, Mr. Wilcox outlined the facts of the job to her in the broadest of terms. After hearing him out, she stated she was interested and would accept his offer of being flown to Delhi, India for a face-to-face meeting to hear the full details of the job, particularly the part about the work that could only be discussed in person.

Landing in India, she was met by Mr. Wilcox, who had flown in the previous day to handle the interview at the Wolf's request. Mr. Wilcox was picked up by the Wolf at the airport in the van and stayed the night at the safehouse.

The next day, Mr. Wilcox took the van to the airport to meet her upon arrival and take her immediately to a reserved room in a high-end restaurant in New Delhi where for the next hour he briefed her on the details of the job and addressed her concerns.

She knew that the man she would be working for was and is a criminal, Mr. Wilcox asked her "if she wishes to continue the interview?" After some deliberation, she said "Yes, if I can feel safe, and the criminal activity is not something I consider nasty like drugs, selling of women or weapons, destroying the environment, or extorting people for money."

Mr. Wilcox could not help but be amused and said, "I can see it would be hard to be a criminal around you." She didn't smile back. "Do you wish to meet this criminal?" he said, "or do you wish for me to take you back to the airport?"

Before she could answer he said, "I would say this, he is not the type of criminal you may imagine, but he can be dangerous and has rules and demands of total loyalty that cannot be broken. This is a lifetime decision." There was a thoughtful hesitation, and she said, "I will meet this criminal."

Later that day, Anton Lupu arrived at the restaurant in his sports car for the prearranged dinner in an isolated room of the same downtown Delhi restaurant. While eating their meal, Anton found Charlotte Hallstrom to be a well-rounded individual, articulate, and very smart. After dinner, Anton gave her the same speech he gave all his other bankers and safe house managers. As his final way of shocking her into a complete reality, he provided her with a copy of his Interpol Red Notice List. She stared at it, breathed in deeply, paused, looked up to meet his eyes, and said, "If I say no, would I walk out of here alive?"

The Wolf answered quickly, "Yes, with conditions."

She cut him off. "Good answer; I think I know the conditions. It appears that your system is designed for everyone to succeed if I can accept your rules and policies as gospel with a lifetime commitment. I can do the rules, and I would take the risk at face value that you care that we all succeed, and I would say you do pay extremely well. I also assume that you would inform me in due time of the safeguards that are in place to protect me if something did happen to you and or your partner." She then said, "If so, then, yes, I accept the job."

The Wolf tasked her to immediately find the warehouse property he needed, emphasizing to her that time was a crucial factor. The Wolf stated that "he requires a large warehouse for conducting experiments in the mixing of various grades of oil" and, in the next two hours, outlined the details in notes and handwritten drawings. He would leave her on her own to accomplish this task as he would be able to tell a lot more about her decision-making and other abilities. The Wolf provided a hotel stay for his new banker in a prominent downtown Delhi hotel while he and Mr. Wilcox would continue to occupy "other quarters." The safehouse location was of no concern to her at this point in their relationship.

∿∿∿∿∿

Petroleum, or crude oil, is one of seven fossil fuels. There are four grades or types of crude oil: Class A, Class B, Class C, and Class D. It is a smelly, yellow-to-black liquid and is usually found in underground areas called reservoirs. The largest share of crude is used for energy carriers that can be combined into gasoline, jet fuel, diesel, and heating oils. Heavier products are used to make tar, asphalt, paraffin wax, and lubricating oils. Most refined products and a lot of high-quality, light crude oils are included in Class A. Class A crude oils are highly fluid, tend to be clear, and can spread at a rapid rate across both water and solid surfaces. This type of crude oil is typically flammable, has a strong smell, a high evaporation rate, and commands the highest market price.

Despite how valuable they are, Class A oils can be extremely toxic to humans, animals, and other organisms and require great attention to safe handling and storage. The density and sulfur content of crude oil are two of the biggest factors that determine its quality. The higher the sulfur content and the heavier the density, the lower quality of the crude oil. Higher-sulfur crude oil is cheaper as it produces larger amounts of toxic emissions than others, it can damage refinery equipment because it has a higher rate of oxidation and corrosion, and a higher sulfur content has fewer hydrocarbons. These components are what allow for the combustion of fuel within an engine meaning that a lower-quality fuel would be less efficient.

The Nigerian oil that the Wolf was used to working with was a Class A fuel, light and sweet and free of sulfur. Nigeria is the largest producer of sweet oil in OPEC. This sweet oil is similar in composition to petroleum extracted from the North Sea and known as "Bonny light." Although the grade of the oil is a major factor in its price there are other considerations in pricing such as where the oil is produced, transportation costs, political and economic conditions in the regions where the oil is sold, and the ease of refining the oil.

~~~~~~

Before they left the restaurant, the Wolf handed her a packet containing $250,000 American dollars and told her to go to PCH Auto World - Luxury Car Dealers in Delhi in the morning and buy an upscale car. He told her she could keep any money left over. He said, "The head of my new company must project a sense of success and wealth." She understood that money was not a concern for the Wolf, except that the source could not to be traced back to him. She was sure he had provided her untraceable cash, but she knew too, that he was very concerned that she maintained a low profile to not draw attention to herself or the Wolf's business. She would know what car was appropriate to buy when she got there and what amount of money to keep, if by chance this was a test of her awareness and decision making.

While she worked on the task at hand, Anton and the Far East banker would jointly review all the Wolf's Middle East financial records and holdings presently left unattended to by the London banker, who currently resided in the Wolf's safe house outside Bangkok, Thailand.

Middle East Holdings

The subsequent review of the financial holdings by the Wolf and Mr. Wilcox showed no improprieties or theft. With the review completed, Mr. Willcox was thanked for his time and was asked to return to his duties in Singapore. The Wolf would drive him to the airport.

Prior to his leaving, the Wolf informed Mr. Wilcox of the safe house in the Maldives that must be closed and of its former manager staying in a rental apartment in downtown Male City. He asked Mr. Wilcox to "discreetly move Mr. Philippe Adnan to manage the Delhi safe house upon Wolf's departure from India, and until that time, keep the safehouse separated from the Middle East holdings and under his direct supervision. He said, "the Maldives manager can move into the safe house with Charlotte if she proves her value to us, and after I finish my business here until Charlotte can successfully close the warehouse and move to Singapore for you to complete her training. We can then decide her new management location."

The final task of Mr. Wilcox, and another expansion of his knowledge of the organization and his duties, was to prepare the necessary arrangements for Wolf's visit to Bangkok, Thailand to visit the London banker when the Wolf had completed his work in India. The Wolf provided him with the necessary information for his contact in Bangkok, Thailand. The London banker was a wanted criminal now and could not be of further use to Wolf's organization, but he had fulfilled his obligations to the Wolf and the Wolf wanted him to be assured he would be protected for his loyalty.

The Wolf would stop in Bangkok when he left India to assure the London banker of his continued support and the banker's need to maintain a low profile with anonymity to stay alive. Although keeping him alive was risky, the Wolf would keep his promises to his bankers and safe house managers if they were loyal and followed the rules.

The Warehouse

India, with the world's second-largest population of 1.3 billion people to that of China's 1.4 billion people and the city of New Delhi with a goodly share of those people, was the perfect hiding place for the Wolf from the prying American 'eyes in the sky.' The overcrowded conditions, poverty, and lack of known CIA agents on the ground offered a more safe and more secure environment for the Wolf.

His new Middle East banker quickly located a warehouse on a property on the Yamuna River in New Delhi that meshed with his operational needs. The eight-hundred and fifty-five-miles long Yamuna River was the major contributor to the Ganges River and solely flowed through India. With over fifty million people dependent on the water of the Yamuna, the Yamuna has developed into one of the most polluted rivers in the world. New Delhi, the capital of India, dumped much of its waste directly into the river, generating almost two million liters per day of sewage. Another issue was that the water remained stagnant for almost nine months a year, leaving the sewage to rot leaving a thick white foam that covered much of the river around New Delhi. It was a perfect location for the mixing of oils as it received little environmental attention from the local government.

The newly purchased warehouse was large enough to accommodate an apartment and office space at the inside back where Charlotte Hallstrom would eventually move from the hotel to directly manage the employees, warehouse equipment buys, and refurbishment details. The office space, when built, would be two connecting offices, one for her and one for the Wolf, with each having direct access to the rear parking lot to accommodate a separate outside backlot entryway. The employees would be provided parking at the front entrance. A common area wait room would be provided in front of the two offices. Anton would keep himself apart from the various contractors and employees as much as possible to prevent a chance of being recognized. He trusted the new banker to be competent in getting what he needed to be done. She would be the boss and face of the company.

With the hand-drawn plans provided by the Wolf, the new banker worked with an architect until final plans were approved by the Wolf. Contractors were then hired by Charlotte to work in twenty-four-hour-a-day shifts to provide the refurbishment needed. Equipment was ordered and contractors were hired to receive and install it. The many large stainless steel oil vats proved troublesome, but with money as an incentive a company was found that was willing to make, deliver and install them.

The six company engineers were hired one year before the company was fully operational to learn from the contractors as the equipment was being installed on how to operate and maintain the various vats, to load and refill the trucks, and to meet safety and environmental concerns in the heating and movement of the oils. It was decided to maintain the three-shift work schedules with the two engineers on each shift. The remaining workers were brought in six months prior to being fully operational to be trained by their shift engineers. All employees were informed that the jobs were temporary, but each employee was guaranteed a minimum of two years of pay plus benefits even if the desired solution was found sooner and the business closed. By the end of 2014, and because of Charlotte's organizational and leadership skills, the warehouse was fully operational.

One newly hired engineer was insistent on knowing the intended purpose of the research before agreeing to work and even threatened to go to the authorities if not told. Charlotte informed him that if he would come back in the morning, maybe something could be worked out, but she needed time to consider what could be offered to him. He agreed to meet her the following morning. Charlotte had made the excuse to talk to the Wolf about what the engineer was demanding as she was not sure how to handle it. With little thought, the Wolf told her to find a lawyer to draw up a paper of agreement for silence by the engineer in return for providing him the information he sought. He added, "be sure you get a nasty lawyer with large financial consequences if he breaks the agreement and leaks the information."

That night, the engineer, in leaving his house and walking to his community red, white, and blue free-standing mailbox, was unceremoniously killed by a hit and run the vehicle. The one neighbor and only eyewitness described the vehicle as a small truck. He said, "You know, the truck with the rear bed and wooden rails that is loaded down with portable toilet tied together." The police reported that neither the driver nor the truck was identified or found.

When the Wolf arrived at his office the following morning Charlotte entered immediately tearing up a piece of paper and saying, "I guess I won't need this letter of agreement with the engineer that I spent half the night finding a lawyer who would open his office for an obscene amount of money and write. He was killed by a hit-and-run vehicle last night. I called him to tell him to come in early today and a policeman answered and told me what had happened after I had told him why I was calling."

The Wolf said, "I want you to quickly respond to his family and offer to pay the funeral expenses and give them a stipend of money, ostensibly to acknowledge his hiring and him being one of the family even though he had not yet started his new job."

The Middle East manager assumed the Wolf was just being generous and it made her proud to be working for him. The Wolf did not know if the engineer had told his family or anyone else that he had threatened the Wolf's company with going to the police, but he wanted to get out in front of this possible issue by having the family thinking positively about Charlotte and the company.

Earlier

Anton had gotten the idea of mixing the different grades of oils from flipping television channels one day in a hotel stay and watched, for whatever reason, an American show called

'Moonshiners.' Master distillers in the hills of Kentucky were using a three-barrel process of mixing different liquor proofs. The result was a final product that retained the higher-grade proof rating, but lowered production costs considerably by absorbing a percentage of the lesser-grade liquor without a drop in the higher rating of the proof. In other words, the distillers had found the perfect mixing ratios through years of experimenting and experience to maximize their profits and the Wolf was determined to duplicate the process using oils.

Anton recognized that the research could probably have been done in smaller portions than the enormously big and expensive vats of oil being used, but Anton wanted to give the final products every opportunity to break down in storage under extreme environmental conditions such as heat as found on a product ship. If the mixed oil had the potential to break down or separate upon storage or delivery, he wanted to know now and not from a customer.

After another year of experimentation with the oils, he found the combination of mixtures he was seeking and knew it would immediately change the world of oil when implemented. He thought, "It was almost two years since he had arrived from the Maldives in India, but the findings were well worth the effort spent here. Before my discovery, oils were merely pulled from the ground and sold for their value as graded. This would not be how it would be done in the not-so-distant future."

He felt the surge of accomplishment that his labs had achieved. The computer would establish for him a matrix of the countries that sell oils, the rating grades of those oils, and the percentage of lesser grade oils that can be mixed with each higher-grade oil to maximize the profit when sold. He found no additional problems in the storage of mixed oils or of them breaking down by applying various degrees of heat.

He thought, "The only factor missing in controlling the international market is having an oil supply on hand to flood the market when necessary to move market prices at will, and that is where China is needed. The ready availability of oil is how OPEC currently controls pricing and manipulates the world market. I am about to put them and their hedge fund managers and the rich people they support into a tailspin with no way out; I have the same grade of oil product, but it would be the cheapest."

The Gala
The Wolf had the Middle East banker invite all the employees and their wives, including the family of the person run over by the truck, to a mandatory business gala with all the trimmings to include different varieties of food, live

entertainment, and an open bar. No expense was spared to include a $1,500.00 stipend in the invite envelope for personal incidentals like in-home babysitting, grooming, missing time at work, or buying a new wardrobe. The business portion was to start promptly at 5:30 pm, with the doors opening at 5 pm. A separate table was provided for each family. On each table was a packet that said, "DO NOT OPEN UNTIL INSTRUCTED."

At 5:30 pm, Charlotte Hallstrom took the podium and said, "Ladies and gentlemen, I've asked you to join me here tonight so that everyone knows how appreciative I am of the hard work you have given this company. The business model that each of you worked so hard to achieve is now a success, and I promise you that it would revolutionize the world in a positive way. I particularly appreciate the attendance of the spouses here tonight and apologize for use of the word mandatory in your invite, as it was inappropriate. But I feel strongly that you are the heart and soul of our success and need to hear the future of our business directly from me as to prevent any possible misunderstandings in communication with your spouse."

She continued, "Tonight, I am closing the doors of my business as we have accomplished our purpose." Murmurs and loud cries were heard in the crowd. "On each family table is a packet that I ask you not to open for a moment as to not disturb others around you while I continue. Every employee was informed when hired that this day was coming. The packet contains the promise I made to each person hired. In the packet in front of you is a check for your payment for the balance of the second year. In that there is only a month left in the second year, I have enclosed a full paycheck for the third year. Additionally, you will find two more checks, one to provide comparable pay for the benefits that you would be losing and the second one just to say again, thank you. You may now open your packet if you have not already done so."

She continued, "At this time and while you are opening your packets, I would ask that the food and beverage servers and the band return to the room. This would close our business portion of the evening and again thank you for being here and have an enjoyable evening." There was no applause as she left the podium as people were stunned and busy opening their packets. She departed the building for her awaiting vehicle with the Wolf as the driver. As she opened the passenger door and entered, he gave her a slight smile and nodded showing her that she did well.

The employees and spouses were in shock and scrambling to find out what is in the packet, all figuring they have been somehow scammed.

But there was no mass explosion of protest when the families saw the size of the checks. There was apprehension among many that the checks would bounce the following morning, but some took heart later from the family of the deceased employee of how well they were treated. Most employees realized that they must wait until the morning and put aside their worry for the moment as having no control of the situation and tried to enjoy the band, food, and drink provided.

The Wolf knew that the wives would not sleep until the banks opened the following morning and their husbands were the first in line, hangovers aside, to see that the checks were valid. The Middle East banker was correct in suggesting that the scheduling of the gala be on a day whereby the banks would be open the following morning for normal business. Having the employees wait over a weekend might have led to unforeseen problems due to stress. A cash handout did not seem appropriate as more people would have partied hard risking something bad happening to them or their money on their way home. Although providing checks was not a perfect solution, it was greatly appreciated when everyone found out the following day that the checks were good.

With his objectives in India accomplished, the Wolf had the Far East banker implement his travel arrangements to Bangkok, Thailand for a late morning departure as it was about a seven-hour flight, and he needed a good night's sleep. He wanted the London banker to understand, if he didn't already, that he was being hunted by almost every major government in the world, and that he was alive because he had followed the rules.

Charlotte had made herself comfortable in one of the bedrooms in the safehouse and he was in another bedroom after a nightcap and general discussion of what was expected to happen in the morning and the following few days. "You will drive me to the airport in the morning in your car. You will then take your car back to the dealership where it was purchased, and it would be bought back from you. I have arranged a fair price and you may keep the proceeds. My black Mercedes van from the safehouse is currently being serviced there, it has been approved for your use after you have sold them back your car. Later in the week, Mr. Wilcox will call and request that you pick up the new Delhi safehouse manager from the airport. He will stay at the safehouse with you. After you have successfully shut down the warehouse, Mr. Wilcox will provide all necessary arrangements for your move to Singapore and the finishing of your training. The new manager will take you to the airport."

CHAPTER EIGHT

NIKOLAI BASKOV,

THE RUSSIAN-THE ROAD TO RUSSIA (2015)

After leaving Japan and having now earned Interpol's most dangerous man in the world classification, General Nikolai Baskov made his way down the Asian coastline of the South China Sea to the Singapore safe house. The time spent in hiding and travel gave the Russian reason to acknowledge that hiding once again in a safe house was not for him. He was an assassin and a warrior and needed the action no matter the risk. Adding to this self-reflection was the knowledge of his burning desire for revenge against the world that hung over him like the Grim Reaper wanted to swing his scythe to reap the souls of sinners. He knew that revenge would never happen if he was hiding in a safe house somewhere. He had nowhere to go that was safe and he picked up the telephone.

On the other end of the line, Natasha answered, "Major Ivanov." Baskov said, "It's

Nikolai," as he heard the choked response of the welcome gladness of him having call. "I am so glad you are alive. I just couldn't let you destroy my Russia and maybe the world when I realized you had chosen death over my love for you and a new life with me." There was no immediate answer and then he said, "You betrayed me."

Natasha instinctively realized from the tone of the response that this experience had further pushed Nikolai towards paranoia. Natasha said emphatically, "No, you betrayed me. I was ready to kill the president of my beloved Russia for you. I was all in and ready to even die for you, but you betrayed ME with that sick plan of yours to destroy the world. Destroying the world and your obsession with revenge was and still is more important to you than our love and a future together. You even dragged Anton down with you against his will. Anton wanted to live! He had found some joy in his life, but you couldn't even give him a future. He belonged to you like a possession. He was willing to die for you, not because he wanted to, but because he believed that he owed his life to you. And for what? So, that you could kill him rather than the guards in that horrible orphanage. You don't offer anybody that is close to you a way out of your spiraling out-of-control cesspool of hate." She realized that her voice had risen to almost a shout, and she shut up.

There was a moment of silence between them, and Nikolai said calmly, "I want to talk to the President. I want back my life in Russia and his trust."

She was holding back her tears as Nikolai had offered her nothing in a personal response to the acknowledgment of her love. She said, "The President has told me to find you, but he didn't say to kill you, but in all likelihood that is what he meant."

Nikolai said, "I realize I was a loose end, being Romanian and leading his armed forces, but he betrayed me. I was loyal. Talk to him. I'll call you back in two days." He disconnected the line.

Natasha thought, "He sounds borderline insane and psychotic at best."

As the phone call ended, Natasha hastily made her way to the president's office. When acknowledged to enter and sit, she told the president about the telephone call from General Baskov. He calmly asked, "And, where is he?" She replied, "He didn't say, but he wanted me to talk with you and would call back in two days for your answer. He wants his old life back to include working directly for you. He pledges his loyalty and feels his straying from you the first time was due to finding out from me that you were going to kill him when he returned from the invasion of the Kuril Islands."

The President said, "And what do you think?"

She replied sadly, "I think he has no other place in this world to go, except Russia, and he is willingly risking you taking his life for a chance at redemption. You are the only one who can provide him sustenance for his vengeful spirit and warrior skills with a country he can freely roam in with some sense of peace."

President Ivanovitch said, "You and him, he is not just returning for love?" mocking her with flamboyant outstretched arms.

She said, "I love him as he is and accept what he is capable of giving me."

He said, So, you want him here?"

She nodded, and he looked at her coldly, paused, and said, "I'll let you know."

When Major Ivanov left the office, the president wondered if supporting her would be a good decision. He thought, "A man like General Baskov, who already tried to kill me once and who without any regret can calmly go about trying to destroy the entire world, is a very dangerous man to keep in line and trust to be loyal." With further thought his best friend comes to mind, Sergei Nilov, who he had sent to Budapest, Romania to oversee embassy security and who had originally recruited the Russian from the Romanian orphanage there and was subsequently killed by the Russian for that very reason. But, at this moment, General

Baskov provided the President with an opportunity to eliminate his biggest critic and political opponent in the forthcoming presidential election. And, if by chance, something did go wrong, General Baskov could easily be blamed as the rouge Russian general responsible for the war and now trying to kill off any further thoughts of Russia becoming a democracy. He made his decision, and the following morning summoned Major Ivanov to his office for his answer.

When she entered his office and was comfortably seated, he said, "I would accept General Baskov's offer with three conditions. One, he would undergo plastic surgery and a complete identity change. Two, a new DNA, the latest capability of our great Russian labs. And three, that you would be held responsible with him for all his actions both as a citizen of Russia and his work for me, to include the successful planning and carryout of his assigned missions, the first being the assassination of Vladimir Potanin.

Vladimir Potanin was a Russian politician opposed to the government of Ivan Ivanovitch. He was liberal and a product of the collapse of the Soviet Union and a supporter of new democratic ideas of government. He was extremely critical of President Ivanovitch and intended to run against him in the forthcoming presidential election.

Natasha did not immediately respond to the President. Her mind was racing, trying to grasp all that is being asked of her, and at the same time give the President an answer. She thought she had garnered the President's loyalty with her good works with RIM and that his fantasy of becoming a tzar was something she could seriously deal with later. But now the President was clearly putting her to the test of her support for him to become tzar on a decision that may not be in the best interest of her beloved Russia. He was asking her to take part in the murder of a Russian citizen and one that may forever kill the democracy effort in Russia. If she did what he asked, her honorable life as a Russian military officer was over and she would be but a pawn of the President. If she did not accept his offer, she knew she would be soon dead, as would Nikolai.

She looked at him directly, knowing that they both knew she had no choice, and replied, "I accept." He replied, "When General Baskov calls, tell him that the three conditions I have outlined would be met after Potanin is successfully killed. If he fails or is captured, he would be arrested as a war criminal and hung. If he is successful and there is no blow-back on me or my administration, and he has completed the three conditions I have outlined, I would welcome him back as a proven asset." He smiled, "It would be good to have my old team back together and working for me this time. Anything else?" She shook her head no and got up and left.

Natasha was ready when Nikolai called the following day as promised. She answered and immediately said, "Your phone may be compromised. During the war, the Americans seemed to know everything we were saying. Go to the nearest Russian embassy and have the Ambassador call me so that I knew where you are. While there I would have you arrested. The Ambassador would facilitate your surrender for war crimes you have committed. I will be in touch." She hung up the phone without waiting for his response. He knew he may be dead by tomorrow, but he must trust that the process before him was for his benefit and was being done in this manner in case the Americans were listening.

By the late morning, the Russian had successfully identified himself to the Russian Ambassador in Singapore, and by late afternoon had received a secured package from Moscow and Major Ivanov with his marching orders. The orders read, "You will proceed to Moscow where you will assassinate Vladimir Potanin. All necessary arrangements for your new identity papers and transportation to Moscow have been arranged. Do not open the envelope found inside your packet until the completion of your mission. The three keys found in your packet are to your temporary safe house, a car for your use that is in the garage at the house, and a locker inside the house that contains your personal weapons and information on Vladimir Potanin's itinerary for his visit to Moscow, February 5th, 2015. The rest is in your hands. I am your handler, and you will report directly to me when this mission is completed." Signed, Major Natasha Ivanov.

Moscow

It was early February and the ice and snow blanketed downtown Moscow. A lull in the weather presented an opportunity for people to emerge from their cocoons for a short walk with their pets or for some badly needed exercise to rejuvenate the senses.

The cold did not deter the Russian as he sat in his car in front of his chosen sniper position from behind a stone wall some one hundred yards on the far side of the Bolshoy Moskvoretsky Bridge, Moscow, Russia, immediately across the river from the hotel where Vladimir Potanin was staying. The Bolshoy Moskvoretsky Bridge is a concrete arch bridge that spans the Moskva River in Moscow, Russia, immediately east of the Kremlin. The bridge connects Red Square with the artsy vibe of Moscow's Zamoskvorechye District. The broken-up ice on the river shimmered from the lights of the bridge and the colorful lights of the city.

Nikolai pulled the thermal blankets tight around him as he could not risk running the car engine with the attention it could draw with the heated engine exhaust against the cold night air. The Russian did not expect to see Vladimir Potanin this late in the evening and in this weather, but would be waiting for his exit from his hotel in the morning.

Potanin was in Moscow helping to organize a rally against the government that was becoming ever more an increasingly authoritarian undemocratic regime, highlighting widespread embezzlement, and profiteering ahead of the Sochi Olympics, and Russian political interference and military involvement in Ukraine. At the same time, Potanin was working on a report demonstrating that Russian troops were fighting alongside pro-Russian rebels in eastern Ukraine, which the Kremlin had been denying.

Potanin was among the few Russian statesmen to vocally criticize the annexation of Crimea by Russia. Potanin stated that he viewed Crimea as an integral part of Ukraine, that he considered its annexation by the Russian Federation to be illegal, and that the people of Crimea and not Russian legislators should decide which country they wanted to live in. He had openly expressed a fear that President Ivanovitch would have him killed.

The unexpected lull in the weather allowed Potanin an opportunity to get out of his hotel just before midnight for a needed stretch and fresh air walk. It was late, but he was not expecting trouble as the weather, security of his travel arrangements, being in the heart of Moscow, and other favorable circumstances dictate a safe environment. The doorman and concierge had gone off duty at this late hour.

He was without escort as he left the hotel entrance and walked towards the Bolshoy Meoskvoretsky Bridge.

The Russian saw an individual exiting the hotel and used his unattached rifle scope to view the person and was shocked but delighted that it was Potanin. This was an unexpected break for Nikolai, and he smiled at his good fortune as the inside of the car was cold and the prospect of warm bedding later was inviting. He gathered himself and his rifle with a silencer attached and further attached the rifle scope in hopes of taking advantage of his good fortune. He didn't believe in luck but knew that good things happened when he was more prepared than the enemy.

He exited the vehicle with no one in sight and turned off the interior door light. He took a shooter's position at the wall bordering the river walkway. He had parked the car as close to the wall as possible, leaving only room for his exit of the vehicle and a shooter's position. It wasn't ideal but did block the view of him from buildings behind and those having additional floors.

He tracked Potanin's progress towards the bridge and his passing of two men enjoying a late evening smoke at the bridge entranceway. When Potanin was a third of the way across the bridge, he saw the two men at the entranceway turn and run towards Potanin. The Russian assumed he has been spotted and the two men were security, but their efforts would be for naught as the Russian killed Potanin with two well-placed bullets to the chest.

The Russian gave one last glance at the two men following Potanin and was confused as they had drawn their guns but showed no concern for him as the shooter. He watched in amazement as they shot Potanin several times in the back using silencers and speedily walked away. Nikolai knew he must get away fast as the unexpected company and their purpose for being there was unknown.

Back at the safe house, he was trying to grasp what just happened, and what part he played in it. It concerned him that he was being set up by the President but could find no clarity as to why this would be necessary. He thought, "Was this possibly a test of my loyalty and the President sent those men to make sure I did my job? It didn't appear that he sent them to kill me and deflect any blame from himself. Maybe, maybe, maybe," he said out loud and to himself. Then he remembered the small envelope that was to be read when the mission was completed and took it out.

The note read in part, "If the assassination is successful, and you can agree to the following: plastic surgery, a complete identity change, new DNA, the latest capability of our great Russian labs, and working for me, know that I would be held responsible for your actions both as a citizen of Russia and for your success in the planning and carry out of your assigned missions, then proceed to 6405 Pereulok-Tupik anytime day or night. There will be an ambulance to transport you to the next step in your process; do as they ask. Your car will be picked up from your drop-off point and returned to your safe house garage."

He questioned the DNA requirement, but decided he had no choice and immediately responded and drove to the address given, a small one-bedroom house with a gated fenced-in storage area containing four cars on blocks and an ambulance parked against the back of the lot. The note had additionally stated, "that if it was nighttime when you arrive, blink your lights twice." He did, and a man came from the back of the lot, unlocked the gate, and directed him to drive his car in and park along the back of the fence line next to the ambulance. A woman exited the ambulance to greet him and escorted him back into the ambulance. When inside, he was given a glass of water and told to drink, and it was the last thing he remembered.

Hospital-Moscow

The Russian awoke and immediately became aware of the sterile atmosphere and the hospital equipment inside the room. Nikolai's mind was clear, and he realized that he was in a real hospital, and he had undergone surgery. He did not expect President Ivanovitch to allow him to live and could only surmise that he must have additional plans for him. He remained perplexed about the two men on the bridge and was anxious to hear or read what was being said about the shooting, but all this was secondary to his new face and DNA as he simultaneously saw the bandages across his nose in the mirror on the table next to his bed.

He now looked for the courage to grasp the mirror on the adjoining table just as his nurse entered the room. He placed the mirror in front of his face, and she said, "I did a beautiful job in wrapping you, did I not?" He said nothing but moved the mirror about his face hoping to find something to relieve his anxiety. She said, "You were a very handsome man before and you would be a very handsome man after the bandages are removed."

At that moment, Natasha Ivanov entered the room, exchanged eye contact with the nurse, and the nurse turned and departed the room. Natasha said, "I hope the new man has a better attitude towards me than the asshole he replaced." She could not see if he was smiling beneath the facial wrappings but felt good that she had her say. He said, "I guess I had that coming. Where am I?" Natasha replied, "You are in a special wing of the Central Clinical Hospital of the Presidential Administration of the Russian Federation. Is that specific enough?"

"Okay, I'm sorry," he said. "My DNA? Replaced?"

She said, "I think he really did not want to risk losing you on an operating table as the technology is not quite there yet. He probably was testing you to really see how badly you wanted your old job back; who knows? He didn't confide in me about such matters."

He asked, "When exactly do the wrappings come off? When will you bring me up to date on the shooting?"

She replied, "Five days for the bandages and maybe two more weeks for some sensitive areas to heal. I told the doctor he didn't have to worry about the sensitive areas as you have none," and gave him a half-smile. He ignored her.

"Concerning the shooting," she said, "You must have done a good job because they cannot tell if there were one or more shooters, why he was outside the hotel at that time of night, and especially without his bodyguards or even if he was actually killed on the bridge?" She smiled and said, "Of course, no one really wants to take on the political arena when things like this happen."

"And what exactly are things like this?" he said. She used this opportunity in their jousting to reply, "Anton is alive."

The news startled him. "Where is he?" His question filled with emotion. Before she could answer, he said, more to himself, "How?"

She handed him both Red Notice Lists. He said, "I saw various media reports about the happenings in the Maldives and heard the rumors that he might be alive, but I saw nothing that confirmed it. Is he really alive?"

"Yes, and it seems he put on quite a show with that CIA agent Sam Mountain. The worldwide media gave the event quite the attention in calling it the 'Figurehead Massacre.' I can only guess that he escaped the sinking of his product ships because his helicopter was already in the air when the missiles were destroyed. We suspect he is either on his way to China or already there," Natasha explained. "In the meantime, you will spend another week here to ensure your surgery wounds properly heal, and then you are coming home with me. No argument as the President has made you my responsibility and wants me to keep a close eye on you. The President would let me know when he has another assignment for you and, no, I do not know what it is or when it will be. He wants to see how things are going to settle out over the next year. In the meantime, you and I would find out where Anton is, and I will get you in touch with him. Deal?"

His nodded affirmatively and noted that she did not comment about the other two men on the bridge and obviously was not aware of that part of the President's plan. He concluded that the President had sent the two men to test him and as assassins themselves were likely not aware of his skills. They took the same advantage he had taken of the improbability of Vladimir Potanin's late-night walk and made sure he was dead as ordered.

CHAPTER NINE

IRAN/YEMEN (2015)

In an isolated Iranian safe house near the Iranian nuclear facility at Bushehr, an attentive but somber individual quietly puffed on his Isfahan Premium Original Tombac 250g, a strong nicotine Iranian cigarette guaranteed for a buzz and not meant for the faint-hearted. He was well known in the dark corners of the world for his brilliant planning of terrorist attacks that kept the western world up at night in anticipating his next move.

Sayat Mansouri had been the Minister of Intelligence for the Iran Ministry of Intelligence Service, MOIS, for five years now. The MOIS replaced the SAVAK which was the secret police, domestic security, and intelligence service in Iran during the reign of the Shah. Mansouri embraced his responsibilities to serve Allah and the Iranian President Ali Khatami but was rarely seen in public to lessen his vulnerability to the American satellites that constantly searched from overhead. He now watched with anticipation from the safe house front window the approaching Porsche.

He was meeting Armik Soruri, the leader of the Houthis, a gorilla group that was making great progress in subverting the government of Yemen and needed Iran's support and financial backing in completing the takeover of the country. Their ongoing two-year plus war with the Yemen government, backed by the United Nations and particularly Saudi Arabia and the United States of America, had drained Houthis finances even though the movement received popular support within the country. He needed help desperately and was looking for a deal. It was the intent of Sayat Mansouri to provide a deal that he could not refuse.

Mansouri opened the door for the Houthis leader and greeted him in Arabic with "As-Salaam-Alaikum," or "Peace be Upon You," to which he responded "Wa-Alaikum-Salaam," or "Unto You be Peace."

Mansouri looked out the door beyond his guest out of habit and took a rare moment to enjoy a deep breath of fresh air not normally available to him. He was assured today that this meeting place was secure from the American eyes in the sky. He had stayed alive by ignoring those lies. Although his death would be considered an act of war against Iran, the American president had shown a willingness to be unconcerned about such.

Armik Soruri initially refused the tea and sweets offered by the male housekeeper as an accepted Iranian custom of politeness, but then accepted the tea and sweets as was custom when offered again. Mansouri joined him. Armik Soruri's two bodyguards were not offered the amenities and remained alert and watchful as did Mansouri's bodyguards. There was no polite small talk as Mansouri came right to the point. "The plan is simple. If followed, you would get the needed money and support for your war and a partner that is willing to fight the Saudis and Americans and their western influence in the region. Three years ago, your protests in Yemen started an insurrection. It has successfully evolved from a localized movement in Sanaa Governorate into the dominant power controlling seaports bordering the Red Sea and most of northern Yemen. You are to be congratulated. However, the Saudis and Americans under the United Nations flag support the Yemen government and relentlessly bomb your country and followers. Coalition ground troops landed in the southern port city of Aden in August 2015 and helped drive you and your allies out of much of the south over the next few months. Even though you are currently at a standoff, they show no sign of leaving Yemen. To the West, it was a war of ideas based upon greed and power and like all conquerors, they must stomp out all opposition to PAX Americana. Your continuance of the war would come at a great cost that you no longer need to bear alone. We can and would be a great partner with you in Islam." He paused and watched as Armik Soruri slowly and thoughtfully contemplated the partnership offer and its consequences down the road. He made his decision and said, "What is your plan?"

Mansouri responded, "The oil product container FSO SAFER, formerly owned by the Yemen National Oil Company, was abandoned in 2015 and is moored in the Red Sea in waters you currently control approximately five miles off the Ras Isa port in the Houthis controlled city of Hodeida, a key entry point for humanitarian aid. You have proposed selling the 1.1 million barrels of oil that remain, estimated to be worth around eighty million, and using the funds to pay public salary payments in support of the Yemen people. The Yemeni government said the oil belongs to them and has rejected all attempts to do so and calls on the United Nations and the international community to put pressure on you to allow the arrival of an international maintenance team to repair or unload the oil from the ship. The ship has been anchored at the same location for more than thirty years without any drydocking or ship repairs and abandoned since 2015. It was beginning to badly rust out and leak gases from the stored oil. These leaks could lead to a massive explosion of the tanker reservoir because of the formation of hydrocarbon gases emitted from crude oil. The Saudis have even stopped dropping bombs and fighting anywhere near the ship as an errant bomb or rocket could set off an explosion. An explosion of the ship would devastate marine life in the Red Sea, would destroy the livelihoods of many locals, and disrupt aid deliveries to the starving people of Yemen. By Iran providing financial resources for the war, you can continue to refuse any repair of the ship and blame the United Nations, the Yemen government, the Saudis, and the United States of America if there is an explosion. We would tell the world your story and how your warnings were ignored; you would become known worldwide as a great Islamic leader."

Armik Soruri responded, "I humbly started my protests and this war to find freedom from government oppression and Western ideas and opportunities for the people of Yemen. Now, you want me to possibly destroy the entire environment of the country and the Red Sea for years?"

Mansouri looks at him hard, "What choice do you have? The only leverage you have here with the Americans is the threat of blowing up the ship if they pay the Yemen government and try to repair it. If that threat evaporates the

Saudis and Americans with the approval of the United Nations would put boots on the ground in force and restore the Yemen government, bombings would be the least of your problems. You and your patriots would be tagged as terrorists, and you knew what the government would do to your followers. Americans would once again be perceived as heroes and Islam would be vilified in the world press and Yemen subjected to Western ideas. I cannot change your circumstance, but I can offer you a way to win. Remember, you are the leader that worked out a deal with the United Nations in 2015 to allow a repair team in to fix the ship and the eighty million to be paid to the people. It was the Yemen government that cried ownership and threatened to blow up the ship if they were not paid the money. Now their media have turned this around and painted you as being responsible. You have a true story that the United Nations would verify and therefore the world press would support. Iran would make sure that your story is told, and the world would demand this ship be repaired and that the people of Yemen be given their money. I can provide the financial resources to include the weapons for you to finish this war and secure all of Yemen for you as their new president. By telling the world your story and how the Yemen president has abandoned his people and is now living in exile in Saudi Arabia, we can directly pressure the Americans to abandon support of the Yemen government and pay you for the stored oil. You would then have your Islamic country with no Western values. For this to happen you must stay strong in your position for payment and call the American's bluff; force them to bend to your demands? Do you really think America's State Department can afford the hatred of the world for letting this environmental catastrophe happen; they would come to you on bended knees. Your story to the world is that the Americans are risking a humanitarian and environmental catastrophe that an eighty million dollar payment is but a pittance in what it would cost to clean up, not to mention that the Americans are acting against a United Nations finding in support of your position and the further appearance that the United States did not care about the starving people of Yemen in that the closing of the Red Sea port would cut off any hopes of possible humanitarian aid. And is it not the people's oil and your revolution in support of a better life for your people? And is not dissent slowly rising in your ranks because your revolution is stalling? How the Americans get rid of the Yemen government is their problem. With worldwide support and legitimacy as Yemen's president, you can accept the eighty million in payment for the oil, open the ports for legitimate humanitarian aid to galvanize the people in support of your success, and fix the ship. And, best of all you can ensure Yemen remains an Islamic country devoid of western influence and values. Your success would depend on the urgency and you yelling loudly to the world in front of the United Nations and the western press in enjoining world support in the correctness of your position. Together we would control the Bab el Mandab Strait and shipping in the Red Sea. Iran would provide you the resources to effectively neutralize the Saudi Arabian intentions of using Yemen as an American puppet to keep the sea lanes open to Western oil tankers and weapons delivery. Along with Iran's control of the Strait of Hormuz, we would control all access to the Region, praise Allah." Mansouri paused again to let his words sink in.

What he didn't say was that this is the best opportunity Iran had in obtaining their strategic goal of a naval base located in Yemen on the Red Sea. "If this weakling cannot find the strength of purpose when America's reputation in the world is at peril, as a last resort I would blow up the ship myself as an errant act of war in a bomb going astray, and make it look like America failed to act in a timely manner to prevent it." He hesitated in taking this action only because it would take years for the Red Sea to fully recover and shipping to become whole again. Yemen would become a spotlight of world focus and that would delay his plans for Yemen. Lost in these thoughts for a moment, he once again focused on the Houthis leader who was slowly nodding his head up and down and finally said "I agree. Allahu Akbar," He said it in a low tone, contemplating what he was agreeing to, and then retorted loudly, "Allahu Akbar."

CHAPTER TEN

ANTON LUPU, THE WOLF,

BANGKOK, THAILAND, (2016)

Bangkok, Thailand is a city filled with ornate shrines, colorful transportation, and vibrant street life. The boat-filled Chao Phraya River runs through the city, flowing past the Rattanakosin royal district, home to the opulent Grand Palace and its sacred Wat Phra Kaew Temple. Nearby is Wat Pho Temple with an enormous reclining Buddha and, on the opposite shore, Wat Arun Temple with its steep steps and Khmer-style spire.

The Wolf had unfinished business here with his former Middle Eastern banker to both ensure he was well taken care of as he was promised and to make sure he knew how important it was for him to keep his identity unknown.

The London banker was housed upon arrival from the Maldives in Wolf's safe house just outside of Bangkok as was agreed-upon protocol with Wolf's prior arrangement with the major general informant in the Thai military. The banker was to be given all the care and amenities requested until the emergency that brought him there was resolved and he could be returned to work or retired in comfort.

The Wolf arrived at Suvarnabhumi Airport, also known unofficially as Bangkok Airport, one of two international airports serving the Bangkok Metropolitan Region. The other one being Don Mueang International Airport, which remained open as a low-cost carrier's hub. The major general brought the Wolf into the country legally as a visiting professor of antiquities with a pending inspection tour of some of the aging Buddha relics to solicit recommendations on how they may best be saved and protected. He was given the proper papers with an appropriately made counterfeit passport. He was met at the airport by the major general to transport him to another safe house owned by his mother and frequently used by the Thailand military to host important or rich visitors as it was well protected.

When in the limousine, Anton asked the major general if the banker was given every amenity as requested and if there were any problems. The major general retorted that he was given everything requested but took exception to him demanding regular protection and transportation to one of the luxury brothels downtown where he was right now. The General stated, "protection is not easy as per the nature of a brothel."

The Wolf said, "Take me to him." The sex trade was run by the Thailand military and serviced visitors from all over the world who had the money and a need for the more exotic sexual tastes offered. For the right price, any sexual activity could be purchased. The Wolf's banker could pay the price. He had left the safe house for another visit to fulfill his needs.

~~~~~~

In the hustle and bustle of the overcrowded streets of Bangkok, one could never imagine the contrast that exists underground below the city. It was a remarkable paradise of marbled walls, elaborately connected fish tanks, and tiled marble floors interspaced with a series of beautifully lighted marble pools heated for baths and sexual play coupled with individual marble chambers that echoed the faint sounds of sex inside that stirred the senses. The only other noises were the sounds of the elaborate waterfalls that filled the pools and the whirling sounds of fish tank motors. It would rival the catacomb baths in the height of the Roman Empire.

At street level, the brothel was just another shop in the landscape of continuous shops offering a myriad of products for sale. If you were new to Bangkok, there was surely nothing striking or fancy about the entranceway, and a madam or a woman on a desk would probe you with questions as to what you were seeking and more importantly could afford, with the understanding it was her duty to get as much of your money as possible, but in an accommodating way.

The men off the street with little money and wanting a quick release before calling it a day made their way without stopping at the desk to the large and open room on the right. There, three feet by six feet smooth wooden benches, like park benches with no backs but four legs were placed in rows. The benches had one two-inch plus round hole drilled in each one a little over halfway down the middle. There was enough room between the benches for a man to pull down his pants and underwear and lay flat on his stomach while inserting his penis into the hole.

Half-naked girls on their backs lie below the benches. Each woman serviced the penises in the holes of approximately five benches with their mouths. After each orgasm and if time permitted, they would quickly get up and take a swig of water from a gallon jug they had nearby and run to the communal sink that ran along one wall to spit.

On the left side and at the end of a hallway and through double doors was an elevator to one of the floors below ground. There, a chain-linked 'house cage' with covering took up approximately half of a football field with bleachers on all four sides. Over two hundred women lived and died in this facility. When not working, they were placed in this cage until their age, health, or refusal to obey their guards suggested a need for their termination.

Spectators sat on the bleachers and watched the women perform the mundane rituals of life when given time away from their sexual duties. They slept, ate, ironed, showered, and used the bathroom in full view of everybody. There was no such thing as privacy. What was noticeably absent was laughter, exercise, or a belief that they would ever leave this place. Drugs were a constant.

Down the hallway behind the woman at the desk was an elaborately decorated archway that led to stairs or an elevator to the chambers below the city where the more affluent chose their vices with payment accordingly. It was not uncommon to find someone that had not been outside the facility in a week or more.

~~~~~~~

A man laughed happily at the attention three women afforded him in a private room of the brothel located beneath the city and away from the loud, and noisy streets of Bangkok, Thailand. The Wolf's London banker lay back on the bed, closed his eyes, and was fully spent for the moment. He felt the bed movement as the three women who had previously serviced him removed themselves.

He opened his eyes to see the women leaving the room and the silencer of the gun flash red. The Wolf said, "I told you that protecting me is a way of life and indiscretion cannot and would not be tolerated." The Wolf had concluded that the now-dead London banker was not stealing from him but felt deserving of a more glamorous lifestyle equal to his perceived new status and needs in life. This was unacceptable.

The Wolf thought, "I was right to kill him. The information he held could not be known and he had deviated from a more normal lifestyle for which he had committed. He had broken my rule; it was only a matter of time before his needs would increase and a loose mouth at the wrong time would land him strapped down in a chair with a blow torch being applied to delicate body parts to obtain every piece of information about my business accounts of which he had knowledge."

The four Thai militaries in the ambulance outside waited patiently to remove the body and clean up the room. The ambulance would take the body and the three women later that night to the specially designed shark tank for disposal that was the fate of all their dead.

CIA Headquarters

Mountain was de-briefing Harry on his trip to the Maldives when Harry was notified of a tip from his major general CIA paid informant in the Thailand military. "The Wolf is using a safe house in Bangkok belonging to the wife of Thailand's Supreme Commander." Harry immediately sent Mountain to Thailand, sniper rifle and all, via the United States Air Force at the highest priority afforded the CIA.

He was flown into Don Mueang International Airport and the plane and crew were towed to a designated area to await further orders. The major general met him at the area to debark and Mountain asked him to take him to where the Wolf could be located and tracked. He was quickly informed that the Wolf departed Thailand two days previous. Mountain was livid and walked away for the moment to gain control of his emotions. He replied, "Then why am I here?"

The major general replied that "our agreement states that you would be notified, and we paid accordingly when the Wolf is found to be in our country. You were subsequently notified." Mountain replied, "Don't you think that timeliness is implied in our agreement?" Before the general could reply, Mountain said, "Take me through the facts as you knew them and show me the areas he visited."

Back at CIA headquarters with Harry, Sam Mountain vented his frustrations by telling Harry, "I confirmed the Wolf was there, but it seemed he was there to kill his banker who couldn't keep it in his pants and was risking exposure, no pun intended, of Wolf's financial empire if captured. As I understand, the Wolf assassinated him at one of the local brothels, and the military was paid by the Wolf to clean up the resultant bodies of the banker and the women who were with the banker, which they did. The Wolf subsequently left Thailand and no one knows or is willing to say where he may be headed."

Harry laughed, "You are full of yourself today. Your story calls to mind the Eagle's famous 'Hotel California' lyric: You can check out any time you like, but you can never leave."

They both laughed and clinked together their glasses and took a sip. Harry said, "Now, enlighten me."

Mountain took a deep breath and replied, "The major general did what was required to take our money. The arrogant jackass scammed us, the CIA. That is not supposed to happen, is it? The Wolf got all he paid for, and we got nothing but a bill." Harry saw that Mountain was getting hot again and, after a moment, said, "Go on."

"He accepted Wolf's money for a safe house for his banker and himself and I was shown only the latter house as the purported safe house. I knew it was not the safe house as it was well known for hosting important visitors, even I stayed there on occasion when his mother was in charge," Mountain said.

~~~~~~

Thailand is America's oldest Asian ally and relations have always been good, however, Thailand is run by the military. Sex trafficking, drugs, the black market, and pretty much anything else you can even dream up can be had for the right price. The wife of Thailand's Supreme Commander has ruthlessly run this vast criminal empire since the Vietnam War and her orderly management of the sex trade industry is respected by all and her rules are followed religiously. The Thailand king is technically head of the armed forces and has a public following but has only moral authority.

She worked closely with the CIA during the Vietnam War, but dollars dictated her allegiance. She accrued her own personal fortune by formalizing a contract with the United States government to provide women to American soldiers at the halfway point in their

Vietnam tour at an R&R site in Bangkok. It was the first time the United States government officially and on paper acted in concert with a pimp, the Thailand government, to purchase women to provide sexual favors to their soldiers.

The men who chose Bangkok for R&R were assigned a woman for the week under a formal written contract and the men were basically told to bring the women back in the same condition as received. If a woman presented a problem to the soldier, he was to notify the nearest policeman and the problem was resolved or a new woman provided. There was never a problem as the women all knew that the alternative of causing one was worse.

She held on to this vast empire as her word was her bond and she was ruthless to anyone breaking her policies or rules at any level of the organization or not standing by her verbal instructions. The shark tank got increasingly bigger over the years.

There is an old saying that humans are not a rational species but a rationalizing species. A reasonable person can survive for three weeks going without food, for three days going without water, and for four-six minutes without breathable air, but only five minutes without rationalizing.

The reality of time had produced more and more usurpers that wanted more of Thailand's sex trade profits and didn't mind breaking the so-called rules to get it. Violence against women increased substantially as did the worldwide distribution of women for prostitution purposes when the cartels got involved. The Supreme Military Commander and his wife grew old with less control of the business. She tried to transfer her business to her son, but he is not rational, but a rationalizer who thought he was entitled.

CIA Headquarters

Harry picked up his telephone and called the major general with Mountain across the desk from him. He started the conversation with, "You are an arrogant son-of-a-bitch, who do you think you are robbing? Do you think you are robbing the local ATMs to pay for your stupidity? If you want to screw with the American CIA, I can dish it out if you think you can rip us off. You cost us just as much money by lying to us in effect by telling us that the Wolf was in Thailand. Before you say anything, your first words had better be telling me you are returning that money, or you knew where the Wolf is right now."

After a long pause and Harry and Mountain personally waiting in anticipation for the answer, he said, "We made arrangements for him to be flown to Singapore." Harry said, "You better not be lying to me again or telling me some half-truth or my response the next time would not be conciliatory. And by the way, where did his papers say he was coming from?"

The major general replied, "Delhi, India."

Harry hung up and turned to Mountain, who leaned over the desk again with his glass, and they clinked again. "It looks like the Wolf is trying to get back to China and is cleaning up loose ends on his way. The banker was from London, and he vanished in thin air after we intercepted Wolf's call of going to the Maldives, as did Wolf's assets before we got to him. So, I think we can assume he was the money manager for the Wolf for some or all his financial operations. I'll get the Embassy people in India and Singapore on this. We are getting closer to catching him. The Wolf cannot stay out of the limelight and our sight for too much longer. "

CHAPTER ELEVEN

Russian Imperialist Movement,

United States-2016

In the United States, Karl Gunter was recruited to the Federal Bureau of Investigation out of Stanford University. Speaking three languages, a top college wrestler, an avid outdoorsman and lover of the big motorcycles, particularly his own Harley-Davidson, and receiving a degree in international law, he was considered a catch by the FBI. With a growing fear within the FBI/CIA of the Mexican cartels buying guns from the Irish and teaming with some of the most violent Neo-Nazi motorcycle gangs in California, and with key officials on American Indian reservations adding distribution and protection, he was asked upon graduation from the FBI Training Academy at Quantico, Virginia, and readily accepted, the assignment to spend the time necessary undercover as a Neo-Nazi and to work his way up in the California organization. He was now a member of the California Atomwaffen Division.

Karl took a cellphone call from an older friend Cal Murphy, ala, Chub, a nickname for the extra weight he carried, who became a Neo-Nazi at the same time as Karl but chose to and was approved to go back home to Arkansas to be a member there. Chub was complaining that he was purposely passed over by younger members for a job in another state. He said, "They tried to soften the blow, but basically, I was told I am too old, too fat, and out of shape for what might have to be a fast in and out. "They hurt my feelings" he jokingly said in pretending it was no big deal, hiding the emotional pain those words have caused him all his life. Karl said, "I can't imagine a job that you can't do, Chub!"

"I was not informed of the details of the job, but it sounds big. They are up at an isolated cabin we have here planning the details now with some Russian guy. To make me feel even worse about myself, I'm packing clothes and supplies for a week to be their cook," he laughed again. "Look, I've been told to not make calls so this letting off of steam is between you and me, okay?"

Karl said, "Okay buddy," and hung up. Karl did not want to push him for further information, but knew he was upset. He passed this information on to his FBI handler.

The FBI saw this information as a possible domestic terror threat and the use of the word job sounded more like an armed robbery. The FBI notified all field offices outside of Arkansas of the possibility that the Neo-Nazis Atomwaffen Division of Arkansas was planning an out-of-state job, possibly a robbery, within the next two weeks. The message said, "press your informants hard and keep tabs on local shooting ranges, bars, and Nazi hangouts for a sudden influx of out-of-state Nazis." For the next two weeks, each state did as ask with no results.

~~~~~~~

Two weeks later in California, a terrorist cell attacked an electric power substation by slipping into an underground vault near a busy freeway and cutting the underground telephone cables. A half-hour later, they used the standard weapon of the Russian Army, the 5.45mm AK-74 rifle to riddle the transformers with bullets . Shooting for nineteen minutes, they surgically knocked out seventeen giant transformers that funneled power to Silicon Valley. A minute before a police car arrived, the shooters disappeared into the night. To avoid a blackout, California's electric-grid officials re-routed power around the site and asked power plants in Silicon Valley to produce more electricity. It took utility workers twenty-seven days to make repairs and bring the substation back to life."

California decided years earlier to move away from nuclear and natural gas energy that instantly provided needed electricity to the densely growing population on command. Renewable energy had merit in that such facilities as the Diablo Canyon nuclear power plant, now scheduled to close in 2025, was sitting on a seismic fault line that could be an extreme natural disaster. However, the decision to use only renewable energies came at a price, in that California must rely heavily on adjacent states to provide approximately thirty percent of the renewable energy required, and baseload power is non-existent.

Baseload power was needed to stabilize grid frequency amid changes in demand and supply. When not available, the grid got unbalanced and power sources could fail. Add to that the possibility of extremes like terrorism or weather, that were statistically unlikely and difficult to predict, the true vulnerability of California's energy grid was now exposed because of this terrorist attack.

A subsequent search for this latest breach of the power system was quietly done by the FBI in order not to scare people and further expose the vulnerability of the power grid to the public. There was the possibility that this was a trial run for a major attack to disrupt the power grid in the United States. These people were not amateurs and the event frightened those in government, especially those officials in the Energy Department. On the fifth day with not a lead to follow, an agent from the Los Angeles FBI bureau, Karl Gunter, posed the question, "Could this be the big job that we thought was going to be an armed robbery in a state closer to Arkansas?"

The idea that Russia, with help from Neo-Nazis, may be behind the California attack had enough merit to warrant a meeting of the CIA/FBI joint task force. In that meeting there were many unanswered questions, such as wherein Arkansas was this cabin, how many men were there, were they there now and how could we be sure that these men were the ones responsible for the attack, what support have the Neo-Nazis in the compound agreed to provide these men, and were all these men local or were more than one Russian?

Harold Thomas, the Deputy Director of the FBI, said to Harry Snead, representing the CIA, "We have knowledge of meals being provided by a cook which indicates the cabin is somewhat close to the compound, but how close? It also tells us that the compound is helping these men." He paused and then added, "If we raid the cabin and not the compound, we chance being outnumbered and outgunned if the cabin is reinforced by men from the compound. And do we even have enough evidence at this moment to arrest anyone?"

Harry said, "What about the undercover FBI agent who gave us the original tip on this operation, can he be of further assistance?"

Harold said, "He is available."

Harry replied, "Get me an hour with your undercover agent and I'll give you a plan that would work.

~~~~~~~

Harry Snead proceeded to bring Sam Mountain up to date on the power plant attack and the tip received from an undercover FBI agent that Russia may have planned the attack using a Neo-Nazi group in Tennessee. He explained to Mountain all the facts as known and they prepared a plan. Harry coordinated the plan with Harold Thomas and a meeting was set with undercover FBI agent Karl Gunter for later that night in Los Angeles, California. Mountain was shuttled to a US Air Force C-40B for transportation to Edwards AFB, California, and a helicopter ride to the Los Angeles FBI building downtown to meet with the agents who would coordinate and implement the logistics of Mountain's meeting with Karl.

That night, Mountain met with Karl in the backroom of a laundromat in Los Angeles as prearranged. Karl was asked to call his friend at the cabin and keep him talking until a trace of his location could be obtained. Karl agreed and suggested just how he could do it. Karl made the call and Chub picked up.

Chub said, "I told you I cannot talk to anyone, and they would kill me, they are that serious."

Karl, pretending to be drunk and not understanding what Chub was telling him insisted on telling his friend about the two women he has just picked up and that he wished Chub was there for the forthcoming party. He expressed anger at the group over how they have treated him and said he would whip their ass if he ever saw them. Chub said emphatically, "I have to hang up." Karl then profusely apologized for calling and drunkenly begs him not to tell the leader that he has called and that he would never do it again. This continued until his friend agreed. The "thank you" continued until the FBI acknowledged they had their trace and knew the cabin's exact location, a half-mile further up the road from the compound.

~~~~~~

Six days following the California attack, in an isolated cabin in the Boston Mountains of the Arkansas Ozarks, and only accessible by off-road vehicles or by helicopter, William J. Sparks, called Jehovah, his middle name, by his many followers including the five sitting in front of him, said, "this week we have struck our first blow in the United States in support of whites worldwide. We started in Europe and now we would expand our influence in the United States. By attacking California's power system, we have demonstrated its vulnerability to others who would follow us. Soon we would be setting wildfires, contaminating the water supply, and killing police. So begins our worldwide revolution. America's political left would join this revolution if it was masked in concerns of racism, global warming, and equality of opportunity. We would join in all peaceful protests and teach them to become more radical. We would break the windows of the storefronts and they would loot the buildings. Our white brothers in groups like Proud Boys will come to understand that there is no will left in the politicians to support law and order and would rise to protect the natural order of the races. Our plan is the start of a greater plan to destabilize the United States government and magnify all problems to force more of our white brothers to take up arms and revolt against the real and frightening lawlessness that is slowly coming to their doors. We would have by then thoroughly mixed legitimate concerns of the American people with our revolution. The newspapers are already speculating about the use of Russian weapons in the attack. Our propaganda is saying that the conservative candidate for President asked Russia for assistance in this attack to scare voters into voting for law and order and for further help in hacking the voting machines in the forthcoming presidential election. This will help solidify the illusion with the political Left of the conservative presidential candidate's connections to Russia. These lies will fuel more direct conflict from the Left and coupled with the growing Marxist movements in the United States of Antifa and Black Lives Matter would force our white brothers to react more quickly. War is on the way. But best of all, history is providing us a perfect storm to conclude the building of the IV Reich in honor of our founding father Adolph Hitler, Heil Hitler."

"Heil Hitler," the men replied.

"Russia has let us operate freely within Ukraine and it would allow us to recruit and grow rapidly, we would then spread rapidly into Europe. I said this is a perfect storm and the growth in Ukraine is the first good news, but the good news continues. China and Iran are getting bolder and are testing the United States in the Pacific and the Middle East and would draw United States attention away from us as would the actions of Russia in the new shipping lanes in the Arctic. And finally, the Islamists and cartels have found a weakness that eventually would aid us in the downfall of the United States government and that is the movement of large numbers of unauthorized migrants across their borders that would overwhelm their equities and ability to govern. You would tell your grandchildren that you were the tip of the spear, the beginning of the new and all-white super race, the best of the best that the world has to offer, and the question is and always would be, Are You Ready? I say again, Are You Ready?"

The answer is a resounding yes after each question.

"Then I say, Heil Hitler."

He got a resounding answer of "Heil Hitler" from the men in the room in return.

William J. Sparks was provided as an alias by the Russian Intelligence Service along with a passport and other credentials, but his cause was real-worldwide white supremacy. He was an Imperial operative of RIM which was the armed forces of the organization. They provided paramilitary-style training to neo-Nazis and white supremacists primarily with pro-Russian neo-Nazi organizations in Scandinavia. The attack on the power grid was seen as Spark's best promise at expanding Neo-Nazi influence in America.

The group's affiliation with Russia had similar goals of destabilizing the American government, but a false narrative that Russia could control them when necessary. RIM supports Czarist leaders, but President Ivanovitch had no royal blood in him and their support for him was an illusion. They needed President Ivanovitch to expand and grow their organization more quickly. With both the United States government and the Ukrainian government in turmoil, they would act in unison with Russia as a distraction in allowing Russia to reclaim the balance of Ukraine with no outcry from the Americans, thus embedding themselves in the recruiting rich European environment.

Spark's followers were recruited from the Arkansas AWD responsible for the murder of a gay Jewish teenager and several plots to attack nuclear power facilities, but now it was just a Russian political pawn to enhance the lies of the American political Left that the conservative presidential candidate was in cahoots with the Russians to steal the election. He thought, "It was a beautiful plan and would grow our following worldwide. How naïve and stupid are these Americans."

~~~~~~~

Harry knew that he needed to get a good look at that cabin and the Neo Nazi compound to understand what the team would be up against if they tried to make an arrest. His first inclination was to use Maxar, a system of satellites that circled the globe every ninety-four minutes surveying two million one hundred and seventy-four thousand seven hundred and ninety-nine miles of the earth every day to capture images that are accurate down to a yard and stored in a massive data set but decided against it as the number of people inside buildings would not show up. Harry knew his best hope was Mountain and met him on his return trip from California. Harry told him that their plan had FBI approval, and he hoped Mountain got plenty of sleep on his return flight from California as he was flying out tonight.

The plan began late that night with Mountain using a high-altitude high-opening jump from an Air Force C-130 Hercules aircraft at thirty-two thousand feet. Allowing himself to freefall for approximately twelve seconds, he opened his parachute at twenty-four thousand feet. He set his GPS coordinates and traveled another thirty miles on the wind to his projected landing point approximately a half-mile north of the cabin.

He knew all the things that made this jump so difficult and dangerous, especially having to use oxygen over 22,000 feet, but landing in unknown mountainous terrain in the dark at a high rate of speed was beyond hoping for a good outcome. But Mountain did not get to where he was by playing it safe where his country was concerned. He came down hard against the extended branches between two large trees on the slope of a hill. When he came to rest, he took a moment to collect himself and assured himself that nothing was broken.

He took off his parachute and unsnapped the specially designed M1950 weapons case that contained his M40A5 sniper rifle. The case was attached to his left D ring next to the reserve shoot and tied down to the main lift web on the front of the harness and Mountain's leg. He checked his GPS then checked in with Harry to let him know he was on the ground and moving downhill towards the cabin. He slowed down as he approached the cabin looking for tripwires or other traps that could alert anyone of his presence. Mountain noted the time as 11:45 pm. He needed to locate a shooter's position above the entry road and front of the cabin before daylight.

An hour later, Mountain advised Harry he was in position. At sunrise, officially set at 6:47 am, twelve FBI agents in three black Toyota 4-Runner TRD Pro vehicles would attack up the mountain to isolate the compound from the cabin. Two of the vehicles would focus on the compound while the third would proceed onward to the cabin to make a peaceful arrest. They would be led by two FBI helicopters with a repel team of four additional agents in each helicopter. One helicopter was assigned the compound and the other the cabin. Both have a coordinated loudspeaker address system that would repeat play to the two Neo-Nazi groups below them, "This is the FBI, come out in the open, throw down your weapons, and lay down on the ground with your hands outstretched in front of you."

At 6:00 am, lights came on in what Mountain thought was probably the kitchen area and was soon rewarded with the faint aroma of coffee drifting upwards from the cabin. At 6:30 am, lights came on throughout the cabin as occupants rose and readied themselves for breakfast. The cabin door opened for two men as they carried their coffee outside onto the porch for a stretch and conversation.

At 6:47 am, the FBI vehicles proceeded up the mountain road as rapidly as possible. As they did, the FBI helicopters loudly swooped in to cover their flanks looking for entry guards that may be posted or other potential barriers to their progress. When the vehicles were considered close enough to the compound, the helicopters proceeded to the front of their advance and to their assigned targets and started their tapes announcing their presence and demands.

Mountain watched as the two people on the cabin porch ran inside at the sounds of the approaching helicopter and the loudspeakers. When they came back out, one was carrying an automatic weapon of some sort and the other a rocket launcher. As the helicopter assigned to the cabin came into full view, both men brought up their weapons for discharge. Mountain immediately took out the man with the rocket launcher with a shot to the head. As the man was propelled backward and downwards, the rocket harmlessly shot straight upwards and exploded in the hills above the compound. The man with the automatic weapon unloaded a portion of his clip into the helicopter before he too died from Mountain's sniper rifle.

The helicopter controls were disabled, and smoke began to billow from its front, but no one aboard was hit. The agent sitting next to the pilot had a cut on his head from hitting it against his weapon in a reaction of bringing it up too fast as a reactive shield in trying to dodge bullets. The pilot brought the helicopter down as slowly as possible and landed hard on the widest portion of the road with the blades effectively trimming the roadside brush and small trees and then hit the slope of the roadside hill on their right with portions of the blades flying everywhere. One large portion of one blade with an accompanying loud explosion buried itself in the logs on the front right-side corner of the cabin. Another Neo-Nazi emerged from the front door firing at nothing and was instantly killed by Mountain.

The four FBI agents and pilot were scrambling to remove themselves from the helicopter as they were now taking fire from a side window of the cabin from two other occupants. One FBI agent took it upon himself to provide cover fire as the other agents and pilot scrambled up the hillside behind the helicopter to safety. He was not rewarded for his bravery as a couple of minutes later the helicopter exploded and killed him.

By then, the other agents were out of harm's way, but the blast and resultant heat was felt by everyone, including Mountain. The heat was intense and the falling debris a danger. These agents were joined by the agents in the SUV following the helicopter to the cabin. It was pure luck that the SUV had stopped behind the hovering helicopter above and the agents decided to proceed from there on foot and being too far behind the helicopter to be caught in the helicopter explosion.

Two more occupants came out of the cabin front door firing rapidly in the direction of the burning helicopter while turning northward to run farther up the road as their best chance of escape. Mountain killed both. One of them was the Russian, William J. Sparks. A third occupant came out of the cabin unarmed and with his hands held high wanting to surrender. With no one there to meet him, Chub sat down on the front steps and did not move.

The Neo-Nazis in the compound located below the cabin did not put up a fight and complied with the instructions provided by the helicopter above them. The occupants appeared unaware of what was happening up the road and showed true bewilderment when they heard the helicopter exploding and later observed the ATVs bringing down what looked like dead bodies. Later, when being interrogated, most said they were not aware of a cabin being up there. The FBI concluded that the raid on the electrical power system in California to be an isolated event in determining the feasibility of further Neo-Nazi and Russian collaboration.

CIA Headquarters

At Langley, Sam Mountain sat down with his friend and boss Harry Snead for a talk following the well-attended funeral of the FBI agent that died in the helicopter explosion. The funeral and eulogy had clearly shown that a good man and hero had died and how truly difficult life afterward would be for the wife and three children. Mountain could relate to similar circumstances following his twin brother's earlier death.

They took a moment in Harry's office to relax. Harry provided Mountain with a much-needed drink of Bardstown, Kentucky's best premium bourbon over ice in an older classical gold leaf Heaven Hill distillery six-ounce glass. They toasted to better days ahead.

The conversation led to a lot of give and take and what-ifs, to see if there was a better way, they could have handled the situation that would have allowed an improved outcome to the subsequent events of the day. They finally agreed that with the short timeframe given and so many unknowns, they did the best they could under the circumstances. The hardest part was not being able to tell the family the entire story. The easiest part was providing a sizable personal check to cover funeral costs and to start a college fund for the children.

Mountain said, "Do we know anything about the Russian whom I killed leaving the cabin area?"

Harry answered, "Interpol tells us his name is William J. Sparks, called Jehovah, his middle name, by his followers. He entered the country under a Russian clearance and passport. He is a member of the RIM group that is currently growing fast and raising hell in eastern Ukraine. We didn't see any connection to Russia until now as they appeared to be another rising rebel group fighting for Russian interests. We now think they are working with Russia to destabilize the region to give merit for a Russian invasion of Ukraine under the pretext of protecting Russian citizens. Sparks may have been a part of a payoff or the payoff in the growth of their organization by opening a new recruiting network in the United States. In any case, they have made us aware of them and they are on our radar."

CHAPTER TWELVE

ANTON LUPU, THE WOLF,

SINGAPORE (2016)

Having completed his business in Thailand and India, the Wolf made his next stop Singapore, one of the most beautiful and prosperous countries in the world.

The island-city state is almost like Hong Kong to the Wolf, and he had spent a lot of time there while setting up his portfolio of investments and Asian safe houses while Nikolai was in Russia training for the war. While there he had mainly stayed at the Marina Bay Sands, a waterfront resort. The massive complex included a hotel, museum, a 76,536-square-feet shopping center, theaters and galleries, an infinity pool, and a rooftop garden overlooking the bay. At the time, when not in his speedboat, the Gardens by the Bay was always a pleasant and calming experience for the Wolf.

He was glad to see again Mr. Fredrick Wilcox III, his Far East banker, and the Wolf thanked him again for finding the most capable Middle East banker for his help in India. and arranging a two-hour and twenty-minute flight on a private jet to Singapore and the necessary papers to enter the country unannounced, a noteworthy feat. The banker informed him that "the Maldives safe house was successfully closed, the safe house manager is on his way if not already at the safe house in Delhi, India and that the Middle East banker would arrive in Singapore next week to finish her training. She is about done in the closing down of the warehouse." They would consider its sale later at a safer time.

The Wolf requested that Mr. Wilcox "arrange her stay in Singapore somewhere other than the safe house and to conduct their business in the confines of a bank." He explained that he did not want Charlotte Hallstrom to know he was in Singapore, nor where the safe house is located. He said, "The less she knows about me and my whereabouts and your operation the better. She is a liability right now in that we allowed her to conduct our business while using her real name. She exposes us all to the CIA if they find out we were in India. When she finishes her training find and secure an agreeable safe house for her in a Middle Eastern country, preferably of her own choosing, whereby she can safely conduct my business without fear of being found. I am sure you are providing her a new alias in coming to Singapore that cannot be traced."

"I am." he replied.

On the first day of reviewing his investment portfolio with Mr. Wilcox, the Wolf found large cash withdrawals and assumed the banker was stealing money from him. He said things he would later regret as he took the banker to task about the missing money. The banker was immediately offended and told him "These withdrawals were made by Nikolai Baskov. He was here in Singapore for several months and recently departed for whereabouts unknown. I did not tell you because your procedure about stays in Singapore is that they are not to be discussed with anyone."

The Wolf was halfway listening as he replied, "Are you saying Nikolai is alive?" "Yes," the banker answers, "Is there a reason why he shouldn't be?"

Anton was ecstatic and apologized profusely to the banker as he fully realized that the banker was being safe and was merely doing as he was instructed. Anton was happy about the system working and elated about Nikolai being alive. He thought that now he could find Nikolai by following the money or possibly, he had already contacted Natasha. The banker showed him the Interpol Red Alert Lists issued on both him and the Russian. Anton already saw the one on him while in India, but not the one on Nikolai. The Wolf informed the banker of how pleased he was with the handling of his affairs and further rewarded him with another cash bonus. He again apologized to the banker and said his overreaction was due to his thinking that his smartest and most dependable person had turned on him.

Moscow, Russia

It was over a year, and after joining Natasha in her home, when Nikolai was informed that the President had another assignment for him. At the time of being told he was extremely relieved as his anxiety for action was again beginning to overwhelm him. At home, and while awaiting the details of his assignment, Nikolai glanced over at Natasha as she answered her cellphone. The caller said, "It's Anton."

"Oh Anton," Natasha said, "You really are alive." She watched Nikolai's eyes widen with anticipation. "I am so happy. I could not let you destroy my beloved Russia. I am so sorry."

Anton replied, "We betrayed you and I hold no animosity, but this is a conversation I look forward to later. I need to find Nikolai."

"He is here with me. Say hello Nikolai," she smiled. She handed him the phone. Nikolai said, "Anton, you're alive." They both began to sob on the ends of the phone. Nikolai somehow expressed the impossibility of the moment that summed up the emotional impact of each having back the one person that may be the part of their soul that keeps them sane and moving forward in life.

While there was silence between them as they recovered from their initial emotions, Natasha quickly reminded Nikolai that they were not on a secure line. Natasha remembered the war and the Americans somehow knew everything that was said. Nikolai quickly composed himself and said to Anton, "We are not on a secure line and the Americans may now know where I am. I have some work to complete here and when I'm done, I'll come to see you, and we'll take a ride in that boat of yours and catch up."

Anton replied like a child reporting a bully to a parent, "That son-of-a-bitch CIA agent either stole my boat or sunk it in the Maldives."

Nikolai said, "We'll find him and cut his nuts off. You cut one and I'll cut the other."

Anton said, "The CIA now knew where I am, as my informant in Thailand said they have successfully traced my travel from India to Bangkok and from Bangkok to Singapore. They knew my contacts are in China."

Nikolai said with emotion trying to cut him off from offering further information, "I am so glad you are alive Anton. It was not a good thing to continue this conversation on an open line. Until I see you, buy yourself another boat and I'll be there as soon as I can." He hung up quickly.

Natasha said, "That was short."

Nikolai replied, "Your line may or may not be monitored by the Americans, but right now, Anton's emotions are ruling his actions. He is as excited as I am I, but we really don't know how much the CIA really knows about our situation and location, and I want to remain on the safe side. I have underestimated this Sam Mountain too many times in the past. Like Anton, I am tired of running but not tired enough to not have my revenge on this Sam Mountain."

CIA Headquarters

Harry was interrupted by his chief of staff while deep in discussion with Sam about the possible whereabouts of the Wolf and General Baskov. He held a classified NSA package that when opened contained a written conversation of an intercepted cellphone call to Natasha Ivanov from Anton Lupu, the Wolf. Harry read the conversation and handed it to Sam to read. When finished, Harry said, "So, we now knew for sure that General Baskov is in Russia and again working for the President and likely in a renewed relationship with Natasha Ivanov, the President's personal bodyguard. It made me wonder if that was not General Baskov's handiwork in Moscow in the killing of Viktor Potanin earlier last year. President Ivanovitch seems to be pushing his luck to keep someone so near to him that once tried to kill him. Anton Lupu appeared to have announced his presence in Singapore and intention to renew his relationship with China and President Li. If we can believe this call is real, then we can believe his intention is to present that oil deal to President Li. The Thailand major general is becoming a problem for both of us as a double agent. The Wolf would soon conclude that the major general was our source for knew the Wolf was in India. He is the son of a powerful Thailand family and consideration must be given to fallout if he is murdered. At a minimum, the Wolf would probably have to give up his safe house there as the major general has ruined it in trying to play both sides of the street. Our India Ambassador uncovered a large oil operation in Delphi that was operated by the Wolf in a warehouse complex on the Yamuna River, and that was recently closed. Some of the engineers and other workers said they were mixing various grades of oil for purposes not known to them. However, it appeared to the workers that whatever the Wolf was seeking was successfully accomplished as all workers were well paid more than their contract for the results of the oil experiments. One engineer died. He was run over by a truck off the job. Some believed he got too curious about the purpose of the operation. It seems it was well known among all the employees that questions were not appreciated, and discussion was to be limited. The Ambassador is trying to locate the safe house, but so far has been unsuccessful. None of the employees have any knowledge of another place she had for a residence after moving into the warehouse. They all thought she had left India. She disappeared without a trace. There is no record of her leaving the country, so the Ambassador assumes she is hiding out in the safe house since the Wolf left India for Thailand. We do know that her name is Charlotte Hallstrom, and she has an MBA in Finance Honor Graduate of the University of Pennsylvania (Wharton). She is recently divorced, no children, and after ten years of nine to five corporate workings in New York moved here. We have confirmed her identity stateside with the pictures contractors have of her from the remodeling of the warehouse and a video of her at the business portion of the gala held the final night before shutting the business down for good. The same photo is on her passport record when she entered India. We have no reason to believe she has changed her appearance. Her assistant was confirmed as the Wolf by the employees when shown a picture of him. Another man, not the Wolf, picked her up at the airport upon arrival. They could not get a clear view of the vehicle plate or his face, but they have the van's color and type of vehicle. They are checking all airport cameras, local and airport car rental agencies, and van ownership records in hopes we can get lucky and find the needle in the haystack. We know she stayed at the Hyatt Delhi Residences Downtown for three months and paid cash, $42,500.00. We assume she had to wait there until the apartment in the warehouse was finished. They found a previous use of what they think is the same van by someone unidentified who stayed in the van to pick up another person at the airport, not Charlotte Hallstrom. They checked all arrivals for that day and found only one, a Mr. Fredrick Wilcox III, that arrived from Singapore that could not be found. His name turned out to be an alias and the address listed on his passport bogus. We think he may be Wolf's contact in Singapore but his whereabouts is unknown."

Mountain said, "The idea of the Wolf having more than one financial adviser suggests that he may have safe houses in various parts of the world and key financial advisors running separate operations in case one or more are compromised. I think we need to find this Charlotte Hallstrom and Mr. Wilson as persons of interest who can provide us the information we are seeking."

Harry replied, "It was careless of the Wolf to expose her in this manner; however, it could be argued that if it wasn't for the greedy Thailand major general, we may never have known he was ever in Delhi, India."

Mountain said, "Good point, but in any case, we need an Interpol Red Notice List on her for the murder of the truck driver. Maybe that would flush her out where we can find her. With her picture plastered on every television and wanted poster she would be hard-pressed to avoid capture."

Harry added, "Let's add Mr. Wilson to that poster, now that we have a passport photo, and really put the heat on the Wolf."

Mountain said, "This oil operation, what do you think it could be?"

Harry said, "We think that firstly, whatever it was, it was preparation for a meeting with the Chinese to convince them to do business with him once again. He has found something in the mixing of these oils that he can sell to the Chinese and believe me, whatever it was, it would not be to our benefit. Our people in Singapore have found nothing to indicate that Singapore was more than a stopover for the Wolf on his way to China where he is making a new deal with President Li. Hong Kong may be another stopover point, where he once lived, bunkered his stolen oil, and raced his boat. Both places are possibilities of where I feel he intends to live."

Mountain said, "Would he be so arrogant to move to Hong Kong where he would be vulnerable?"

Harry said, "We knew he is obsessed with speed boat racing and being part of a high society so running and hiding did get old after a while and could make him careless in seeking his past freedom of movement. China is not exactly a high-profile place whereby his ego would be properly stroked. I would put money on Hong Kong, and if not there, maybe a place like Macau. If he is in China, we do have a problem. He has proven himself arrogant or careless in the past and maybe the next time would prove his downfall."

"How so?" said Mountain.

Harry answered, "I consider it very arrogant or careless to have allowed us to tap his calls in entering the Maldives and now Singapore in him exposing us to the whereabouts of Nikolai Baskov, the Russian. He has additionally left his work in India exposed and even his stay in Thailand could have ended badly if the major general had decided in our favor. He is juggling too many balls and it was only a matter of time before he loses control of at least one of them."

Earlier

The Far East banker arranged private air passage to Singapore for Charlotte Hallstrom, the new Middle East banker, with a new identity, a passport that reads Angela Murphy with all supporting credit cards, a birth certificate, and other needed background papers. She would stay in Singapore until she is trained and can take over her responsibilities as the Middle East Banker. The Far East banker agreed with the Wolf that she left quite a footprint in Delhi, India that left her vulnerable, and he wanted to be sure she was protected, as well as her not leading Interpol to his doorstep. He would ensure her travel to Singapore was not traceable. He would take the same precautions with her travel later when she picked another country to call home.

The Middle East banker was enjoying her first week in Singapore and the company of the Far East banker. There was intense training that morning and she absorbed a lot of information, but the Far East banker additionally wanted her to enjoy the sights of his beautiful city and fully appreciate what the job offered in total. So, with that in mind, in the afternoon he became a tourist guide and escorted her to various sites of interest.

She admitted to herself that she was physically attracted to the banker as they shared so much in their common knowledge and likes and dislikes. He was a gentleman and was never out of line with her, and she had no illusions that any affair would be seen as only problematic by the Wolf. She was never told that she could not indulge in sex or even get married, but she knew enough that the business always came first, and it would always be a priority. She knew a safe house was never to be used for personal sex and any ongoing relationship would prove difficult for her in this regard. A woman could not go out and have sex randomly like a man without creating notoriety or a bad reputation. Her stay at a swank hotel in lieu of the Singapore safehouse served as a reminder to her that shared information among bankers was an exception and not a rule, and she should maintain her lane and only know what she was supposed to know.

The banker was all business as he drove her around Singapore. Like a tour guide, he answered her questions. They soon found themselves enjoying the day and each other's company. She was admittedly lonely, and despite knowing better, she was freely flirting with her banker and secretly enjoying the increasing bulge in the front of his pants as he tried hard, so to speak, to avoid it.

She tried but could not resist the increasing turn-on she was experiencing and told him that she wanted to return to her hotel for a drink and then change for an evening out. She said, "You would show me the beauty of Singapore at night, and you cannot say no." She admitted to herself that she was preparing her lamb for the slaughter, or in this case, a night that he would never forget. She was emotionally high on her perceived control of him. When they entered her hotel room, she began to undress in front of him while slowly walking towards the bedroom dropping her clothes as she goes. She turned slightly to see him following her and saw that the bulge was now stretching the front of his pants. At the bed, she fully turned to show him all her nakedness and listened to his last meek effort to say no, but it was all for naught as she reached forward and pulled him towards her by his belt.

It was nighttime and they were soon exhausted from their intense and enjoyable sex. They both felt an overwhelming sense of completeness with each other as the physical and mental had meshed to complete the whole. They realized instantly that whatever happened, from there on out, that they were in it together and in talking it over felt they could even better serve the Wolf as a couple. They knew they must face him together and tell him the truth and the consequences may be harsh, but they had no choice. The Far East banker decided to contact him immediately for a meeting the following morning at the safehouse, only saying that it was important but could wait until morning.

The following morning, the Wolf came downstairs from his safehouse upstairs bedroom and was startled to find both his bankers waiting for him at the kitchen table. He was firstly shocked and then livid that Mr. Willcox had completely disregarded his orders and was disappointed as he had come to trust and depend on him. He yelled, "You better have a good explanation for this!"

The Far East banker said, "Please, hear us out." Both expressed regret for what was perceived by the Wolf as a betrayal but held firm that they were loyal and made the argument that as a couple they could handle both areas of responsibility and provide a more normal and settled home life, thus less worry about situations like what transpired in Bangkok with the London banker.

"Yes," the Far East banker explained, "I knew about that situation since the major general there informed me of it when I arranged your stay there. And yes, it would take some adjustments on both our parts to make all this work, but in the end, you would not be disappointed, and we would continue our loyal support as a couple. There is no one that knows your organization and its needs better than me. Let me do this and you will not be disappointed."

The Wolf now wondered how he was still alive with the things that were going on behind his back and a major general that couldn't help but shoot off his mouth. At that moment, the in-house fax machine beeped and spewed a Red Notice List for Charlotte Hallstrom, for murder and international money laundering, and a Mr. Fredrick Wilcox III as an accomplice. It noted that the murder regarded an employee of the oil company she managed in Delhi, India. He now knew that the major general sold him out to the Americans about his time in Delhi, India and the CIA was hot on the trail of his accomplices for the information they could provide about his location and overall operations and assets. He could not figure out how they knew about Mr. Wilson, but he understood that they were close to locating the safehouse in Delhi and maybe the one here in Singapore. He thought, "They would not have included Mr. Wilson on the Interpol Red Notice List if they had found it."

The Wolf turned and handed the Red Notice List to the couple and watched as both their faces turned to panic as they looked back to the Wolf for absolution. The Wolf calmly said, "The CIA knew I was in Delhi and is hoping to use you to get to me. They cannot locate you or they would not be trying to scare you into running so they can find you. If you want a life together, we need to straighten this mess out."

He said to Mr. Wilson, "Get her a new identity and one they cannot trace, plastic surgery if necessary or marry her if that's what it will take. Both of you need to be somewhere safe until you can assure me and yourself that you cannot be recognized or found." He grabbed the Interpol List Notice and pointed to the pictures of both on the sheet and said to Mr. Wilcox, "Make me not have to worry about all this and I will accept it. Close down this safe house and the one in Delhi as soon as possible and tell the Delhi safe house manager to disappear for at least six months until we can determine that the Delhi safe house has not been compromised. The major general knows you are in Singapore, and the CIA will be looking hard at a safe house here, so understand that the threat is real and take every precaution. Now, let me shower and get dressed while you finish eating and we will continue our discussion."

While showering and dressing, Anton thought, "The Far East Manager would be hard to replace but would be useless without his new love it seems. So, it was a choice of saving both or none. This thing called love has complicated Nikolai's life in having Natasha and now my life with these two. I fully understand hate, but not love, even though I admit to an inner yearning for Natasha that I cannot define." He opened the drawer of his nightstand and took out his handgun and attached the silencer. He calmly descended the staircase and walked to the kitchen where they had finished their breakfast and were cleaning up like two

211

comfortable married people. Without hesitation, he killed them both.

He took out his cellphone and dialed 33-91- and the ten-digit mobile phone number for the Delhi, India safe house. When the former Maldives safe house manager answered, the Wolf said, "This is the Wolf. The CIA is in Delhi, and you have little time before the safe house is compromised and you are found. Follow shut down procedures and lock it down. Clean the vehicles thoroughly of fingerprints if you have used them. I would contact you when I feel we are safe. I'll provide you with further directions at that time. There is a small wall safe behind the painting in the master bedroom. Use the money stashed there." He gave him the combination to the safe and hung up.

Now feeling confident about his finances in the Middle and the Far East and having all his financial records and knowing that Nikolai was alive and well and with Natasha, the Wolf made it known to his Chinese contacts that he wanted a meeting with President Li. He stressed that he was in immediate danger from the CIA and needed safe passage to Hong Kong and a safehouse there until the meeting with President Li was held.

While anxiously awaiting word from China, he piled the two bodies from the safehouse into the trunk of his car and drove them to a car crushing facility in one of the many industrial parks of Singapore. Fifty yards in and at the front office he reported himself to the supervisor as a teacher wishing to learn about and observe how the crushing machine worked to possibly set up a field trip for his students. He was introduced to a Mister Wang who supervised the operation of the car crusher. Mr. Wang permitted him to observe if he stayed out of the way and wore the proper safety gear. In less than an hour, the Wolf was a forgotten man as he watched and talked to people.

He learned that the car crusher was a baling press type, with which the automobile was compressed from several directions until it resembled a large cube. He was somewhat fascinated to watch the massive hydraulic pistons used, powered by a large diesel motor that pushed hydraulic fluid to drive the pistons, and how quickly several large cars could be turned into a much smaller remaining metal cube, succumbing to 2,000 psi and more than one hundred and fifty tons of crushing force.

By day's end, most workers had left, and he had met the people intricately connected to the car crusher operation. He felt confident of the person he could approach to have his car crushed with no questions asked for the right amount of money.

Working for Mr. Wang and operating the loader was Mr. Zhao who had finished loading two automobiles into the crusher and was about to load a third. The Wolf saw that Mr. Wang was on the other side of the lot working on another project. The Wolf flagged Mr. Zhao down and said, "I have ten thousand dollars cash if you would crush my car as your third car with no questions asked." The man hesitated and then looked about for Mr. Wang. Seeing glimpses of him on the far side of the lot amidst the stacks of broken-down vehicles and equipment he said, "It would cost you twenty."

When the Wolf agreed, he said, "Go say goodbye to Mr. Wang, and when you drive out from the front office, park, and leave your car beside the loader and walk out. Do not come back. Avoid contact with anyone. Do it quickly while he is busy."

The Wolf did as he was told and walked approximately forty yards through the stacked vehicles and parts to say his goodbye. He shook Mr. Wang's hand in appreciation for his time and promised to get back with him to arrange a time for his students to visit. With that accomplished, he walked quickly to the front office and his car. He started the engine and drove approximately twenty-five yards down the road to the car crusher and abandoned the vehicle. He left the money on the ground beside the car after holding it up to show Mr. Zhao where it was placed and walked away. As swiftly as he exited the vehicle, the loader moved in from the passenger side and lifted the car into place in the car crusher. Mr. Zhao quickly got out of the loader to check that the cash was in the bag and started the car crusher. Mr. Zhao saw the finished cube and the red coloring seeping from it, so he quickly grabbed the water hose nearby and washed it clean before loading and stacking it with the other metal cubes.

When back in the safe house, the Wolf personally cleaned up the worst of the blood on the kitchen floor and called a restoration and repair company to come in and restore it the rest of the way back to the original. He explained that his dog was run over and he had tried everything to save him, but he had lost too much blood.

Immediately, the Wolf was rewarded with an invite to come to Hong Kong and told that time would be made for a conversation with Chairman Li. Safe passage would be provided and he was asked to go at once to the Chinese embassy in Singapore and present himself to the Ambassador.

China

President Li was pleased that the Wolf had reached out to him. He thought, "The Wolf's arrival would add to our oil profits and understanding of the West. I want to personally hear what he has to say. This meeting must not ever be known, as even allowing a criminal

215

wanted by Interpol into my presence would create a worldwide scandal, but this man is brilliant and has always been honest and straightforward in his dealings with me." He secretly smiled at the use of the word honest in thinking about a conversation with the Wolf and thought, "For some reason, I trust this man more than I do President Ivanovitch."

CIA Headquarters

Something in the India Ambassador's report had gnawed at Harry for over a week. His mind could not quite grasp what was bothering him until James Dean entered his office that morning asking him if he wanted a donut. He had said no thank you when James Dean laughed and said, "They sure are good. I can only hope my wife did not find out that I am making a detour most mornings to get them, or she would find a way to monitor my diet."

Harry jumped up. "I could just kiss you, Mr. James Dean. Get me a conversation with the India Ambassador!"

When the Ambassador answered, Harry said, "You said you did not find the car that the Wolf drove or the van that was used to pick up Charlotte or Mr. Wilson at the airport. Did you find the car that Charlotte Hallstrom was driving?"

The Ambassador replied sheepishly "we did not think to look for her car."

Harry said, "Then maybe she is still driving it and maybe one or all of these cars are parked at the safe house location. Find for me where she rented or purchased the car, and we can maybe use the seller's GPS tracking device to find the car and maybe her? She was using her real name and there is no reason she would have used another name in renting or buying the car."

"I'll get on it," the Ambassador replied.

Three days later

"We located the car," the Ambassador told Harry. "We found the paperwork at a high-end dealership where she had purchased an Austin Martin Advantage N420 for slightly over $100,000, fully loaded including a GPS finder. Believe it or not, the car was still parked in the lot as she had sold it back to the dealership. The dealership gave us a description of a black Mercedes van she departed in that was arranged to be held there by the Wolf for her use. The manager recognized him from the warehouse pictures I showed him. It was the same van we have been searching for. Her car's GPS led us to the safe house as you hoped it would.

The house manager was newly hired and said he knew nothing about Anton Lupu, this so-called Wolf, or this being a safe house for a worldwide criminal enterprise. When he has fully explained the facts of what he had gotten himself into, he fully accepted what he and I already knew, he was a dead man unless he gave up everything he knew about the Wolf and his organization for a promise to be placed in the American witness protection program. The extent of Wolf's operation shocked me, even though I was hearing about only a portion of it. He did say that he drove Charlotte Hallstrom to the airport for a flight to Singapore under the name of Angela Murphy. We found a flight to Singapore by an Angela Murphy that same day."

Harry said, "Hopefully, she rented a car when she got to Singapore, and we can find her and the safe house. I'll get my people on it. Thank you!"

A brief time later, Harry was informed by the American Ambassador in Singapore that airport cameras had her being picked up by a Mr. Fred Wilson, the previously identified person she met in Delhi, India. He had a local bank account, and they got an address from it. "We are sending the local police in as we speak."

One hour later it was reported that the house was empty, the utilities were on the minimum, and a card for maintenance and a cleaning company was left on the kitchen table as the responsible party for the house. The Ambassador said, "We called the company, and they were given a three-month retainer and were told that they would be notified at that time of the owner's intent. When shown pictures of the Wolf, Charlotte Hallstrom, and Mr. Fred Wilson III, the Wolf was identified as having set up the three-month maintenance contract. The other two persons were not known or seen by the maintenance company personnel. There was no evidence of where the three wanted individuals had disappeared to."

CHAPTER THIRTEEN

NIKOLAI BASKOV, THE RUSSIAN,

UKRAINE (2016)

Shortly after his conversation with Anton and receiving final clearance from his doctor, Nikolai Baskov was ordered to St. Petersburg, Russia with orders to infiltrate the RIM with the intention of determining RIM'S positive or negative support of President Ivanovitch as the next tzar of Russia. The organization operated a paramilitary training facility in St. Petersburg with a training course they call 'Partisan.' The training program included instruction in urban warfare, firearms, bomb-making, and cold weather conditions. The purpose of the program was to train private Russian citizens to fight alongside pro-Russian Ukrainian separatists as part of an affiliated paramilitary unit, the Imperial Legion.

Nikolai was told by Natasha of President Ivanovitch's desire to re-establish a ruling tzar class with him being the first of the House of

Ivanovitch. Nikolai thought it bizarre, in that it implied wife and children and a whole myriad of other ideas he did not associate as being a part of President Ivanovitch's life, also. He was also not considered a young man in Nikolai's eyes. Frankly, Nikolai didn't really care about the why of the matter and only cared that he was doing what was necessary to get his old life back. His thoughts now were squarely focused on his mission.

He started by reading RIM's 'Statement of Purpose' from the 'Partisan' brochure provided, "RIM is an ultranationalist, pro-monarchist organization based in Russia that seeks to re-establish the Russian empire. The group emphasizes twin pillars of authority: political power vested in the tzar, and spiritual power vested in the Russian Orthodox Church. The organization embraced a form of Russian nationalism grounded in ethnic identity and calls for the state to maintain influence or control over all territory in which ethnic Russians reside." Nikolai agreed with the President that his attendance at the training program would give him a good feel for RIM's organization and growth potential. It was now up to him as to how he gained membership.

His time with Natasha was initially good as they punched, counterpunched, for a balance in their relationship, but his eagerness to see real action once again was always a barrier to calm and reason and a chief source of his discontent and restlessness. She didn't say it out loud, but the changes in his looks did not please her. She felt she was making love to a stranger and one that was hard to like.

He could tell that Natasha still loved him deeply despite everything that was happening between them but was herself distracted by her work as she became more involved in the President's wishes for a new tzarist Russia. Rim provided an opportunity for them to at least work together when he received his orders for Ukraine.

∾∾∾∾∾

Andrei Balan, Nikolai's newest alias, was a reporter with the Moscow News, former Russian Spetsnaz, and an avid supporter of the white race. Andrei decided the best course of action in infiltrating RIM was to drop in at a local bar known for being a RIM hang out and get a firsthand understanding of their tolerance for newcomers.

Andrei entered the bar with a forceful push on the solid wooden entrance door that almost hit a person on the other side. "What the hell man," the person said. "Watch what you are doing."

"Or what?" Andrei said.

"Or this," the man retorted. He swung an overhand right that found nothing but air as Andrei had adroitly ducked under it and stepped in with a crushing right-hand blow to the lower right-side ribs that sent the individual down writhing in pain. Nikolai bent over and offered his right hand and said, "Come on, let's get you some ice. I tried not to break anything." By now a crowd had gathered to see what was happening and to support their friend.

The individual looked up from the floor at the extended hand and thought about slapping it away when Nikolai turned both his hands over with palms up and said, "Come on man, give me a break, I just reacted." The individual thought about it and took his hand and let him help pull him up. Nikolai whispered quietly to him as he was being pulled up, "Go ahead and hit me if it would help."

Before he could get the rest of the sentence out, the man did just that with a straight right to the jaw. Nikolai's instincts immediately clicked in from the floor, but before he could act, a hand was extended, and he was pulled upwards to his feet. "Your apology is accepted," the individual said as he smiled. "It's okay folks, the show is over," he said.

The individual continued, "That is a nasty right you carry, my friend. Formal training I assume?"

Nikolai replied, "Spetsnaz."

The individual said. "What are you doing here man? This is out of your territory." He smiled again knowingly. "By the way, Lev Volkov, I own the place."

"Andrei Balan," Nikolai answered. "I really do apologize, especially since you are the person I came here to meet. To answer your first question, if what I am hearing about RIM is true, I want to join the movement. I am no longer in the military and work as a reporter for the Moscow News. One thing was very clear to me while serving. All this bull about inclusion in our military of ethnic minorities and equality and such was what led to the downfall of the old Soviet Union. This would not have happened if a tzar had been in charge. I think RIM can make good use of my talents for a renewal of the tzar and the dominance of the white race. I am a believer and I know my skills are valuable in support of the right cause."

"How do I know you are not just after a newspaper story?" Lev asked.

Andrei replied, "I can assure you that I am and the stories I would write would be of your successes and the progress towards meeting our goals of a white race-dominated world."

Lev said, "Join me in a drink and we'll discuss the future of the white race and see if we are the right cause you are seeking." He smiled again. "Afterward, give me a month to have you checked out and I'll let you know something."

"Checked out?" Andrei asked.

Lev said, "You know, to see if President Ivanovitch has put you here to keep tabs on RIM's loyalty or to determine whether we are growing too fast and cannot be controlled. He may feel threatened."

Andrei paused and then replied, "If that is the case and since I've never met the President, and since you have gone out of your way to offend me, I assume as a way of apology you would be buying those drinks?" Nikolai smiled back at him.

Lev laughed and said, "You are smooth, my friend. We have a new training class starting next month, and if there are no problems found in your request, you can then decide on how committed we are to the cause. It looks like you could probably teach the course." He looked down at him while getting up from his chair and smiled at him again. "I guess one way or another I owe you that conversation and the drinks, so follow me."

Nikolai's background information in his file was carefully comprised and vetted by the Federal Security Service, an agency responsible for counterintelligence and other aspects of state security and who directly reported to the President. Russian intelligence personnel ensured it would pass a cursory review by someone being paid to risk getting a quick glimpse of it to verify Andrei's history. It would also tell them if RIM or anyone acting for RIM was a spy in their agency.

As such, Andrei's file was made rife with problems encountered before, during, and after his time spent in the Russian military as Spetsnaz. He became known during his various assignments and deployments for his vocal displays in support of the dominance of the white race supported by filed copies of papers he wrote criticizing the government's position on recruiting non-whites and ethnically different people that supported his position. His file was thick and indicated that he could be a person of future interest as an extremist and a possible future threat to the Russian government.

Otherwise, he was an elite soldier, both a fighter and a thinker. As a result, RIM's leadership was pleased he had shown up on their doorstep. Russian Intelligence was pleased they now knew the spy in their organization who would give up all he knew about RIM when this operation was over. Russian Intelligence would provide a credible story of accidental death to satisfy RIM for their missing man.

Although RIM's goals with Russia were adversarial in the long run, this knowledge was not yet understood by either party. In evaluating Andrei Balan's request to join RIM, the RIM's leadership's thinking was, "What is there to fight about? There are too many common areas of agreement. If he isn't who he says he is and is working for the Russian President, what is his objective? Did he see us as a threat to the Russian Orthodox Church with our support of the Anglian Church? And, if so, would not President Ivanovitch have said that at the beginning of the relationship? Maybe he is concerned we are growing our membership too fast and becoming a threat to his rule?"

Johann Wolfgang Bayer, a German-born from Bavaria that moved to St. Petersburg, Russia early on, and one of the three founders of RIM, and the contact Major Ivanov negotiated with on behalf of Russia said, "I am not too concerned that Andrei's paperwork, credentials, and history are exceptional, and that Andrei Balan might even be a Russian spy. It was a mutual relationship of benefit to both parties and Andrei would be an asset in Ukraine. What can Andrei Balan discover that is not already known? The knowledge that we would not support President Ivanovitch for tzar is only known by the three of us in this room and he can't find that out in Ukraine. The bottom line is until we know what he wants, we don't know, so I say let him join. There may be a chance he is for real, and we are just overthinking this." The others nodded in agreement and Andrei Balan was approved for membership.

RIM training camp, St. Petersburg

The training time Andrei Balan spent in St. Petersburg proved uneventful to the gathering of any information of value. Nikolai's reputation as a fighter and strategist was quickly revealed and he was frequently called upon to contribute to the class and occasionally teach. His class of six was about average as the ones selected to participate had to be disciplined, a believer, and have teachable skills. Quality in building the organization was emphasized from the beginning and each member felt special to be a part of it. Members also had to have a willingness to kill, which was not evident immediately to the teachers, but asked of them soon enough.

Upon graduation, four of the six men, including Andrei, were ordered to join the conflict in the Donbas Region of Ukraine. The other two men were sent to Sweden where they and an accomplice participated in the bombing of a café and migrant center in August 2016 and tried to bomb a refugee campsite before being killed in a firefight.

~~~~~~~

Nikolai Baskov, alias Andrei Balan, arrived at Boryspil International Airport, one of nineteen international airports and the largest serving Ukraine, and the main airport of three serving the capital city, Kyiv. Kyiv is the Ukrainian spelling; Russia insists on using their version, Kiev. His papers listed him as Andrei Balan, a Moscow reporter. President Ivanovitch had not added any new mission requirements to the three previously ordered: determine if RIM supported him in becoming the newest tzar of Russia, determine the effectiveness of RIM and their efforts to undermine the Ukrainian government, and take any action he deemed necessary to brought about Ukraine's return to the old pre-revolutionary Russian empire. Andrei Balan's entry papers to Ukraine were immaculate and there was no indication by customs that he was recognized as Nikolai Baskov or as the person wanted by Interpol.

Russia continued its occupation of Crimea and much of eastern Ukraine's Donetsk and Luhansk regions. The conflict in Ukraine risked further deterioration of U.S.-Russia relations and greater escalation of the war if Russia expanded its presence in Ukraine or into NATO countries. Russia's actions raised wider concerns about its intentions elsewhere in Eastern Europe, and a Russian incursion into a NATO country would solicit a response from the United States as a NATO member. The conflict heightened tensions in Russia's relations with both the United States and Europe, complicating the prospects for cooperation elsewhere including issues of terrorism, arms control, and a political solution in Syria.

Nikolai noted there were eight ways to travel to the Donetsk region of Ukraine, but all would take a minimum of ten hours even if the bus, train, taxi, or airplane runs on time. It was a three-hundred-and-seventy-one-mile trip in less-than-ideal travel conditions. He decided to take the recommended option of a combination of bus, train, and taxi for a time of thirteen hours and two minutes. Andrei wondered why the two minutes had any meaning whatsoever to the person having compiled the information.

After a successful entry into Ukraine, Nikolai changed his attire and demeanor into his reporter persona interested in viewing the war and talking to soldiers on both sides of the conflict. His glasses, notebook, pen in the breast pocket, lively bow tie, and old-time plaid dress jacket supported his profession. If stopped, he carried his passport, as did all visitors to Ukraine, that listed him as a visiting Russian reporter. This cover story allowed him some explanation for his nosiness, lack of fluency in the Ukrainian language, and a constant quest for more information. Nikolai Baskov, now Adrien Balan, felt it was the perfect cover for what he needed to accomplish.

A major portion of the three-hundred-and-seventy-one-mile trip occurred on the first leg bus portion. The rigors of the seven-hour bus portion of the trip were offset somewhat as the bus was relatively new with roomy seats and the roads acceptable, whereby the Russian could relax and get some sleep. A pamphlet about the trips offered in a rack at the bus terminal read in part, "In 2016, many of Ukraine's major provincial highways are in very poor condition, with many of the roads in need of repair. The time needed for the scheduled trips to the Northeast requires extended time due to deteriorating safety conditions and concerns ever-present because of the ongoing conflict there. These trips should not be viewed as tourist attractions. We cannot guarantee your safety."

The following approximately three-hour train portion of the trip out of Dnipro to Donetsk was getting into the active war areas where Ukrainian pro-Russian forces joined with active duty and contracted Russian forces had control of the Donetsk and Luhansk regions and conflict was sporadic and continuous. Andrei had settled in and slept during most of the bus portion of the trip. He was now in the third rail car of nine rail cars for the train portion of the trip. He sat alone as he was in the first row facing the bathrooms. The seat was made a little wider and the flooring indented to allow anyone waiting for the bathroom to not block the aisle. Andrei did not mind the sometimes inconvenience of a hovering body in exchange for the roomier seat and being alone.

The trip was uneventful until an unexpected explosion on the tracks ahead occurred approximately one hour-and-a-half into the train portion of the trip. Andrei had just returned from the bathroom, sat down, and buckled up from habit when the explosion ahead occurred. It may have saved his life.

As a result of the explosion, the train engine brakes were fully applied, and everyone tried to brace and hold on to whatever was nearest to them as the train made an unsuccessful effort to stop before running out of rail. Even at twenty-five-miles-an-hour, the inertia of the two ton plus train carried the engine and the first passenger car to the point of the explosion and the derailment. The engine and first rail car were now laying on their sides with the engine still running and wheels still turning. Smoke and debris filled the air.

The train was nearly full, and the people caught standing or unbuckled became human projectiles. The ones caught standing in the aisle were the most vulnerable, and some died instantly. One of the elderly women had split her head open on one of the seat armrests as she flew by Andrei during the initial slamming on of the train engine brakes and was grotesquely plastered against the sidewall of the bathroom in front of him that he had just used. He watched haplessly as her crushed body quickly came free of the inertia holding her to the wall as the train car stopped, and she slid down the wall in a heap to the floor, leaving the wall painted in red. The injured now created their own rising tune of misery as the screaming for help and sobbing sounds echoed throughout the train as the rail cars fully stopped.

When Andrei unbuckled and rose from his seat, he noted that he has a few cuts from flying objects and bruises and soreness from his seat belt that had held him back from being the first mixture of blood and brains on the bathroom wall, but he was otherwise okay. Outside his train car window, Andrei saw approximately twenty what he assumed to be pro-Russia soldiers fast approaching the train engine and first train car and assumed there were about the same number of soldiers on the other side of the train doing the same. When he left his seat and stepped into the aisle, he could see the intact second car in front of him and through its window more bobbing heads and panicked people and open space in the front of that car where the first car and engine were supposed to be but were now gone.

At that moment, he heard the first sounds of automatic weapons. Soon he heard what he knew was sporadic return fire as more returning soldiers to the conflict seated in the rear rail cars were scrambling free from the wreckage and taking up the fight. Andrei pushed through the screaming people that were stepping on or over the injured and dead and retreating to the rear of the remaining train where they sought safety from the gunfire. He exited his train car to the platform between his and the second car in front of him and forced open the outer exit door to his left.

He saw that the civilians and a few soldiers in the overturned first rail car that had survived the crash were now trying to escape out the skyward pointed train windows and being slaughtered. Already dead was the train engineer who was limply draped over the train engine's topside exit railing. The second rail car was mostly composed of more well-off citizens, plus women and some children, as the seats were more expensive and roomier. They were now in a panic and running over one another trying to make their way to the rear rail cars and possible safety.

The Ukrainian soldiers, both experienced and new to the conflict, were mostly in the less expensive rail cars at the rear. They were now debarking under fire and becoming a fighting force. Fully automatic weapons were being indiscriminately fired from mostly young and scared troops, and, coupled with the attacking enemy fire, made the entire environment a kill zone.

Andrei immediately saw one soldier running towards the now opened door to breach the defenses of the train. When the soldier pulled himself up the two-metal train entry steps and entered, Andrei grabbed the barrel of his gun with his left hand and quickly neutralized the soldier by stepping in and throwing a right elbow to his nose, followed by stepping back and throwing a right cross that caught the soldier flush, and then quickly pulled him in while turning his body and breaking the soldier's neck from behind. He pushed the now dead and limp soldier with his foot back down the steps from which he came where he lay in a heap on the ground outside the train, the bloody cloth mask covering everything but the nose and eyes oozing blood onto the ground.

Andrei now had a weapon. He looked out the exit door and saw two men firing towards the rear of the train from about twenty yards out from him. Two short bursts from Andrei's automatic rifle fell both. A bullet hit above Andrei's head coming from the other side of the train and another bullet from the same source killed a lady behind him in the aisle. The many screaming and panicked passengers from the second rail car were now so compacted in the aisle behind him that two more men died from bullet fired from the soldiers trying to breach the rail car on the other side.

The compacted stream of people now turned from the gunfire towards Andrei's exit door. Andrei, in seeing this, jumped out to the ground in front of them, turning quickly to face the train and flatten himself in a dive to the ground to fire at the legs of the soldiers on the other side of the rail car trying to breach the door. He shot one soldier straight in the face who had stupidly gotten on his knees to look under the rail car to see where the gunfire was coming from. He killed two other soldiers writhing on the ground in pain from being previously shot in the legs. Their bodies blocked two others wounded and crawling away.

When he assured himself that the threat was minimized, he jumped up and directed the passengers to hug the side of the rail cars in their fleeing to the rear, not because he cared they might get shot, but they blocked the friendly fire of the soldiers from the rear cars. Some were listening, but a number ran away in pure panic from overwhelming thoughts of dying. Andrei knelt to provide covering fire, thankful that the friendly soldiers did not initially fire at him exiting from the train. He guessed that he was followed out so quickly by civilians jumping and being pushed out the door that it became obvious that he was one of the good guys.

One woman was laying on the ground screaming in pain from a broken leg where she had been shoved out the door and fell the wrong way. Another woman fell dead running straight out from the rail car, but the subsiding of gunfire was becoming noticeable. The attacking soldiers had begun to withdraw knowing that the battle was lost, and the war was not. He watched the soldiers retreating into the adjoining hills from whence they came. Andrei quickly moved back up the stairs and through the rail car to the exit door on the other side to assure himself that a similar withdrawal of soldiers was taking place on that side of the train. He was not disappointed. Soon, everything was once again very calm, except for the continuous cries of the injured and the wailing from still fearful and distressed passengers.

People were now slowly and cautiously exiting the train from every rail car, with most of them sitting down on the ground outside trying to regain some dignity for their actions. Others turned their attention to the wounded or injured from the wreck. Andrei placed the weapon he had back in the dead soldier's arms and returned to the train to gather his personal carry items. He successfully found his briefcase with his papers, cell phone, and camera bag. He carried them out and sat down on the ground with some of the other passengers.

Soon, there were helicopters landing with troops getting out and forming a perimeter around the area. A ranking officer was now barking orders and soldiers were posting guards/lookouts with guns on top of the train rail cars in case of another attack. The dead were being carried to one location and the wounded/injured to another. Andrei took out his camera and started taking pictures of all the different scenes. There were seventeen dead, five wounded, and two captives from bullet wounds. The two captured had lower leg gunshot wounds. Added to the total dead from the attack were twenty-three dead from the train wreck, and numerous injuries from lacerated body parts to broken bones.

After a period, a soldier approached Andrei and said that the Commander wished to talk with him. An administrative tent had been set up to the train's rear and Andrei entered after the soldier announced his presence. After introductions and shaking of hands, the Commander said, "Russian troops with heavy weapons accompanied by tanks have joined with pro-Russian Ukrainian rebels to expand pro-Russian held territory in the northeast. We are in an undeclared war with Russia for our country. If they are successful and the world doesn't respond to help, they will continue to push on until our country is no more. It was the nature of this tyrant." Andrei could only guess why he was being told this.

The man continued, "Some of the passengers said that you were a major help in stopping the attack, and some are calling you a hero. Are you a soldier?"

Andrei replied, "I am a reporter for the Moscow News, and yes, former Spetsnaz. I hold no allegiance to the present Russian government and believe their intrusion into Ukraine is unjust. I try to report the news in an unbiased way so that the facts are there for people to make an informed decision. It was difficult to do that in Moscow given the present government and the attack upon our new democracy. Am I being separated out in some way for what I did here today?"

The Commander smiled. "Yes, but in a good way. I wanted to personally thank you for what you did in protecting our citizens, and frankly, your actions deserve praise."

Andrei did not reply.

The Commander said, "Do you have an opinion on the attack?"

Andrei said, "Only that it was designed to be much worse, and something went wrong. The explosives were too weak or went off prematurely to derail the entire train as planned and that allowed the soldiers in the rear rail cars time to recover and provide a defensive action. I think the statement they made is bad enough, but it was meant to be a total massacre."

The Commander said, "But why?"

Andrei said, "Fear that if you stand against us as a soldier or as a civilian, whether man,

240

woman, or child, you would be killed. It was meant to jolt the senses that you had better choose the right side in this war that you say is now upon us."

The Commander pursed his lips and rubbed his chin, giving thought to what Andrei just said. He continued, "Thank you, and since you are

a reporter, and I am thinking you want to report on the massacre you just witnessed. Would you like to join me in my helicopter for a ride to wherever you are going and a tour of the war zone if you so desire? I was heading that way when I was directed here. A tour might give you a better perspective on events in our country and what happened here today. I need a copy of your photographs for my report."

Andrei said, "It would be my pleasure, sir, and I must confess, I was not looking forward to another bus ride from here."

The Commander rose to his feet and Andrei followed him out.

CHAPTER FOURTEEN

ANTON LUPU, THE WOLF,

HONG KONG/CHINA (2016-2017)

Anton Lupu, the Wolf, smiled as he viewed Hong Kong harbor from his former safehouse and residence in the prestigious Victoria Peak neighborhood where homes sold upward from ninety-four million dollars. His thoughts were on the ocean water in front of him, the former good times there with his race boat, and the mesmerizing panoramic views of Hong Kong harbor. He wanted to announce his presence in Hong Kong and take his rightful place in the yacht club but recognized this for the dream it was at present, even though he was now under President Li's protection. He promised himself that he would buy the best speed boat available to celebrate his newfound joy in life, but for now, he would call his former madame to send over some women while he awaited his long-sought-after meeting with Chairman Li.

Later that week

The Wolf was looking forward to an afternoon meeting with Chairman Li as he was being driven to an awaiting helicopter for a flight to an unknown location away from Hong Kong and somewhere within the mainland of China. He was well prepared, and he carried the materials needed to support his proposal. An hour later he was debarking at a remote location on the lawn of a small quaint-looking house that would serve as his place of meeting with the President. He was met by a military officer and escorted into the house.

After a search of his person and briefcase, he was given tea, cheese and crackers, and a comfortable chair for his wait. Approximately forty-five minutes later, the Wolf recognized the sound of another helicopter, maybe two, landing near the house. He stood as Chairman Li entered the house and then the room where they would meet and talk.

After a quick introduction and an expression of pleasantries, Chairman Li apologized for the personal search conducted and asked how Anton Lupu, the Wolf, could be of assistance to China. For the next half-hour, Anton provided charts and narratives to support his proposal. He suggested the mixing of the lesser-graded Iran oil with the higher-graded Iraqi oil and selling the mixture as Iraqi oil at the higher graded price in Iraqi flagged ships not subject to American sanctions. He provided the details of how this would be done and what it would mean in terms of increased profits. He concluded by saying, "this mixing of oils would produce one other stream of revenue. The second revenue stream would be accomplished by taking a percentage of each shipment of oil and storing this unrecorded oil in storage facilities here in China. This oil would be built up and eventually used to flood the oil markets at specific times to manipulate the price of oil stock. We would buy low and sell high in much the same manner as currently being used by OPEC and their hedge fund managers. The OPEC and the rich, men like the approximately twelve hundred Russians, including its President, that controlled approximately thirty-five percent of the Russian economy, are now able to set oil prices and be assured of their financial gains. Their blatant and uncontrolled manipulation of world markets to make millions and even billions of dollars off one oil buy are how the real criminals operate in today's world to escape 'The Scarlet Letter' of Interpol. With oil in hand, I would be able to control this manipulation, but unlike OPEC, I can always guarantee the best grade of oil with the best price." He concluded by saying, "I offer the majority share of these profits to you, Mr. President, and my loyalty."

Chairman Li responded affirmatively to Wolf's briefing and said, "I trust that without more specifics presented that you could do this without exposing China's collaboration in this."

The Wolf replied, "Yes, and of course, we both must always be aware of America's eyes in the sky, particularly in dealing with large ships and storage facilities. Timely transfers must not be exposed and recorded, if possible, as it might lead America to the boarding of Iraqi ships and sanctioning of them. America is playing a dangerous game in policing the world using sanctions. We would not be cheating our customers with a lower grade oil, and the world understands each country's need for oil, so most of the non-oil producers consider America's sanctions as more of a political problem and would not look favorably on the USA if it results in a loss of oil to them."

Chairman Li said, "I hope you would be my guest and remain in China. I wish you to keep your safe house in Hong Kong for as long as you want. I cannot currently protect you there, but you are welcome on the mainland if you so choose."

The Wolf responded, "Thank you, my gut tells me it won't be long before Hong Kong would be as completely safe as is the mainland, so I will make my homes there and in Macau with your permission."

Chairman Li said, "Of course. We have made an open expression of our intentions in Hong Kong, and it is also no secret that we wish to secure the resources of the islands in the Asia Pacific Rim and have control of their waterways for fishing, minerals, and commerce. Taiwan and America's interests there are key."

The Wolf slyly smiled and said, "In the yesteryears, your army would have simply placed diseased bodies in catapults surrounding an enemy castle or strong-hold being attacked and slung the bodies over the walls and awaited the forthcoming disaster and their surrender."

Chairman Li paused and thought, "What was he really saying? I need to give some thought to his comment before I even express that idea aloud." He then abruptly changed the subject and said, "How far would America go to defend Taiwan?" When the Wolf hesitated, President Li said, "I know this is not why you are here, but I have looked forward to hearing your thoughts on this matter."

The Wolf replied, "I can speak broadly to the nature of America and the unique blending of good and evil men from which it was formed, to the concepts of freedom, equality, justice and their cowboy ways for which they are famous, but in the end, it matters only that half of America is always itching for a fight and the other half would bend over backward to

247

prevent/avoid one. What matters now is that it was an election year, and they would respond if embarrassed. If you approach Taiwan anytime as an invasion force, the Americans will fight."

Chairman Li replied, "So, you would not consider invading Taiwan?"

The Wolf hesitated and knew it was an honest question and not meant to trap him, and replied, "With all due respect, I would consider a more subtle approach. The key is to make it a regional issue that escalates gradually where conflict spontaneously erupts between neighbors and is not seen initially as an invasion. My suggestion is to use fishing rights as the primary issue for conflict with Taiwan." The Wolf proceeded to outline his thoughts.

Chairman Li was impressed by Wolf's words and the amount of detail in a plan his mind had put together in minutes. His voice and the answers given were like the 'Howl of the Wolf' echoing off the cranial cavity of his skull. The ancient emperors of China all talked at once and clamored in unison of their support. Chairman Li added, "When you say you can be loyal to me, what do you mean?"

The Wolf replied, "It was a word I have used only twice before in my life and means that I am all in to help you achieve your individual goals and those you have for China. I fully appreciate my new home and the opportunity you have provided. I have no ambitions other than to safely race my powerboats in whatever world you wish to create. I only hope that you would allow me to express a true opinion when asked. Whatever decision you make would always be supported and never undermined in any way."

Chairman Li said, "And, your attempt to destroy the world?"

Anton responded, "I am loyal to Nikolai Baskov, the man you knew as the Russian who was the general who led President Ivanovitch's invasion of the Kuril Islands, and like I am, currently wanted by Interpol. I owed him one attempt. I am also loyal to Natasha Ivanov. I would not support any action that directly jeopardizes his or her lives or yours."

Chairman Li said, "Who is she?"

The Wolf continued, "Natasha is the personal bodyguard of President Ivanovitch." Chairman Li smiled, "So, the war was stopped because of personal involvements even though we were winning?"

Anton said, "I can only assume that when the CIA closed down our illegal oil operations in Nigeria and found our history of being Romanian orphans, that the USA President threatened President Ivanovitch with exposure of Nikolai as being Romanian and leading a Russian army."

Chairman Li said, "Yes, that would be unacceptable to the Russian people. Thank you, your words give me a lot to think about. I'll have your helicopter readied for your return." He shook Anton's hand.

When President Li heard Wolf's helicopter departing, he was left a little anxious, as the Wolf presented solutions that were beyond normal answers to situations and problems. Chairman Li thought, "With his solutions, you either become ruler of the world or look around to not find a world to rule."

Chairman Li was a grinder, and like an endurance runner, he would find a way to be there at the end of the race. He had an ability to diagnose which was important in disciplines such as medicine and the ruling of a country. He knew Wolf would be an asset and probably loyal, but Wolf demonstrated to President Li all the emotional symptoms of acedia, an ancient Greek word referring to feeling without care, concern, or grief. Chairman Li thought, "I must be careful in accepting his solutions to my problems. Ss compelling as they are, the fallout from potential mistakes can be catastrophic for me, China, and the world."

CHAPTER FIFTEEN

NIKOLAI BASKOV, THE RUSSIAN,

DONETSK REGION, UKRAINE (2016)

The battlefield, from the Commander's Mil Mi-24 Hind helicopter, viewed like a scene from World War I. "Trench warfare" was Nikolai's first thought as opposing forces with identical army trenches fifty to two hundred and fifty yards apart paralleled each other and stretched out across the landscape for miles. He thought, "These trenches served the troops well for many months while Ukrainians fought Russian contractors and pro-Russian citizens to a standstill, but now Russian tanks and heavy armor may change the nature of the conflict. Contracted Russian troops are moving the boundary line in the North in their favor. It would take everything the Ukrainian military has to stop the advance."

The Hind 24 helicopter had been around since 1972 and was made famous by Sylvester Stallone as John Rambo in the 1988 film Rambo

III. Rambo mounted a one-man mission to rescue his friend Colonel Trautman from the clutches of the formidable invading Soviet forces in Afghanistan. The Hind 24 is currently the favorite of militaries in thirty-six different countries as an attack helicopter with the unique ability to carry eight troops into combat. Like the American B-52 bomber and the A-10 Thunderbolt II, affectionally known as the Warthog, the Hind 24 never found a war it didn't like.

The Ukrainian commander was now using the helicopter for reconnaissance and was unaware that he and Adrien were viewing Ukraine's future of a sniper war between trenches for at least the next six years. Afterwards on the ground and in the Commander's administrative headquarters Adrien Balan thanked the Commander for letting him tag along and asked to use his communication system to report his story of the attack on the train to the Moscow News. The Commander had no objection as Adrien had proved himself in a battle to be at least sympathetic to Ukraine. Adrien was given time alone and contact was made with his agreed-upon Russian contact who would write the story for the morning edition of the paper. He provided the facts and pictures and left out his actions, centering the story around the first battle in a new war between Ukrainian troops and an invading Russian mercenary army.

When he was done, he let the Commander know and the Commander said, "I hope you don't mind, but I have ordered us dinner here and I have made ready a tent for you to use tonight as it was getting late. You would find the necessary toiletries and bedding inside your quarters when you are ready."

Andrei said, "Thank you, Commander. Your hospitality is greatly appreciated."

The attack on the train was already a big story on social media, and by breakfast the following morning, Andrei was being hailed as a Ukrainian hero. One woman passenger was now on television explaining how he saved her life by taking a machine gun away from one Russian trying to board the train and killing him with his bare hands before the Russian could shoot her and the other passengers. She said, "he then protected us while fighting off more attacking Russians and getting me and the others to safety at the rear of the train."

When Andrei came out of the tent for morning breakfast, he was approached by several of the military men who want to shake his hand and clap him on the back. This attention was all new to Adrien and unnecessary, unwanted, and not understood. He had retired early the previous night as he was worn out and the story of his heroics had gained worldwide attention on social media by morning. He was now a celebrity and there was no way to undo it or deny his heroics as men were congratulating and thanking him as he walked to breakfast.

One person persisted in having an autograph until Andrei had to either stop and give it to him or decide to shoot him. It was a close call, but the individual got his autograph. The Commander had come out of the breakfast tent at hearing the commotion and made the comment to Andrei as he held the screen door open for him to enter, that he was glad he had chosen not to shoot the individual as if he had read his mind. At breakfast, the Commander explained to Nikolai what had happened on social media while he slept that had made him famous.

By mid-morning, the Ukraine President was addressing the nation about the attack and using Andrei as a rallying cry for the nation "to rise up and defeat the Russian mercenaries invading our country. If Andrei Balan, a Russian, can see the need for an independent Ukraine and would willingly fight on our behalf, then we as a free and independent people must find the will and courage to follow his lead. Long live Andrei Balan and a free and independent Ukraine. Throw out the Russians for what they are, insidious leeches that wish to suck out the resources of our nation in the name of a growing autocracy!"

CIA Headquarters

Harry was being briefed by his staff on what social media has dubbed 'the Ukraine massacre.' Harry, like the rest of the world, was fascinated by this new superhero of the Ukrainian people. He asked James, his lead staffer, "What is the story on this guy?"

James said, "They say he is a reporter for the Moscow News, former Spetsnaz, and in favor of Ukraine remaining a democracy."

Harry said, "Get me a history on him, as maybe we can use him. We need someone close to the action there who also has a Russian connection." This former soldier and now a Russian reporter sounded too good to be true. The article he wrote about the event said nothing about his personal experience which was unusual and certainly not self-serving as would be expected.

Russia

President Ivanovitch was briefed on the 'Ukraine Massacre' and wondered how Nikolai Baskov became a featured player in the news and was now a hero in Ukraine. He could only conjecture that whatever he was up to would benefit Russia in the long run. He decided to take a wait-and-see attitude at this point. He called Major Natasha Ivanov into his office and had her briefed on the situation. Once they were alone, he said, "A reminder that I hold you responsible for Nikolai's work." He dismissed her before she could reply.

Natasha contacted the Russian ambassador at the Kyiv embassy to have him pass on to Adrien Balan her need to talk with him immediately. The ambassador knew who he was as did most of the people in the country by now, both Russian and Ukrainian. The ambassador assumed Mr. Balan would receive a stern reminder that he was a Russian citizen and employed in Moscow and traitors were not welcomed back in Russia.

CIA Headquarters

Harry was being briefed on Andrei Balan and was not surprised his history had been created by Russian intelligence, but for what purpose. Certainly, his actions at the train favored Ukraine and that made no sense unless he was on his way to the war zone for another purpose and simply got caught up in a survival situation. Russian intelligence had gone to a great length in providing him with a viable background history, but such things as comparing the news articles contributed to him to the real news of the day's events easily proved that the articles on his life were fake. There was no doubt he had serious military training and probably was Spetsnaz, but as there were no records available of his having completed Spetsnaz training, it added to the idea that his file was being manipulated by Russian intelligence.

Harry remembered a statement made by Nikolai Baskov in the intercepted telephone exchange between him and the Wolf, "I have some work I have to do and afterward, I'll visit, and we will ride in that boat of yours." Harry said out loud and somewhat apologetically to himself at the possibility, "Could this be Nikolai Baskov, the Russian? The timing is right!"

Harry picked up the passport photo of Adrien Balan that was used to enter Ukraine and carefully examined it but saw no resemblance. He said quietly out loud and unenthusiastically to himself, "plastic surgery is a possibility."

At that moment James Dean pushed his head around the entrance door to his office and said, "We got him. He is a new member of RIM and graduated in their latest 'Partisan' class at their training facility in St. Petersburg, Russia. Two of those six graduates were the ones recently killed in a firefight in Sweden in a bombing of a cafe and migrant center and trying to bomb a refugee campsite."

"So," Harry said to James reflectingly, "President Ivanovitch created this Andrei Balan as a disenchanted ex Spetsnaz and currently a

Russian reporter for the Moscow News to infiltrate their organization RIM, but why?"

James had learned over the years that he was not really being asked to answer Harry but provide a needed presence for Harry to better focus. "Is President Ivanovitch getting a little antsy about Rim's rapid growth in both the Ukraine and Russia and their continued allegiance to him? Or is he wondering if he is still getting true involvement by RIM in Ukraine as had been fully provided to him in the Crimea? Maybe President Ivanovitch wants an assessment of the war effort and or Andrei's thoughts on whether the time is ripe to fully invade Ukraine. In any case, I knew that whatever Nikolai Baskov, alias Andrei Balan, is after, it was not in the best interests of America."

James Dean looked at him questioningly and it suddenly all came together for him, and he said, "of course! Nikolai Baskov."

~~~~~~~

Nikolai Baskov, the Russian, was fighting his normally calm demeanor as he assessed the now run-away train that had become his life. He smiled at the analogy but understood that a true spotlight on Andrei Balan by reporters and the CIA researching his past would soon expose him at minimum to be a fraud, and at worst, to be one of Interpol's most wanted criminals. He had unwillingly become a public figure and a hero for the enemy of his two benefactors, the President of Russia and RIM leadership. He could not think of a worse possible scenario for an assassin that depended on the life of anonymity and the support of his employers. He was particularly mad that the plastic surgery he underwent would have all been for nothing, a shallow thought considering the pandora's box opened since being outed.

Nikolai admitted to himself that he was somewhat confused as to what his next move would be considering his situation and knew that he had little time before someone came for him. He was now a recognized figure to law enforcement worldwide and ironically, he was about to be awarded Ukraine's highest civilian medal for heroism by the Ukrainian President at a ceremony in Kyiv this month. Unknowingly, he was about to get some help when he was contacted by the embassy in Kyiv to immediately contact Major Natasha Ivanov.

~~~~~~~

The three leaders of RIM were particularly upset about Andrei's heroics on behalf of the Ukrainians and expressed to each other how unhappy they were about Andrei not joining the Russian mercenaries in the attack on the train. They could not think of a single scenario where his decision favored Russia or RIM. "Did he even know why he was there?" one of them asked.

The RIM leadership contacted Lev Volkov to express that this was on him as the one who vetted and trained Andrei and told him, "Andrei is now a problem, and that problem needs to be eliminated. ." Hearing the urgency in the message, Lev Volkov immediately sent a message to the last three graduates of Andrei's 'Partisan' class of six that were sent to Ukraine at the same time as Andrei "to immediately take all necessary action to kill Andrei Balan as a traitor to the cause."

~~~~~~

Two former classmates at the RIM training school in St. Petersburg, Russia, and now RIM members on the frontline of the Ukraine war were somewhat shocked when they received notice that Andrei Balan was a traitor, and that the leadership wanted him dead. The thought had already occurred to the two men after finding out that Andrei had become a hero for his pro-Ukrainian actions on the train and killing a man with his bare hands by breaking his neck, a man that was Andrei's former classmate and their third friend who participated in the raid that day and did not return after the fight. They were also very aware of Andrei's skills and the difficulty of the task being asked of them. The two men pledged to do whatever was necessary to carry out their orders.

Their current duty was the daily running of the pro-Russian trenches on the war's front line looking for anomalies suggesting enemy buildups or incursions by the Ukrainians during the previous night. This was a necessary routine in response to the closeness of the enemy trenches and the need to make it difficult for snipers to establish fire positions. When done for another day, they requested a meeting with their commander.

The commander heard them out on their orders from the Rim leadership for an assassination of a prominent Ukrainian, the name they were not allowed to provide. This placed the commander in a tough position as he could not verify these orders nor knew the name, but he realized that he was working with pro-Russian nationals, Russian military regulars posing as mercenaries, Russian military advisors, volunteers from other countries, and RIM mercenaries, not to mention his own military men. They all had the same enemy, but different motives for being there. He said, "You get two weeks." They looked at each other and nodded as if saying, "let's get it done."

Major Natasha Ivanov, President's Office, Russia

It had been a week since Natasha asked the Kyiv ambassador for help in contacting Andrei Balan on her behalf. She was livid with the lack of a rapid response to her ask. The ambassador was apologetic, but explained that Adrien Balan was informed, and the non-response was on his end. He explained further that Adrien Balan was a civilian and there was only so much he could do. She wanted to slap him up aside the head but understood that from his viewpoint and knowledge of who Adrien Balan was that he was correct. She was unhappy with Nikolai and felt disrespected as his handler.

When the call finally came in from Nikolai, he was in the Russian embassy in Kyiv. He had no problem losing his two Ukrainian bodyguards for a couple of hours as the public was not yet aware of him being in Kyiv, so there was no one yet seeking him out. He had never been a threat in abandoning his bodyguards, so he was not closely watched.

She answered testily and asked, "Do you understand I am your handler, and that the President is holding me responsible for your actions and how embarrassing it was when I cannot tell him why you are now fighting for the other side?" Before he could answer, she added in a hurtful and sharp manner, "How could you disrespect me like this?"

He said hotly, "It wasn't intentional. This whole nightmare wasn't intentional. I was fighting for my life like everybody else on that train. What I did merely to stay alive was perceived by the passengers as me doing it to save their lives. I'm in a serious situation here and I must proceed cautiously. It's only a matter of time before the CIA and every other government intelligent service dig into my background and my affiliation with RIM and recognize that I am not who I say I am. I could not chance to call you on an open Ukrainian phone line from the middle of a war zone seven hours away and I could not request a flight to the embassy or a secure line from the Ukrainian commander without raising some suspicion of my motives. Hell, the only reason I am in Kyiv now and able to sneak away from my Ukrainian handlers to call you is that the President wants me here to present me a medal next week for my so-called heroic actions. He is about to use my face as propaganda of a reasonable Russian who accepts a separate and free Ukraine."

"Okay," Natasha said, "I get the picture. Give me two days to put together an extraction plan for you."

Nikolai exploded, "An extraction plan? That only adds to our troubles. President Ivanovitch would be blamed for my disappearance and ultimately you would be blamed for damaging his relationship of trust in agreements the President has with RIM. President Ivanovitch would have to kill me as a traitor to Russia to cover his ass, and you would quietly disappear!"

Natasha did not answer immediately, as if thinking over what he has said, and then replied, "two days." She hung up silently. Natasha now understood that three things must happen: Andrei Balan, the hero, must die, Russia must be absolved of all direct responsibility for his death and the relationship with RIM repaired.

Natasha picked up a secure line and called RIM leader and her initial contact Johann Wolfgang Bayer. After pleasantries, she asked, "Was any of this fiasco on the train with Andrei Balan a part of a RIM plan, or was RIM otherwise involved?" Expecting the shock of being accused and negative reply received she added, "So, what is your take on Andrei Balan's actions? I know he was trained by RIM in your school in St. Petersburg and became a member upon graduation. We follow him closely as he has always been a rebel. We assume you sent him to Ukraine?"

Bayer replied, "He received no direction from us except to fight on behalf of Russia in Ukraine as was specially requested by him when he came to us. We have always assumed he worked for you, but you have no reason to mistrust us, so we felt no threat."

Without addressing his comment, she said, "What actions, if any, are you taking to quiet this man?"

There was a pause as he knew there was no way around the truth. "I have ordered him killed," he confessed.

She replied, "That is good and generally would be sufficient, but my President is not happy with being embarrassed by this man, and timing and perception are critical so that Russia would not be blamed when he is killed. I need to know who, when, and how this is supposed to happen."

Bayer knew she was right. Whether Andrei was a Russian spy or a true RIM follower, Andrei was now cannon fodder for political expediency. He said, "Two members of Andrei's graduating class are currently serving on the front lines of the Ukraine war and were given orders to kill him immediately, whatever it takes. The how was left to their discretion. I am not in contact with them as communication lines may be compromised and RIM's participation cannot be revealed."

She replied hotly, "I guess leaving Russia to be perceived as responsible for his death is acceptable to you, and if by chance these men are caught or killed, you risk the exposure of the entire operation to include Russia's support of RIM in the Crimea if our working together can be shown. Is this what you want?"

Bayer was caught off guard by her reprimand, but just now grasped the full consequences of his order. She said, "Here is what you are going to do and there will be no argument." She outlined her plan to him.

Two days later, Nikolai was again in the Russian embassy and reported to Natasha as asked. While the bodyguards were manning the outside hallways for people seeking to see Andrei, he waited for his opportunity and disappeared from his room leaving a note saying he would return in two hours. Luckily, there were only twenty minutes left of the two hours when he was discovered gone and he was able to return on time while avoiding the gathering crowd outside the hotel now chanting his name. The bodyguards were upset but had not reported his absence as it would mean their jobs. Andrei was most apologetic, but stated he had to meet a girl he had met on the train.

It was three days before the big day for the presentation of his medal by the Ukraine President. He hoped that Natasha had a plan that would work. He listened as she outlined her plan. It was complex and asked a lot from everybody involved and had many moving parts that could easily go wrong, but he knew he had no choice but to make it work. He thought the plan could lead to further plastic surgery, but if the plan was successful, it may not be necessary.

Andrei's Hotel Room

Two days later, both Ukrainian bodyguards were in his room as Andrei had requested a meeting on security concerns of the gathering crowd outside the hotel. The bodyguards were previously posted in the hallway to stop people wanting to meet Andrei and thank him for his actions on the train. As the crowds increased, it quickly became necessary to clear everybody off his hotel room floor as people were trying anything and everything to get near their hero.

There was a knock on the door, and one of Andrei's bodyguards quickly jumped up to respond gun in hand. He was already upset that this was an unnecessary meeting and now people were getting onto the floor unannounced. He peered through the glass peephole and instantly turned to see if Andrei was still in the room as the man outside looked exactly like Andrei. He said, "The man outside looks exactly like you."

Andrei replied, "Let the man in. I hired him when I snuck out the other day. He will be my ruse, a double if you will, meant to draw the people away from the hotel for periods of time for me to have some peace and quiet in the next few days."

The bodyguard said, "How can I protect you if you keep doing these crazy things?"

Andrei said, "Why do you need to protect me? The people out there love me. Put the gun away and the three of you sit down for a second and let's talk about these security concerns so you can return to your duties."

As the three took their seats, Andrei rose from his to address them. At that moment, there was another knock on the door and Andrei quickly answered before the bodyguard could react. Two men barged in with silencers and shot the two bodyguards and lastly, the Andrei look-a-like. The shooters looked at Nikolai as if they wanted to shoot him but did not.

Adrien smirked as he recognized his former Partisan classmates and shoved past them to the refrigerator and retrieved the quart of his blood previously stored there. He walked to the Andrei look-a-like and poured his blood on his bullet wounds and around the body and replaced the Andrei look-a-like's ID with his own. He then went back and grabbed one of two bottles of acid previously stored in the refrigerator and poured it on and around the Adrien look-a-like's face so that whatever remains looked like Andrei, if not too closely examined. The two shooters stood transfixed in a stupor as Andrei went about his business.

Andrei then went back for a third time to the refrigerator, and with his back turned to the two shooters, removed a gun with a silencer from the meat tray. While bent over, he turned his head to the right side keeping the refrigerator door blocking their view of his gun, and said over his right shoulder, "Check the hallway to see if anybody has heard anything." The second they moved, Nikolai killed them both. He took his gun and placed it near the hand of the Andrei look-a-like ensuring that the real Andrei's prints would be found and identified.

He took the remaining bottle of acid from the refrigerator and poured it on both hands of the Andrei look-a-like and particularly the fingertips to remove the look-a-likes identity. He carefully removed a handwritten note from his pocket as to not leave his fingerprints and placed it in the hand of one of his former Partisan classmates that said, "You died for killing our friend on the train."

There was another knock on the door and Andrei saw through the glass peephole that it was the bellman with a trunk on a baggage carrier as planned. He recognized the bellman as being one of the two gunman that shot Viktor Potanin on the bridge in Moscow. He quickly let the bellman in, opened the trunk, and climbed in.

In the lobby, the bellman quickly headed to the hotel exit pushing the luggage carrier with the trunk in front of him. When outside the hotel, he pushed through the crowd and headed to the small U-Haul truck approximately twenty yards up from the hotel entranceway on the right. With the driver helping the bellman, they loaded the trunk and luggage carrier into the U-Haul and drove away with no one the wiser. Later that night, Nikolai would recognize the driver as the other gunman that shot Viktor Potanin on the bridge in Moscow.

~~~~~~

The next day, the Ukrainian President was livid that a Ukraine national hero invited to Kyiv by him and protected by his military personnel was murdered by two Russians, not because it was ordered by the Russian president, but as revenge for their friend being killed by Andrei as one of the train attackers. The nation, upon hearing of Andrei's death, was in mourning. The President must console them while somehow explaining how this all could have happened on his watch.

CIA Headquarters

James Dean briefed Harry on all the reports pertinent to the reported death of Nikolai Baskov, alias Andrei Balan, and shook his head as to how this cold-blooded killer came to be beloved in a country not his own.

Harry said, "It was true, that probably through no effort on his own part, what Andrei Balan did was a good thing for which he would be memorialized in Ukraine, if he is truly dead." Harry wished he could get ahold of that body and examine the crime scene. But Harry knew that the Ukrainian President had allowed their hero to be murdered and he was not about to double down by blaming it directly on the Russian president. It would make him appear weak in trying to divert responsibility without proof and further divide his people. He may even prove Andrei a fraud or that the murder was an inside job, but to what end?

The President read the note left in the pocket of the dead shooter to the cameras and reporters and said, "Adrien Balan died because he humanely protected the innocent Ukrainian citizens on the train even though he was a Russian citizen. The assassins stated he was killed because he betrayed them as his friends. Even though I feel the assassination of Adrien Balan was not the immediate responsibility of Russian President Ivan Ivanovitch, he is responsible for the dead Ukrainians on that train and the fourteen thousand plus people killed to date in the continued war that he underwrites in our country's Northeast. I thank Adrien Balan for his clear thinking, bravery, and resolve to do what was right at the time. Know there will be consequences. Rest in peace Adrien Balan. Know you will be forever a hero of Ukraine. Thank you!"

He walked away from the shouts of approval and additional questions wanting to be asked. What now appeared to the public as the revenge of the murder of a friend and not an assassination would be the President's official position. As such, Harry knew that all evidence would be destroyed as soon as possible.

Harry said to James Dean, "Work with NSA and see if we can locate Natasha Ivanov. She seems to be an important player in all this."

CHAPTER SIXTEEN

IVAN IVANOVITCH, PRESIDENT OF RUSSIA (2017)

In his Kremlin office, President Ivanovitch reviewed pictures of his newly refurbished gold-plated swimming pool and underground spa in his one billion-dollar-plus palace on the Black Sea. Started in 2007, it was now nearing completion. His beady eyes, like black pearls, only smiled inward in appreciation and contentment with himself. He thought, "I may not be Tzar Ivanovitch yet, but the old USSR with myself as the first tzar of the Russian House of Ivanovitch will happen and this palace would be befitting of a tzar's home."

He was pleased that Natasha had reported that Nikolai had found no indication in Ukraine or in any of his dealings with RIM to suggest that RIM was not living up to their support of Russia or President Ivanovitch's desire to be the next tzar. He also was pleased with Natasha's successful extraction of General Baskov from Ukraine and her relationship with RIM, a relationship that he felt would ultimately bring Ukraine back to Russian control and further undermine America's support at home and abroad for a war in Europe. He was also pleased that his proxies in Libya and his mixture of Special Operation Forces and Spetsnaz units in northeastern Ukraine, referred to as his 'little green men' because they were in unmarked green uniforms, were successful. He thought, "If Nord Stream II can be completed and opened, Europe would prove defenseless to my influence and expansion plans in providing them their needed energy."

One victory that President Ivanovitch took great pride in, but received little attention in the world press, was Russia's achievement of its strategic goal of a warm water port on the Mediterranean Sea at Tartus. He thought, "My armed forces showed superior training and performed a snap mobilization by air and sea into Syria to save the Syrian President's reeling regime. If it wasn't for that idiot Syrian president using nerve gas on his own people and forcing the United States, whose president clearly wanted to pull out and abandon Syria, to respond and effectively close the air space to all Syrian airplanes, the war would have been over by now. This was the warm water port we have so desperately sought after since the end of World War II and would easily multiply our military capability."

THE HOWL OF THE WOLF

On 18 January 2017, Russia and Syria signed a formal agreement, effective forthwith, whereunder Russia would be allowed to expand and use the naval facility at Tartus, Syria for forty-nine years on a free-of-charge basis and enjoy sovereign jurisdiction over the base in return for Russian military support in Syria. Tartus would be the Russian Navy's only Mediterranean repair and replenishment point and is the Russian Navy's only overseas base.

He continued his thoughts, "The Russian agreement with Syria hinders America's ability to track our submarines as they would no longer pass through the narrow straits of Iceland to the Atlantic Ocean. We would be able to repair our nuclear vessels, sparing Russia's warships the trip back to their Black Sea bases through the Turkish Straits. As a part of our five-year military upgrade, nearby Khmeimim Air Base would house our new hypersonic Mach-5 aircraft and our Mig-15 fighter jets that can travel up to twelve hundred and fifty miles with nuclear or conventional weapons attached. Both the Kinzhal air missile and the Avangard ground-launched missile can traverse the atmosphere at ten times faster than the speed of sound with the capability of carrying nuclear-tipped missiles and can change directions in flight."

From President Ivanovitch's perspective, China, Russia, and Iran seem to be doing everything right in hampering America's efforts in policing the world. The axis of three, as they were now called, were rapidly expanding their influence, territorial claims, and economic capacity. He said out loud with emphasis and to himself, "It is Russia's time to flourish." President Ivanovitch could now foresee a clear path to ruling Russia as a tsar in the new world order.

CHAPTER SEVENTEEN

HO LI CHUNG, PRESIDENT OF CHINA (2016-2018)

For the week following the Wolf's visit, President Li gave much thought to his two earlier suggestions. The catapulting of diseased bodies into the strongholds of the enemy to achieve victory was a realistic proposal cleverly shrouded in a double entendre if considered inappropriate or unacceptable to him. The Wolf was suggesting shutting off travel to and from China and sending infected diseased carriers worldwide, like creating a pandemic to advance China's economic and military goals for new world order. He thought, "The suggestion is doable and worth the research." He rationalized that the research could be canceled before implementation of the disease if there were unacceptable problems like no ability to control it by not having a cure.

For the years 2016-2018, time, money, and effort were placed into the hands of the Wuhan Center laboratory scientists to make a controlled pandemic possible. There was an additional concerted effort by the Chinese government that provided the World Health Organization and their inspectors large sums of money for favorable treatment of inspection results.

Wolf's second suggestion on how to invade Taiwan had a lot of merits using fishing rights as a basis for a regional conflict. Chairman Li saw how easy the narrative would be to develop a plan for American interference in siding with Taiwan as meddling in a neighborhood spat. He made the decision to proceed with further research and development and set in motion a plan for possible implementation later. Like the plan for the pandemic, it too can be called off at any time if deemed too risky or unacceptable.

Wolf's plan for a future invasion of Taiwan was simple: steadily increase the number of fishing boats in waters off Taiwan until the boats were accepted and seen only as a nuisance by the Taiwanese military. Occasionally ram a Taiwanese fishing boat as a provocation caused by Taiwanese fishing in China owned and occupied waters and proclaim a need for military protection of China's fishing fleet.

"Induce reactions from the Taiwanese military where possible that would give the illusion that Taiwan is the aggressor and China would one day have their fill of being bullied and see a need to retaliate. Send an occasional military cutter boat into Taiwanese waters to ostensibly break up fights whereby the Taiwanese military becomes used to their presence in helping Taiwan prevent further escalation of incidences and over time did not interpret the China military boats as a threat for an invasion. Steadily increase the fishing boat numbers and push the fishing boats ever deeper into Taiwan's waters and increase the conflict that would require more of a Chinese military presence to keep the peace. Make increasingly more overflights of Taiwan with an increase each time in numbers and types of aircraft."

"In the meantime, build a fleet of small military boats that appear as fishing boats and intermix them with the fishing fleet. These boats would have speed and hidden guns attached to a rotating flooring platform that acts as a deck when fishing and as a gunboat with rotary cannons with a flip of a switch. Use a Gatling-type rotating barrel assembly that delivers a sustained saturation direct fire at a much greater rate of fire than single-barreled autocannons of the same caliber. Design and build bigger fishing trawlers that can carry troops in the hull in lieu of fish. When the time is right the small military boats would break away from the fishing fleet and spearhead the takeover of Taiwan followed by the troop carriers."

"The question is not whether the military can successfully invade Taiwan, it can. The true question is whether it can be done fast enough to prevent American and allied coalitions from responding. The first objective would be to dismantle all major weapons and communication systems to include military airports and designated people of leadership and their homes and work facilities by a simultaneous missile strike just before the first troops land. The second objective is to get onto the island amongst the population to negate American and allied air support. The third objective is to provide the Americans an excuse to not respond and save face by not allowing a controlled Taiwanese ground offensive or defensive area that can be supported by additional American or allied ground troops. The fourth objective is to control the media narrative with a coordinated campaign that this invasion was all brought about by Taiwan's illegal fishing in China's waters and left China with no other choice but a military response. Further, explain that China has no territorial ambitions except that which has been taken away in the past. Place maximum pressure on the Americans that this is a regional conflict and nothing more." The Wolf concluded by saying, "Finally, have the Americans facing the one and only decision left, which is all-out war with China to have the island returned to Taiwan or the capitulation of Taiwan to China. They would not choose the former.

Chairman Li recognized that there were many in Taiwan that supported an invasion and a return to their roots. He also recognized in his experience with Hong Kong that as each year passes that the younger generations and a lot of the old would come to feel less of or no attachment to the mainland. He thought, "If Taiwan does not wish to return to control by the mainland, why do they not defend themselves more effectively in the sense of the Israelis? Are they so naïve to think the Americans would come to their rescue when Taiwan's population of twenty-three million people can reliably out-number any invading force? They can readily adopt a universal short-term conscription program with intense military training and place their soldiers in a ready reserve with periodic training as needed if they really were worried about being under China's rule?" Their major weapons, communications, and leadership are highly vulnerable to missile attack, whereas small cells armed with portable missiles and the right communication equipment and distributed throughout the island could survive an attack and even provide an incentive for the Americans to help if there was a force on the ground to support and keep the war regional. I can reduce the Americans ability to help by building a militia fishing fleet big enough to dominate all the waterways of Southeast Asia to hinder the movement of their fleet."

CHAPTER EIGHTEEN

ANTON LUPU, HOME AT LAST, THE VISIT (2017)

The Wolf was pleased that Chairman Li approved his plan for the mixing of oils and his living in both Hong Kong and the administrative district of Macau.

On December 20, 1999, Macau became a special administrative region under Chinese sovereignty, as Hong Kong had in 1997. Macau was a special administrative region of China, which maintained separate governing and economic systems from those of mainland China under the principle of "one country, two systems." The period since reunification had been peaceful and marked by increasing prosperity.

The Delhi safehouse manager and former Maldives safehouse manager, now in the Philippines awaiting further orders from the Wolf, picked up his ringing cell phone and heard, "This is the Wolf, report to the Chinese Embassy in Singapore using the name Ma Chen.

Your orders await." The Wolf pushed the red button on his cell phone ending the call. The Delhi safe house manager's CIA handler smiled happily that the call had finally come as expected and there was no extended conversation.

The Delhi safe house manager knew he was in a dangerous game, but he had been promised full immunity and a new life in the United States against certain death if the Wolf found him out. He figured he has no choice but to work with the CIA. The cover story of his having waited for Wolf's call in Manila seemed foolproof to both him and the CIA handler as he left Delhi India as the Wolf had requested. In fact, he was told by the CIA to travel to the Philippines on his own with the CIA handler traveling separately and to set up housekeeping as if it was a normal move. Once he was moved into the house, the CIA had come in and wired the house and cell phone for any calls or visitors.

Four days after receiving the call from the Wolf, Ma Chen was led out the back door of the Chinese Embassy in Singapore to an awaiting limousine that took him to Singapore Changi International Airport for a private jet to Chek Lap KoK International Airport or simply known as Hong Kong Airport. The better part of three hours later, he was landing in Macau, China.

Upon debarking from the airplane, he was met by the Wolf.

"Do I dare ask?" said the Wolf, "How was your flight?" He smiled and shook his hand. "Welcome to your new home!" He turned to his right and swept out his right hand at the airport and buildings in front of him. "I purchased a safe house here and I hope you will be happy in living here.

The manager replied, "I can't wait to see it."

In the passenger seat of what the Wolf said was the manager's new right-hand-drive Mercedes-Benz vehicle, he was asked to pull out and open the envelope enclosed in the glove compartment. The Wolf said, "Inside you will find your new passport, driver's license, bank accounts, and the credit cards you will need immediately to buy yourself some clothing and other personal items you need. I hope the monetary figure in your checking account meets your approval." The Wolf waited a moment and then glanced to his right to see the safe house manager's eyebrows go up and the slow pursing of the lips and the slow nodding of the head to show agreement. Macau kept driving on the left because of its close ties with Hong Kong, even though Portugal and all its other colonies had switched to driving on the right in 1928.

The new manager had played his new role well and was happy after seeing his new home.

He was most happy that there was no sign that the Wolf thought there was a problem. The safe house was in an area open to the South China Sea and came complete with a boathouse that now housed the new racing boat that the Wolf would take back to Hong Kong in the morning.

The hiding of traceable assets and a disciplined approach to life in keeping a low profile was key to his survival with the Wolf. He knew too that any hint that he was now working with the CIA meant certain death. If he is careful, he just might survive.

The Visit

In mid-2017 a Chinese Embassy limousine arrived at the safe house and two individuals, a man and a woman, got out. After leaving Ukraine, Natasha had arranged for Nikolai to visit Anton on their journey to their next assignment. President Ivanovitch had made the case for the visit with Chairman Li after Natasha had made the case with him about the importance of the promise Nikolai had made to visit Anton. Natasha had emphasized the emotional dependence of the two in remaining effective and focused. Thus, President Ivanovitch had capitulated.

At that moment, the noise of a speed boat could be heard in the back of the house pulling into the dock indicating that Anton had arrived. The safe house manager welcomed the two unknown visitors when Anton appeared running from the rear of the house. He jumped into Nikolai's arms for a long-awaited hug. Natasha was next and everyone was in tears as they could not seem to get enough of each other. The safe house manager looked on in amazement but was soon dragging the suitcases inside as the three made their way to the house as the limousine drove off. He heard Anton say to Nikolai, "I hope that is really you I am hugging as you have changed your appearance completely!"

"It is me," Nikolai replied.

The manager has heard about this other partner of the Wolf's, but the woman called Natasha was a new name to him. The following week went by quickly, and the highlights seemed to be the boat rides on the ocean and the nightlife in Macau.

Macau is located on China's southern coast, thirty-seven miles west of Hong Kong, on the western side of the Pearl River estuary. It was surrounded by the South China Sea. An area of twelve square miles, it was the most densely populated region in the world. A Portuguese territory until 1999, it reflects a mix of cultural influences. Its giant casinos and malls on the Cotai Strip, which joined the islands of Taipa and Coloane, have earned it the nickname, "Las Vegas of Asia." It has become a major resort and a top destination for gambling tourism, with a gambling industry seven times larger than that of Las Vegas. The city has one of the highest per capita incomes in the world and the territory is highly urbanized; two-thirds of the total land area is on land reclaimed from the sea.

The Chinese limousine arrived at week's end and departed with the two occupants. All things returned to normal for the manager who had successfully pulled a copy of the house security cameras on the last day before erasing the system. The CIA received the tape and his report on the safe house and occupants the following week.

Headquarters CIA

Harry said to James Dean after reviewing the safehouse security film. "It looks like General Baskov survived Ukraine. I assume the Wolf has garnered President Li's support for this visit as part of the deal he has made to sell and receive these mixed oils. President Ivanovitch must also be involved if Natasha Ivanov is there. They are flying on government airplanes with diplomatic privileges, it was why they are not showing up on NSA's radar. I don't like this buddy system the Chinese and Russians are suddenly getting comfortable with. James, please get on this and see if we can find out where they are heading for their next assignment."

CHAPTER NINETEEN

RIM, UNITED STATES OF AMERICA (2017-2019)

TUCSON, ARIZONA

The prison yard was full and the Neo-Nazi white brothers were compacted together with Cal Murphy, known as Chub, in an area next to the outside fence separating the guard towers and institution from freedom. The intense heat from a relentless sun offered no relief for the men outside in the yard. All around was the never-ending desert that comprised most of Tucson and the southern portion of Arizona.

At the far end of the fence line on both sides of the Neo-Nazi group were guard towers overlooking the grounds of the Arizona State Prison Complex, one of thirteen prison facilities operated by the Arizona Department of Corrections. Inmates tried to stay busy by lifting weights, exercising, having conversations, small games like checkers, and just enjoying being outside. Latinos, Blacks, Neo-Nazis,

289

individual gangs, and other groups were aware that violence could erupt at any time and were constantly observing their surroundings and any changes or disturbance in the everyday sounds or routines normal to them.

When the Neo-Nazi leadership determined that Chub was the only one that could have divulged the location of the cabin, his death warrant was signed. The location of the traitor, as Chub was now called, was quickly found by friends of the Neo-Nazis in the Arkansas state government. It was ironic that Chub was sent to Arizona for incarceration as it was not done out of concern for his safety, but to be closer to Karl Gunter. The FBI felt if Karl Gunter was close enough to visit him occasionally, he might be able to obtain additional information from him about the Neo-Nazi organization.

Randal Jones, age eighteen and a pending member of the Colorado Neo-Nazi Atomwaffen Division, was found to be serving time for armed robbery at the same prison. He was raised as a part of this group by its leader, his father, and taught from birth the supremacy of the white race. He was given the opportunity to become an Angel of Death by killing the traitor. If successful, he would be awarded a special tattoo of the former Nazi surgeon Josef Mengele, the true angel of death, for whom the award honored. Other perks included, once he was released, would include a free bar, women of his choice, a one percenter motorcycle patch for his leathers, and an assigned first year lackey to do his bidding.

Randel Jones couldn't care less about the perks. He was a believer through and through. Randal thought, "If the FBI thought moving the traitor West for incarceration would protect him, they were wrong. The traitor cost five devotees their lives, and for that, I will make sure he dies today. I feel no regret or remorse for taking this man's life."

Chub sat against the fence unaware that he was being moved against for his perceived betrayal. His tattoos glistened from the sweat falling off his fat body. The tats, inks, on him and those around him were a kaleidoscope of violence known only to the individuals wearing them, other group members, and some outnumbered and assorted law enforcement.

Billy Joe Bailey, a white supremacist from the small town of Alice, Texas, near Laredo, got up from the group as planned and slowly worked his way towards another group of five men. The five men were members of the Sons of Silence, a small Colorado-based motorcycle gang with the reputation as the most terrifying gang in the nation. As he passed by one gang member, he slipped the money to buy the shank. On the return pass from a different Sons of Silence member, he received the shank that was specially made in the machine shop and looked like an ice pick. He returned to the group and handed off the shank to Randal Jones. All hell was about to let loose.

On the go signal from the leader of the white supremacist group, one of the men got up and purposely bumped the first man with whom he came in contact. The man reacted and was instantly punched. Everyone in the yard was hopelessly sucked in towards the fight as if a door had been blown open on a commercial jet at 50,000 feet. There were now fights everywhere and tear gas canisters descended from the control towers. Police with riot gear began entering the compound information with batons swinging. The rifles in the towers were aimed at the compound areas marked as off-limits, the so-called kill zones. The inmates knew that if anyone entered a kill zone for whatever reason, he would be shot. Those were areas with direct access to the outside and the guards must consider the brawl a ruse to facilitate a prison break if these areas are violated. There was no plan B.

When the initial brawl began, everyone responded except for five individuals. Two white supremacists grabbed the traitor and penned him to the ground while two more blocked the prison camera angles to the ground area. Immediately, the fifth man, Randel Jones, kicked the man in the throat and then the teeth and fell on top of him. He thrust the blade in hard underneath the rib cage and upwards several times until the blade found the line to penetrate the heart. They held him down while he bled out and died. Jones wiped the handle with the bottom portion of the man's shirt and left the shank on top of the body. Once finished, the five men walked away together and joined the brawl.

Karl Gunther-Undercover FBI-Los Angeles, California

In the adjacent state of California, Karl Gunther heard the news about the death of Cal Murphy, Chub. The Neo-Nazi organization in California was now celebrating his death and ran rampant with rumors and stories on how he deserved everything he got and more. Karl was sad to hear of his friend's death and somewhat surprised at the reach of the Neo-Nazi organization in finding him and pulling off the assassination. Chub's whereabouts were supposed to be unknown. He considered Chub a friend even though they were on different sides of the law. There were several key moments when Chub had made Karl's transition into the Neo-Nazi lifestyle easier, so his death has saddened him.

Karl Gunther had maintained a low profile in the California Neo-Nazi organization as an FBI plant, and in the succeeding years gradually garnered the trust of those around him. He was known for his quick wit, leadership, and ability to solve problems. He had not met with Chub since his arrest as the FBI considered it too risky. There was not much that happened in a prison environment without the inmate's knowledge, and exposure as being an FBI agent was not worth that risk. But that was all about to change.

RIM-Miami

Several months after leaving Ukraine and visiting with Anton in Hong Kong China, Nikolai found himself in a safe house purchased years earlier by Anton on Miami Beach, Florida. Natasha's plan and agreement with RIM leader Johann Wolfgang Bayer for RIM's sacrifice of their two men in Ukraine called for Adrien Balan to be moved to the USA to replace RIM operative William J. Sparks and do the work there for RIM that Jehovah had started. To provide further cover for Nikolai's new alias, Natasha agreed to accompany him for the first two years. Russian intelligence provided all the necessary paperwork for background and entry into the United States for both Natasha and Nikolai.

Nikolai entered the United States under a J-1 visa in the Teach USA cultural exchange program as a secondary teacher. Russian intelligence established the credentials to meet national and local teaching requirements and Natasha was listed as his wife and a marriage license was provided. The names on the marriage license were Mr. and Mrs. Lev and Sasha Petrov. His paperwork was pushed through by a United States Secretary of State Department supervisor in Florida given a $100,000 bribe. English was not a problem for Nikolai (Lev) as his time in Nigeria proved invaluable. Natasha (Sasha) spoke enough English to get by but proved a quick learner in the first six months there.

Nikolai got through United States customs with a shaved head, nerd glasses, goatee, ill-fitting suit with bowtie, and an additional thirty pounds provided by a faked stomach attachment for the passport photograph coupled with the State Department's employee meeting him and Natasha at the entry point to push for an expedited entry. There were no red flags as seen by customs. Three months later, the State Department employee was unfortunately found dead in a boating accident off the Miami Beach coast.

The first year in the United States was the happiest of Natasha's life. She and Nikolai worked side by side in a common cause for her beloved Russia. The time with Anton was extra special and all seemed well with the world. Nikolai and Natasha met with over seventy groups considered to be white supremacist groups, like the Ku Klux Klan, Proud Boys, Aryan Nations, and the Patriot Front, and slowly built a loosely united national organization of similar interests that provided needed structure in recruiting through social media, and goals for individuals and the organizations.

The one goal every member seemed anxious to support was a call to action in the streets as a unified group in a serious effort to overthrow the United States government. Members were tired of only talk of a fourth Reich, the growth and expansion of Blacks and other minorities in America's society and sitting on the sidelines while socialists were making headway by action in the streets. Lev and Sasha also met with many anti-American socialist groups on the left like Antifa and Black Lives Matter to determine their willingness to support an all-out war in the streets to achieve the overthrow of the government. They would sort out their differences or divide the territory gained later. Lev was about to offer all of them the ultimate plan of action in one masterful effort to overturn the American government.

California

Karl Gunther was surprised when the leadership of the California Neo-Nazi Atomwaffen Division requested his immediate presence at a prearranged meeting in San Francisco. He was to be provided a protective motorcycle escort of five other members, two of which he considered friends, from Los Angeles to San Francisco and back. He had never met with any other neo-Nazi groups or members, nor had any leadership role since joining the party, so it worried him why he was singled out for this meeting.

Upon arrival in San Francisco, the coordinates given to the group ended at a gated structure with a small building within that probably served previously as a used car lot. There were ten motorcycles within the fenced area and one more motorcyclist who was left outside at the entrance gate as a guard. He opened the gate for the group to enter. Leaving their bikes at the front of the building where the other bikes were parked, they were graciously met and welcomed by four of the San Francisco Division Atomwaffen members. Karl was told that he was the only one allowed inside the building. The others remained outside, and a folding card table, chairs, and beer were provided.

As Karl entered the building, he noted on his left a small common area that housed a bar and refrigerator with two four-top tables with chairs. Behind the bar was a storage area and restroom. To his right was an enclosed meeting room where he knocked on the entrance door and entered when granted permission. Within, six people in motorcycle uniforms with helmets on the table in front of them sat around a specially designed and constructed ten feet by four feet rectangular table with the leader seated at the head. The table was old and specially constructed from thick pieces of hand-carved oak with the Nazi swastika in black in a white circle over a red background carved into its center. At the far end of the table and in the corner of the room was a free-standing Nazi flag. Several pictures of Adolf Hitler were on the walls with crowds giving the Nazi salute for the words he was providing.

The leader stood and welcomed Karl into the room and introduced him to the others in the room. He said, "I know you are wondering why you are here, and it was time I provide answers for your concern. Our organization has been requested to meet with the newest RIM representative to the United States, a Russian named Lev Petrov. If you are unfamiliar with the Russian Imperialist Movement, you will be brought up to date soon enough but know that RIM is at the forefront of worldwide growth and resurgence of the Nazi party. We are to work with him to build a nationwide plan to further grow the Nazi party and to formulate a plan for an insurrection for the takeover of the United States government. This meeting will be held in Miami Beach, Florida, on December 14th, 2018. It would be our first step in coordination with RIM in the rise of the Fourth Reich in the United States of America." He made sure Karl was paying attention before continuing. "I have met with the affiliates in our national organization and sold them on you being our representative to this meeting. I know you are wondering why you were specifically chosen, but that question has no relevance. I have watched your development and know that it is now time for you to step up and fulfill the expectations we have for you. You have carte blanche approval from myself and our affiliates for any action needed, including open warfare in the streets if it would move the needle towards a Fourth Reich. Congratulations."

The leader was looking directly at Karl expecting him to say something. Karl quickly gathered himself and said softly, "For whatever reason you have chosen me, I am humbled and grateful. Know that I will do my best for you and the party." There was a pause as he slowly rose to his feet, and he suddenly slammed down on the table with his right fist. He gave the Nazi salute and said, "Heil Hitler." They looked at him a little stunned as he again said in a forceful manner, "Heil Hitler." He watched as they quickly came to their feet and smartly saluted him and answered, "Heil Hitler."

He looked around the table forcefully at each man until he was assured that each one was committed to him in his new role as leader. When he was satisfied, he smiled broadly and reached out his hand to accept the mantle of leadership and congratulatory acknowledgments from the others. He knew now he had the lead role in his party and his decisions would not be questioned.

Virginia-FBI Headquarters

Upon being briefed by the FBI's staff of Cal Murphy's death, and later being informed by Karl Gunther of another Russian RIM operator in the United States, FBI Deputy Director Harold Thomas took action to notify CIA Director of Operations, Elizabeth Downing. She handed it off to Harry Snead to respond. He agreed to personally attend a meeting of the CIA/FBI task force.

On the edge of the Mojave Desert in a cabin outside Los Angeles, California, Director Thomas met with Harry Snead, Karl Gunther, his FBI handler, and a briefing staff of three. After pleasantries were expressed and Karl and his handler are recognized by the Director for the job they are doing, they received a formal and combined CIA/FBI briefing on RIM. It included its organization, leadership, suspected agreement with Russia to act as a mercenary fighting force in Ukraine in return for Russia's commitment to supporting RIM's growth in Europe and the United States, and RIM's latest involvement in Ukraine with General Baskov and the attack on the train.

As another part of this briefing, Karl was told the history of the Wolf and the Russian, their relationship to China and Russia through their relationship with Natasha Ivanov as the Russian President's personal bodyguard, and the Russian President's use of RIM to justify the war in Ukraine's northeast. He was told of their former efforts to assassinate the Russian president and destroy the world. He was shown the security camera footage obtained from Wolf's safe house of the stopover in Macau after their storied time in Ukraine, and pictures of all three and particularly Natasha Ivanov, a person of interest as being the nexus between RIM, China, and Russia and possibly having sent this new RIM operative to the United States. Director Thomas emphasized his belief that Russia's agreement with RIM for their fighting on Russia's behalf in Ukraine has led to a bold Russian move to aggressively support RIM in growing their cause of white supremacy in Europe and the United States and to seek internal overthrow of the United States government. The FBI Director said, "Natasha Ivanov is the key to unraveling the mysteries of what we are facing."

They all came to an agreement that the Russian Rim leader was in place and actively meeting with neo-Nazis, socialists, and other organized American haters across the country and Karl's group was only one of many.

Informants had told of meetings attended that was led by a Russian married couple. One FBI informant in attendance at one of the meetings said that it was a membership type rally, but his friend and leader later told him that all leaders were being tasked for a part in the biggest event in Neo-Nazi history that would be explained in detail to the members as the date approached.

When there was a pause, Karl said what to him is obvious, "Is there any chance this married couple is Natasha Ivanov and Nikolai Baskov and this was the next assignment for them that you referred to after the Ukraine and Macau?"

Harold and Harry looked at each other perplexed. Harry shrugged his shoulders giving Harold the intense questionable look with eyebrows up. This was neither Harry's nor Harold's area of responsibility as Customs falls within Homeland Security, but if this was them, they both realized that there had been a major breach in the system especially with them being wanted by both the FBI and Interpol.

Harry recognized that Harold deserved the right to answer first. The FBI was vastly more powerful than the CIA, especially regarding ordinary citizens. They primarily operated in the United States and had the power of arrest. Their mandate was much wider than the CIA's and they had far greater discretion in following the law as there was no one to really investigate them. Harold answered, "It was a good observation, and taken at face value it truly made sense. Maybe we did not want to see a connection because we do not want to think our system can be that vulnerable. We trusted Homeland Security to do their job. In any case, our rationalization failed whereby your fresh eyes on the situation may prove invaluable. I promise you that my staff and I will follow up with Homeland Security."

Harold thought, "We probably would have found this out sooner or later and especially at the time of the face-to-face meeting with Lev Petrov in October, but this would give us a few more months to plan if it was them. How could I have missed something so obvious? This kid is sharp. I need to recruit him into the CIA and let Mountain train him as his future replacement!"

Karl Gunther thought, "Unbelievable, can all this really be happening unknown to the average citizen and those in charge of our security?"

Harry and Harold agreed that Karl would play a key role in the future outcome of events. The Director said, "Karl, you may literally be the most important person to the United States and maybe even the world in the decisions you would make in the forthcoming months, are you ready for this?"

Karl looked hard at the Director and slowly nodded affirmatively. "Yes Sir." What else could he say to what he knew now?

Washington D.C., Homeland Security

Back in Virginia, Harold Thomas immediately contacted Jonathan Summers III, Secretary for Homeland Security, Washington D.C., for a face-to-face video conference. When connected, Director Thomas voiced his concerns that one of the most wanted men in the world by Interpol and the FBI, General Baskov, and the Russian President's personal bodyguard and a Russian military officer, Natasha Ivanov, may have slipped through Customs and was now in the United States making plans for an insurrection to overthrow the United States government. After several minutes of allowing Secretary Summers to absorb the possible ramifications of such information, Harold asked the Secretary to investigate, but if confirmed, hold until his office and the CIA can meet with him to provide a plan of action for the President. The Secretary reluctantly agreed but understood that all three agencies had responsibilities in this matter: Homeland Security for counterterrorism, the CIA for possible covert actions, and the FBI for protection from espionage and terrorist attack.

By the following morning, and after due diligence given by Homeland Security, the illegal entries of both parties were confirmed. Also discovered was the involvement and murder of a State Department employee connected to the illegal entry into the country by General Baskov. With this information provided to Harold by Secretary Summers, Harold immediately notified the CIA and asked for another joint meeting of the FBI/CIA task force in Washington with Homeland Security before taking the knowledge gained up the chain of command to the President.

At this meeting, and after much discussion, two major concerns emerged in addition to Customs possibly having to air their security lapse to the American public. The first was with the legal system. Their arrest would present jurisdiction problems and Russia might demand their return for trial as war criminals. Their trial would be the media's dream scenario for sales and sensationalism that could drag on potentially for years. There might be riots and calls for retaliation against Russia for their perceived interference in American politics, and certainly, there would be great costs, both in time and money, and in their arrest and trial.

Secondly, Nazi leaders of the pending insurrection could be charged and arrested, but there was no meat on the bone, so to speak, for prosecutors to win or even hold them, as currently there was only talk. The publicity generated in their arrest would only serve to advertise their cause, give rise to their membership, bring about protests and more riots, and further waste the court's time and money. There would again be an immediate outcry against Russia, but Russia would claim that General Baskov was a known wanted war criminal and Natasha a willing partner. The world would eventually continue as before, leaving only the American public and politicians demanding 'a pound of flesh' from Russia, but at what cost?

With all this in mind, the central question remained: if General Baskov and Natasha Ivanov were immediately arrested, would it be enough to stop the planned insurrection? They just didn't know.

The participants quickly decided to recommend to the President that Karl Gunderson be allowed to attend his meeting with Lev Petrov in Miami to gain more information. Hopefully, he would find that the term insurrection was overblown, or at minimum, he would gain enough information that presented an opening for a way out of this mess. When briefed, the President agreed. It was also agreed that the fewer people who knew about this situation, the better the chance of stopping it. Leaks in the White House were proving common and troublesome.

Miami Beach

On 14 December 2018, General Baskov met with Karl Gunderson in Miami Beach, Florida. Karl recognized him immediately as Nikolai Baskov upon being introduced to him. He looked exactly like the man in the newest Interpol Red Notice List that had both General Baskov's picture from the killings in Japan and his time in Ukraine as Adrien Balan. He also recognizes him as the man in the security camera at Wolf's safe house in Macau. He no longer hid from the world with a bald head, nerd glasses, goatee, or a big stomach. Karl saw how exceptionally fit he was, and how he dressed for power in the latest designer ads. Karl thought, "I guess he thinks he is among friends and feels safe."

Karl did not see Natasha Ivanov. Later it was determined that she had returned to Russia via the Russian Ambassador and his diplomatic immunity channels. There was now the added concern that General Baskov might also choose to leave the United States after placing his plan in motion.

In private conversation, Lev Petrov outlined a plan to Karl for an insurrection against the United States government to take place on Halloween night, 2020. He requested that the fight in the streets be initiated by the Neo-Nazi Atomwaffen Divisions located in major cities across the United States. He said, "The Neo-Nazis would start the evening by killing police officers at individual police stations and innocents in the vicinity of the police stations in as many major cities as men and weapons can be provided. Socialists would join your groups and provide the rioting and burning down of the cities. The idea is to overwhelm and inhibit the immediate response of local authority to include fire and medics. This would force more local citizens to take to the streets with guns further confusing the bad guys with the good guys. This would result in unnecessary violence. At that point, the national guard/military would be forced to be brought in. If the military can be coaxed into the fight, then it would naturally escalate until the country burns. I would see to it that you are provided stinger missiles that would provide the necessary firepower for the National Guard to request help from the active-duty military. Do not use the stingers until the National Guard first shows up."

Lev thought, "Even my Taliban friends furnishing the stinger missiles view these Godless Nazis as truly evil. We would see how they get along when all this is over."

Nodding his head slightly up and down with a half-grin, he continued, "You would determine and provide all the other strategy and firepower needed with one exception. This exception is the key to our manpower needs to continue the fight. In the early morning of the second day three, specially trained teams in coordination with Nazi guards would attack three prisons in California. I would coordinate and handle the attack on the prisons. The three teams would be armed with stinger missiles, grenades, and automatic weapons. I would provide the additional weapons needed for the prisoners we free who would join us in the fight. There are thirty-five prisons in California with some one hundred and twenty thousand plus inmates housed in facilities meant to hold eighty-five thousand. All are affiliated with local gangs, cartels, or other malcontents. These prisons and their associates are where we will find the manpower to build our army. They will want to join us. We will start our recruitment with the three prisons holding the meanest and most despicable people on the face of the earth and thank the police for getting them together in one place for our convenience.

Halloween night was chosen as it will put a lot of people in the streets partying, especially in places like New Orleans and Las Vegas, making for many available targets. There would be a panicked public response nationwide when the shooting starts exacerbated by parents outside with vulnerable children to protect, people in costumes not knowing who the enemy is and who are the candy seekers, and the police's inability to respond and help. Our followers would wear bright red latex gloves with their costumes, all others should be considered targets."

Karl thought, "This plan can very well work, and at a minimum would be disastrous for law and order in our country." Karl said, "We will do our part. We will gladly initiate the violence in the cities and use the stinger missiles against the military. Are we agreed?"

Lev said, "Agreed."

Karl said, "Give me the details on the stingers ASAP, as the numbers available will determine our capability, especially if your first priority is the prisons."

Karl extended his hand to shake with Lev Petrov and turned and walked away.

General Baskov thought, "This guy is smart. He will get his stinger missiles, but no more than two or three if he is lucky, and nowhere near the numbers I will promise him. When he realizes what I have done, it will be too late to cry foul, and he would still be the cannon fodder that I needed to start this insurrection. The key to a successful insurrection is the freeing of the prison inmates and getting them armed."

Virginia, FBI Headquarters

Karl briefed the FBI, CIA, and Homeland Security Directors on his private meeting with Lev Petrov. All three listeners shook their heads side to side at the scope and depth of the plan and knew that any part of it unfolding would be a devastating blow to the country. When finished, Karl stepped out of the briefing room while the three of them considered their options to prevent it.

Harry said, "Karl's first words in verifying Lev Petrov as General Baskov was expected, but the possibility of him escaping again as it seemed Natasha Ivanov had done, was daunting. It was possible that General Baskov in taking responsibility for the prison break-ins was meant only to provide the planning, and he too would soon be leaving. His escape would be a major blow for everyone concerned."

Harry said, "Now we have the worries of stinger missiles. That is a totally different ballgame in terms of security and the national structuring, and organizing of neo-Nazis, socialists, and other malcontents under one leader and the beginnings of an army."

There was a discussion of the merits in letting the plan all play out so that all the problems could be resolved at once, but that option had many moving parts that could each potentially take on a life of its own.

Harry knew Harold exceptionally well, as did Harold knew Harry, but the Director of Homeland Security was an unknown with two strikes against him for allowing General Baskov and Natasha Ivanov into the country illegally and being reluctant in agreeing to a Homeland

Security plan before running to the President to be first there to possibly cover his ass. So, Harry and Harold gave each other the look that they had better find out if this guy was going to push to have it all play out for a heroic ending that would save his job or if he was open to other options.

Harry led the way and commented, "Director Summers, what do you suggest?"

Summers shook his head slowly showing that there was no easy answer. "Letting it all play out provides us the possibilities of some major victories, but frankly, this guy is no ordinary criminal. He tried to destroy the world, for heaven's sake, and still is clever enough to walk between the raindrops. I want him arrested, but in today's world I'm not assured I still wouldn't be looking over my shoulder at every opportunity."

Harry and Harold look at each other and both laugh out loud. Harry said, "Welcome to the inner sanctuary. Let's all work together and find something that will work for the American people."

Before they left the room, a plan was decided with all in agreement.

CHAPTER TWENTY

IRAN, THE BATTLE FOR CONTROL OF THE RED SEA (2019-2020)

In mid-2019, Harry Snead and Sam Mountain were waiting in Harry's office for a State Department briefing on Yemen. Harry said, "I am glad you are keeping safe my friend, but the world obviously waits for no man. Maybe time will allow us a drink over dinner later? I have a lot to run by you."

In the briefing room downstairs, the Department of State briefer started with introductions of attendees from the CIA, NSA, and United States Department of State. The State briefer used pictures and charts to present an overview of the Yemen war and the environmental problem posed by a dangerously close to exploding oil product container ship, the FSO SAFER. The briefer expressed that State and the United Nations have been negotiating unsuccessfully since 2015 for a compromise that would allow the removal of the ship's oil from the abandoned tanker.

The United States offered to pay the eighty million dollars demanded and split the money evenly between the Yemen government and the rebels, but each side wanted all or nothing. Iran was holding fast to its support of Yemeni rebels by providing weapons and training for the rebels to keep fighting. The crux was that the American President was fed up with the impasse and wished for the CIA to resolve the situation. In layman's language, the President was the only one that could authorize a CIA covert action.

That afternoon, Harry and Sam had their own sit-down and shook their heads at each other knowing there was no easy solution to this problem.

Harry said, "What is not being said loudly enough is how important Yemen is in the scheme of choke points that control the world's shipping lanes. If we lose Yemen, coupled with China's plan to control the Asian Pacific Rim and their current ability to close down the Panama Canal, Russia's plan to control the newly opened shipping lanes of the Arctic, Iran's ability to close down the Suez Canal, and now Iran's further plan to gain control of access to the Arabian Sea by establishing a military base in Yemen and having control of both the Strait of Hormoz and the Strait of Bab el Mandab, all shipping from the West can be impeded. The secret sauce to them controlling these chokepoints that is not being addressed is that the container ships have tripled in size and are becoming a possible weapon to use in blocking shipping lanes and subsequently international commerce. If we give in and pay the Houthis rebels, the Red Sea is saved from an environmental disaster, but Iran gets the Red Sea port they covet. If we don't give in, the United Nations has repeatedly warned that delays in taking action to fix the FSO SAFER could lead to a man-made environmental disaster in the Red Sea four times greater than the Exxon Valdez oil spill in 1989. If the ship exploded, we get blamed for doing nothing to prevent the environmental disaster, lose Yemen to Iran anyway, and our shipping lanes are cut off. Iran is already furnishing the Houthis financial aid and weapons to include increasingly more accurate and sophisticated missiles. This would make it more difficult to remove the rebels the longer we wait."

Harry continued, "There is also the problem of our dependence on Saudi Arabia. Right now, the old king is dying, and the young prince is an unknown. He is aggressive and smart and currently put himself in a position to assume the throne, but he has a taste for opulence, a hunger for money, and a need for power. To give you an idea of what he is about, Mountain, he followed you into the Maldives after you left. In July 2015, he rented the Velaa Private Island for a month for fifty million dollars. There were over one hundred and fifty female models from as far away as Russia and Brazil. He also bought the Serene, a four-hundred-foot yacht rented by Bill Gates the year before for four hundred and sixty-six million, as well as a chateau near Versailles with a fountain and a moat for three hundred million. His security guards assassinated the journalist Jamal Khashoggi in Istanbul, and he thought nothing of it. This situation is not good and leaves us but one choice, and the reason the President put this in our lap. We will assassinate Sayat Mansouri, the Iranian Minister of Intelligence for the Iran Ministry of Intelligence Service, and send MOIS and Iran's leadership a message to stay out of Yemen. Agreed?"

Sam said, "Agreed."

Harry ordered all available resources towards locating Sayat Mansouri as a priority one. "I will get NSA on board, and while Iran is in disarray from the assassination, we will take care of the situation in Yemen." Harry thought of something that H. Keith Thompson said, "Ideals are peaceful, but history is violent."

Sam remembered an earlier time in his career when Sayat Mansouri's name was mentioned. The FBI Director had requested CIA help earlier through CIA Director of Operations Elizabeth Downing as Sayat Mansouri was bringing his terrorism in the form of assassinations to American soil. Harry was busy with events in the Ukraine and Sam was asked to take his place in New York City and meet with FBI Director Harold Thomas.

In New York, Sam remembered Sayat Mansouri's name first being surfaced by the CIA as an accomplice in the 1983 suicide bombing of two hundred and forty-one American army men asleep in their barracks in Lebanon. This was a true American tragedy ignored by succeeding fainthearted American presidents since the inaction in the 1979 takeover of the American embassy in Iran with hostages held for four hundred and forty-four days had emboldened Iran's terrorist stance and had America walking away with its tail between its legs ever since. Mansouri was rewarded and promoted gradually up the chain to Iran's second-in-command, head of the Islamic Revolutionary Guards Corps Quds Force, and the architect of Tehran's subsequent proxy conflicts in four continents that have killed thousands, including Americans.

At that time and still today, at least two attempted Iran-backed assassinations were in New York courts in ongoing trials. One was an attempt to assassinate the Saudi Arabian Ambassador in Washington DC with a restaurant bomb, and the other an attempt by four Iranian terrorists to kill an Iranian American journalist for her coverage of a lack of women's rights in Iran. Sam remembered filing a full report of his meeting with the FBI with Harry. It was forwarded up the chain of command to the White House hoping for further action on Sayat Mansouri as an Iranian terrorist. Sam thought today as he thought then, "His death would be my privilege one day."

~~~~~~

The Iraqi Consular Section is located on the U.S. Embassy compound on Al Kindi Street in the International Zone in Bagdad that overlooks the Tigris River. In late 2019, Ambassador Harold Crawford Biltmore was transmitting the information the CIA had been waiting for, Major General Sayat Mansouri would be visiting Iraq on 3 January 2020.

On 3 January 2020, Mountain was in the Democratic Republic of the Congo at the request of their government when the morning news reported that "a United States drone strike near Baghdad International Airport targeted and killed Iranian Major General Sayat Mansouri while purportedly on his way to meet the Iraqi Prime Minister in Baghdad." It was further reported that "The drone strike also killed five Iraqi nationals, including Abu Buhdi al-Mohandas -- the deputy head of the Iran-backed Iraqi Popular Mobilization Forces, and tension between Iran and the United States is at the highest level seen in years."

Sam Mountain saw the news and thought, "There is nothing clandestine about that drone strike. I guess the right President finally read my report on the man and wanted to send Iran a very clear message and I wasn't the one with a big enough bang stick to send it."

Following the assassination of Iran's security officer, Supreme Leader Ali Khatami stepped up advanced uranium enrichment at the Fordow nuclear facility south of Tehran in violation of the 2015 nuclear deal and seized a South Korean-flagged oil tanker and its crew. The Iranian Foreign Minister responded to the airstrike by saying that "the Iranian Nuclear Deal would never be renegotiated. Period."

In response, Israel exploded a limpet mine on an Iranian ship used as a base for the paramilitary Revolutionary Guard off Yemen. No one was killed, but the ship required major repairs. At Natanz, Iran, power was cut off across the facility, which was made up of above-ground workshops and underground enrichment halls. This followed a mysterious explosion at the Natanz advanced centrifuge assembly plant, now being rebuilt deep inside a nearby mountain.

Yemen (2020)

In Yemen, Houthis leader, Armik Soruri, made a mental note that his effort to remove the Saudis and their allies from Yemen was not working. Iran's weapons were slowly being received and used and were increasingly more sophisticated, particularly the missiles, but progress was slow. He was amazed the FSO SAFER had not exploded, and more amazed that the world community, especially the environmentalists, had not considered the ship a problem. The effort to convince the world of the importance of this environmental issue had fallen on deaf ears. The American press had become the American 'less,' as it appeared that raising this issue might somehow work in the American President's favor in seeking re-election at year's end if he somehow saved the day.

Even among his own people, Armik Soruri was now being considered just another terrorist. He had taken over all the means of communication, torture had become the means of extracting information and getting rid of rivals, and the people were starving as he would not allow the ports to open to humanitarian support. He thought, "Mansouri is right, the Americans are playing a waiting game and would not attack me in force as long as I have the ship to explode. What I did not consider is that the American president would willingly sacrifice the Red Sea environment and blame the Houthis when it did happen, justifying a ground war to eliminate us and to prevent Iranian control of the Red Sea. The American President may be playing a game of bluff, but right now he is winning."

CHAPTER TWENTY-ONE

SAM MOUNTAIN,

DEMOCRATIC REPUBLIC OF THE CONGO. AFRICA, (2020)

THE CONGO

Sam Mountain was in the Republic of the Congo at the personal request of President Marion Pascal Mokoco. President Mokoco was told of Mountain's abilities by the President of Nigeria, Jonathan Patience, who Mountain helped out in late 2013 with the president's problems with Hezbollah and Islamist terrorists in the north of the country. On President Patience's recommendation, Mokoco requested the United States President to lend a hand with the problem, a loosely affiliated group of local militias under the umbrella name of Mai-Mai that were battling for power and resources, mainly oil, in eastern Congo.

Mountain was in Africa on several occasions as a Navy Seal when on active duty and assigned to the United States African Command located at Kelly Barracks in Stuttgart, Germany. He also spent time in Nigeria in 2013 fighting Boca Harem. He was glad that Harry had requested a Navy Seal fire-team assigned to African Command to back him up in case of trouble this time around. The team was flown into the Congo Republic via a Chinook to await further orders. The helicopter was armed with two M134 7.62mm electrically operated, air-cooled mini guns and two M240 7.62mm belt-fed machine guns mounted on either side of the fuselage at the forward and rear sections.

Christian-dominated countries like the Congo, ninety-seven percent Christian, had become targets of jihadists. Islamic State was collapsing in Iraq and Syria, but from the jungles of Eastern Congo, a jihadist appeared on YouTube to declare that the so-called caliphate was regrouping in Central Africa. He said, "I swear by God this is the abode of Islamic State." He was initially dismissed as a headline seeker, but three years later, his group of Congo and Mozambique militants had soared in numbers estimated to be around fifteen hundred members.

Known as ISCAP, the swelling band of Congo and Mozambique-based militants, once fighting for autonomy from the central government, had this year become one of the terror group's deadliest franchises. Led by a veteran Ugandan jihadist, Musa Baluku, the Congolese militia previously known as the Allied Democratic Forces, or ADF, killed over 849 civilians in 2020 alone, according to the State Department. Islamic State's new local ally, the ADF, sprang out of a 1990s rebellion by Muslims in Uganda who felt persecuted by the regime of President Yoweri Museveni. Under pressure from Kampala, the group took refuge in Eastern Congo, a hotbed of armed groups that have long fought over rich mineral resources in a region with little central government control.

No longer vowing to seize and hold territory, Islamic State instead had embraced guerrilla tactics, improved local leadership, and dramatically improved training, tactics, and propaganda—and giving the impression it can strike at Western interests in unexpected places. ISIS provided funding and training but didn't direct its day-to-day operations.

In Sam Mountain's view, why this request for his service was granted was not the ever-on-going loss of life over poverty versus dollars, although hundreds of park rangers and visitors had been killed over the years, but it was because the violence was taking place in Virunga National Park. The Park is the oldest national park in Africa and second oldest in the world behind Yellowstone Park, and home to around one thousand of the remaining mountain gorillas, the famous silverbacks. People have always pulled for the underdog, and for the gorillas to hold on to this land would require decisions to keep the land undeveloped which is not necessarily in the best interests of the people living there.

There were issues of ownership going back to 1925 when the park was established, and like the Amazon rainforest, this land contributed to reducing the greenhouse effect, biodiversity, and a stable climate by absorbing the dioxide, and releasing the oxygen that we as the world, depend on for us to survive. The United States President had sided with the gorillas and other endangered primates over the developers and ordered the CIA to do what it could to assist the Congo Republic's president. Harry and Mountain were assigned the task.

Sam Mountain was a vanishing breed in the CIA, with twenty-one official kills and other non-official kills too numerous to remember, he was old school CIA married to his job and a stone-cold killer of bad people. He brought integrity and honor to an organization that once lost its way.

At the end of World War II, General MacArthur found out through interrogation of Japanese prisoners captured in the Philippines, and them exchanging information for their lives, that General Yamashita, the Japanese commander in the Philippines, buried a vast amount of gold and other treasure accumulated during Japan's conquest and looting of Eastern Asia. Emperor Hirohito and his top military commanders concocted a plan called the Golden Lily to bury looted treasures in the Philippines from conquered countries in the Far East for use after the war. Americans captured during the invasion of the Philippines were used as slave labor to bury the treasure valued in the billions in one hundred and seventy-four separate burial sites. The Americans were then buried alive with the treasure when the sites deep within the Philippine mountains were sealed.

MacArthur informed President Harry Truman of the information he obtained from prisoners about the treasure and Truman met with him in Asia and agreed that the information was credible. Over the next two years, the CIA supposedly found four treasure sites worth billions in gold and other treasure recovered. President Truman agreed with MacArthur to keep the treasure as no one knew who owned the assets and it would probably clog up the courts forever in a lawyer-feeding frenzy. Truman had in mind another purpose for the money.

President Truman recognized the need following World War II for a new, fully functional post-war independent civilian intelligence organization within the executive branch, as Russia and communism were becoming the new threat. So, in 1947 he signed the National Security Act creating the Central Intelligence Agency. He saw the treasure found in the Philippines to finance the CIA without accountability to Congress. A trust fund called the Black Eagle Trust Fund was secretly created and money used as seen fit by the CIA Director, a civilian operating independently of Congress, to keep America safe as he saw fit. The Black Eagle Trust Fund stored its treasure in one hundred and seventy-six bank accounts in forty-two countries.

Truman's intentions were good, but he turned loose an unaccountable group that led the United States to engage in sixty-four covert and six overt attempts at regime change during the following 'Cold War' years. One of these CIA operations included the United States and United Kingdom-orchestrating the 1953 Iranian coup d'état to put the Shaw in power, a decision still being dealt with today.

The CIA's independence from Congress was reined in somewhat later on with such missteps as joining with the American Mafia to invade Cuba; trying to assassinate Cuban President Fidel Castro; threatening the deaths of John and Bobby Kennedy, if not actually killing them; using African American men as experimental subjects for new drugs without their knowledge; starting the Vietnam War with the fake Gulf of Tonkin incident; selling drugs from Vietnam by shipping them into the United States in body bags of dead Americans; selling and distributing opium from Afghanistan's poppy fields as needed to sustain their economy and the list of abuses goes on and on.

Mountain dedicated his life to a renewal of integrity within the agency and doing his job in the best interests of his country, the President, and the American people. He took no personal gain and blended his mantra of ethics to what he knew worked in both the moment and in the long term. Torture, for example, had its moments, but did not work in the long-term interests of America. He only hoped that he could make a difference.

He was straddling the equator near Burundi in the Virunga National Park, and the African heat was beginning its relentless toll on all breathing things, including himself. In observing the sun slowly climbing upwards overhead, he was reminded that like the sun, his kills had been climbing, especially in recent months. When he had last talked with Harry and mentioned this to him, Harry had asked him a question about his work that gave Sam some perspective on both their jobs.

Harry had said, "Sam, am I making decisions on who lives and who dies because I am getting too cynical for this job and simply choosing death as the easiest solution for resolving problems and ignoring the longer-range solutions that require more effort?"

Sam thought about what Harry was asking and concluded that Harry had come to a point in his life that he needed assurance that his decisions were thoughtful and that he is still doing what is right and best for the people of the United States, particularly his staff, who he personally placed in harm's way.

Like Sam, Harry knew that the President was a final authority for a kill. The latter required a leap of faith by the President in his CIA Director to make the right decision to protect the office of the presidency, as there was a CIA history with Congress and the American people that had evaporated trust and the wrong decision could bring a government down. Sam replied, "No Harry, you are just hitting your stride in knowing with confidence the best decision to get us through all this."

Harry replied, "Thanks."

Sam's thoughts continued, "The new generation thought more in terms of themselves and their personal career, money to be made, and time spent in quality-of life issues such as their annual ski trip; they think that they deserve it all without sacrifice and willingly move problems down the road if an immediate solution is not available to them. The future is their wall. James Baldwin said it best in his book "I am not Your Negro" even though he was talking about a different wall, *"You don't know what's happening on the other side of the wall because you don't want to know.* is not."

Iran was a good example. Iran with a nuclear bomb was not a problem for the new generation of CIA as they didn't see Iran as an immediate threat to the United States, but only to Israel. Mountain thought to himself, "Would Harry and I have played second fiddle to Israel in our recent adventure with Iran if Iran was considered an immediate threat to the United States? My answer would be that this problem would have disappeared a long time ago. But I, like Harry, can find some hope that government employees at all levels are on a pace to eventually see the need of looking at the potential of an escalating problem considering the future. The wall requires a view of both sides of it."

Sam, in his growing discomfort in the heat of the camouflage, thought, "and I am in the Congo Republic trying to get all of us through this because I must believe I am also hitting my stride and doing my best for the American people. I love the CIA and I love my job, but decisions of history deserve some review and Congress has oversight but has failed us by making all reviews political. We are subsequently the number one intelligence agency in the world in the gathering of information but ranked below Israel in our ability to act upon it."

Mountain peered from beneath his camouflaged covering that he had been under for two days and was now starting his third day. He was tired, sweaty, dirty, and eaten up with insect bites, but he maintained his discipline. His nest was the result of a four-day circuitous and grueling hike south deep into the Congo's Virunga National Park in hopes of finding some answers to the problems presented by the militants. He had entered the park overland via Uganda.

He brought his M40A5 sniper rifle with a suppressor up from the bottom portion of the camouflage and searched the area for targets, but it was early, or maybe it would be another day of no shows. His chosen place of hiding was limited in visibility due to the thickness of the lush flora surroundings and hillsides, but he did have an overview of a game trail and small watering hole.

Seeing the movement of flora on the trail below and to his left, Mountain dismissed all thoughts and brought his focus back to his mission at hand. He brought his sniper rifle up from the camouflage and his scope to bear on the target. There were three of them, all armed. There are nearly seven hundred rangers based in the park that covered an area three times the size of Rhode Island. They were considered police officers and were authorized to carry a weapon and make arrests, but these three men were not park rangers.

He decided to watch them and knew that this was risky in that they could quickly disappear in the dense flora but killing them would solve nothing as the leaders that sent them would only think they were ambushed by another rebel group or park rangers. So, Sam let them pass hoping they would return, so they could be followed to their camp.

When the morning of the following day arrived, Mountain realized he probably made the wrong decision in allowing the three men to pass but decided to wait until the afternoon to abandon his site just in case the three men were purposely staying out all night and returning today. By late afternoon, Mountain decided he was wasting his time and the three men probably didn't even have a permanent camp and stayed on the move due to the skill of the park rangers.

He took one last view of the area to his left and saw nothing, but when he brought the gun and scope back to the right to brace his elbow to rise from his camouflage, he glimpsed movement of the flora down the hill coming towards him. It was three different men heading in the opposite direction of the first three men who passed yesterday. Mountain said to himself, "I was wrong, the camp is on the right of me, and the first three men were returning to camp from night patrol and these three men are leaving the camp to go out on night patrol." When the men passed, Mountain knew that if he is correct, the men would be returning to camp the following morning and he would follow them. He bedded down once again in his camouflage and waited patiently for their return.

Mountain thought back to his college days and the fun he and his twin brother had together. Mountain was the more serious one and the one more highly recruited by the University of Georgia as a five-star football player. His brother played but loved to party with the women, and later, after marriage and children, it would eventually lead him to an embarrassing death in a Kroger parking lot while having sex with a woman who was not his wife.

Mountain's time in the military as a Navy Seal, and later with the CIA, had isolated him from finding the right woman, although he had fallen in love once. While serving as a sniper on special assignment to Iraq, he had helped an injured soldier to a temporary support hospital and met Amie, an Army nurse captain on her first deployment. He had stood there like a dummy while she tried to coax enough information out of him to find out what had happened to the wounded soldier. For some reason, the normally coherent thoughts and words were not coming forth. In frustration she finally commented, "You do talk, don't you?" And, in an insulting way, he answered, "yes I do." She quickly replied," Go get me a soft drink and sit down somewhere outside and I'll be on break and join you in five minutes."

The rest of the day became his most cherished memory. He often asked himself how so much commitment and sharing could have come from so little time spent together. There was no rational answer. They simply fell in love. The next morning, he was on the way to the hospital to say goodbye when the rocket attack began. He watched in horror one rocket descend in a direct hit on the hospital.

With first daylight, Mountain forced himself fully awake, and approximately an hour later his expectation was met with the reality of the three men returning from the night patrol. When they passed, Mountain strained to make his body respond to movement, and slowly and surely, he shed and packed his camouflage skin and followed the men on the trail. An hour later, he smelled the aroma of coffee in the air and decided to leave the trail when he detected the faint conversations of an encampment in front of him.

For the next hour-plus, he slowly and cautiously crawled towards the sounds and looked for any opening he may find, whereby, he could access the encampment. The flora was so thick that every inch felt like a victory. In what seemed like an eternity, he came to an opening on the edge of a plateau area and a deforested view that Mountain had determined by GPS to be the border of Burundi. There he found what he was looking for: an encampment of militants. He carefully looked and listened, for the sound of dogs but heard and saw none.

Half the jihadists were a ragtag bunch of young men, mostly older teens, interspersed with grown men and women. There were no children. Mountain counted thirty-five militants in this group. Most of the older men and some of the women carried some version of the AK-47 Russian Kalashnikov assault rifle on a strap sling slung against their body. The younger ones carried a pistol and machete, if not a rifle.

What he did not expect to see were five people in the right corner of the camp in a cage. Mountain thought they must be the five visitors to the park kidnapped a week ago. The two men and three women look beaten, haggard, and in need of food and water.

Mountain slowly moved backwards into the flora to find a good spot to wait for nightfall with a good view of the camp. One thing that Mountain did not want to do was underestimate the youth in the group. They had been raised hard and experienced the slaughter of others by or with the older members of the group. Some may be ten to fifteen years of age, but they were hardened in what they have had to do to survive. Mountain reminded himself, "I cannot treat them like normal children."

Mountain had crawled far enough away from the camp and notified the Seal Team leader of the strength of the camp, its location, and the five hostages being held in a cage within the camp. Mountain and the Seal Team leader quickly put together a plan that started with a 2 am Seal Team HILO drop and parachute sail into the eastern camp area away from the dense flora. Mountain input his best guess at where the camp's night patrol would be at the time of the drop. This type of approach would mute the helicopter noise and allow selective combat in protecting the hostages in lieu of the helicopter randomly destroying the village and all occupants.

The Seal Team would walk in the remaining half-mile from the drop, initiate their attack at 0300 using night vision goggles and grenades. This should provide the Team and Mountain an advantage against the numbers, but that was another one of the many unknowns and not taken for granted. The helicopter, at the time of the attack, would swoop in and put their lights on the village for the forward guns and give time for discarding of night vision glasses before mop-up began.

Mountain suggested using a loudspeaker demanding the surrender of the jihadists in the same manner as the CIA used in Tennessee for the Neo-Nazi operation. Mountain would provide oversight protection for the hostages during the battle and anticipate the return of the night patrol at the sounds of the battle, or if by chance they saw or heard the helicopter approaching and returned earlier.

Mountain crawled back to the edge of the camp for the next few hours in a protected spot with a good view of the hostages to watch for the direction of anybody arriving or leaving the camp, particularly the night patrol or a raiding party. In the late afternoon, he watched as three men departed in the same direction as the three men he followed into the camp and assumed they were the new night patrol. Mountain removed himself from the edge of the camp and slowly crawled away and spent the next couple of hours finding a perfect shooter's location for meeting his mission responsibilities. He patiently waited further back from the camp until nightfall to move into the new forward position.

Mountain pulled himself up to a sitting position against a tree and leaned back to rest a moment. He donned his night vision goggles and almost swallowed his tongue in a silent scream as a nine-foot black mamba snake crossed under the heels of his boots where he had pulled his knees upward to rest his weapon. The snake's head popped up about a foot in the air as it came out the near side of his legs and stopped to observe its new surroundings. Mountain was breathless and rigid in fear.

The snake, his regal grey head sleek like the portrayal of ancient Egyptian gods, turned slowly and majestically towards him. His coffin-like head's mouth opened to show the black interior for which he was named. As the second deadliest snake in the world, his venom could kill you in forty-five minutes without treatment, and seven hours with treatment. He was lithe and athletic and could travel with speeds up to twelve miles an hour, and unlike Mountain, he had not made a hunter's mistake. The snake was motionless for a split second which was a lifetime to Mountain but determined his prey unworthy. As quickly as his speed suggested, the snake turned and disappeared into the flora.

Mountain knew the snake jolted his senses and subsequently his reflexes. He was completely caught off guard and the recovery processes that he had depended upon over the years were foggy as he slowly regained his composure. He thought, "I screwed up. I cannot afford to mentally relax or be vulnerable for even a moment. I assumed I was safe. I got cocky. Mistakes like this would get me killed and worse yet, others that think I am such a professional that they have placed their lives in my hands." He thought, "What would I have done if the snake had attacked? And why didn't it attack?" Mountain was questioning everything and was particularly upset because he knew he was just plain lucky. Mountain understood that in his world luck was a word that could never be rational thought. Hope was for the afterlife.

Mountain's approach to discipline and combat was shaped by Admiral James Stockdale's Vietnam experience. Listening to the account of his story had impacted his life and allowed him to cope with the loss of Amie and find meaning in serving his country. He had embraced every word like a lifeline to continue and live by them, and now he had to admit to luck, the ugliest word in the dictionary, to save his life.

James Stockdale

"September 9, 1965, was a life-changing day for James Stockdale. It was the day that his Douglas A-4 Skyhawk was shot out of the sky, forcing him to eject to save his own life. The North Vietnamese detained Stockdale at the Hỏa Lò Prison, the infamous "Hanoi Hilton." He soon established communications among the American prisoners of war, and a code of rules to organize the prisoners and boost their morale.

When the abuse of American POWs reached a climax in 1969, Stockdale was selected by his captors as a trophy for their propaganda. Knowing that he wouldn't be paraded if he was disfigured, he cut his own scalp with a razor and then beat his own face with a wooden stool, foiling his captors' plans.

After Stockdale found out that several POWs had been tortured to death, he slit his own wrists to show that he would rather die than capitulate to his captors. From that night on, the practice of torturing American POWs stopped in the facility. Stockdale finally returned home to the United States in 1973. In 1976, he was awarded the Medal of Honor for his heroism.

Once, Stockdale had invited Jim Collins, a management scholar, out to lunch. Collins asked Stockdale about how he persevered while in Vietnam. "I never lost faith at the end of the story," replied Stockdale. "I never doubted not only that I would get out, but also that I would prevail in the end and turn the experience into the defining event of my life, which, in retrospect, I would not trade."

Collins then asked about the kinds of people who didn't make it out of the Hanoi Hilton. "The optimists," came the response. And then Stockdale explained. "Oh, they were the ones who said, 'We're going to be out by Christmas. And Christmas would come, and Christmas would go. Then they'd say, 'We're going to be out by Easter.' And Easter would come, and Easter would go. And then Thanksgiving, and then it would be Christmas again. And they died of a broken heart." After a moment of silence, Stockdale finished his thought. "This is a very important lesson."

"You must never confuse faith that you would prevail in the end — which you can never afford to lose — with the discipline to confront the most brutal facts of your current reality, whatever they might be."

The Attack

Mountain took the time to ensure the snake was gone and there would be no more surprises. He knew he did not anticipate the snake as a part of his environment, and it was a mistake in the discipline that he would not make again. He rebooted, given the second chance, met his fear head-on, and settled in to provide coverage for the hostages and prepared for the later attack on the village the following morning. He cleared his mind and generated various scenarios that could take place when the attack began so there would be no hesitation or lack of a decision on the necessary action to be taken. He understood that the fewer variances in battle decisions reduced the chaos that was always present in war.

The American Seal Team began its attack as planned at 0300 with silencers killing a couple of sentries, two others by the campfire still conversing, and two women taking a bathroom break together. This assault opening was followed immediately by grenade explosions that took out the five nearest tent occupants. The tents were mostly individual and easy to pack and carry, but some were larger for supplies, for eating of meals, administrative functions, and two for officers.

The camp was suddenly fully awake and responding to the attack. One tent flap opened, and a man hurried out lifting his rocket-propelled grenade launcher to the now fast-approaching helicopter. Mountain made an exception to his responsibilities and killed him.

As guns were starting to fire throughout the camp, and the grenade explosions and resultant fires provided the vision for the militants, the helicopter lights were turned on blinding the jihadists and their shooting accuracy, allowing the Seal Team members and Mountain to remove their night goggles and adjust their eyes to the lights. A loudspeaker came on telling the jihadists to cease-fire, put down their weapons, lay down on the ground with their hands out in front of them, and surrender. To make the point that surrender was the best option, the forward helicopter gun with one burst took out eight more tents and its occupants. Some militants responded instantly and did as told, but one commander took a group of five from the back tents and disappeared into the flora.

The remaining six jihadists were retreating away from the helicopter and backward towards the caged captives. With relief, Mountain saw the remaining jihadists stop and throw down their weapons and lie down on the ground. They all surrendered, except the one remaining commander who had found his way back to the hostages and was now preparing to fire. Mountain killed him.

When Mountain was convinced the terrorist was dead, he quickly shifted his attention to guarding the camp against the potential return of the three jihadists out on night patrol. He communicated his location to the Seal Team leader and his concern for the six jihadists that escaped into the flora, including a probable commander from the rear area of the camp.

The Seal Team leader quickly gathered his prisoners and their weapons in one spot. He then ordered the helicopter to fly a perimeter check for the remaining jihadists and for two members of his team to secure the camp and check on and free the hostages and find some water and food, if available. Mountain remained alert.

A short time later, Mountain spotted on his right the three-night patrol men running towards the camp and notified the Seal Team leader. Mountain had time for one clear shot and killed the lead man. The second man dove headfirst into the flora to his left and screamed unknown words at his attackers. The third man rushed into camp firing wildly at nothing and was killed by a Seal Team member. Mountain waited patiently until the second man stopped screaming but was concerned that the jihadist had gathered himself and was now trying to retreat or was making his way towards the camp to avenge his friends.

The Seal Team was now vulnerable, so Mountain decided that he must immediately find and kill the jihadist so there were no surprises. He told the Seal Team leader his intentions and exited the flora into the camp and turned right to get on the easily accessible path used by the militants. He laid down his rifle and gently removed his pistol from its holder. He knew he was extremely vulnerable now, but he also knew that in all probability, this jihadist was inexperienced, new, or not properly trained, otherwise he would not have been on patrol duty. Mountain thought, "He would stand up to fire his weapon, thus giving me a chance." At least that was how Mountain justified the breaking of other procedures and being reckless.

He shortly saw his first kill on the path and proceeded more prudently. When he neared the dead man, the bush on the right violently rustled, and Mountain unloaded his handgun in response. When all again was quiet, Mountain proceeded to the bush responsible for the movement. Continuing his breaking of protocols, he parted the bush for a first look and quickly jumped back. He collected himself and looked again and saw what could have been him several hours ago.

The now-dead jihadist had dived headfirst onto the nine-foot black mamba and was snake-bitten to death. The snake was still curled around the body, but a lucky shot from Mountain killed the snake in place. Mountain said out loud, "I hate that word lucky." He took a picture of the scene and sent it to Harry, a first, and the caption read, "Make mine a double."

Harry replied, "You got it, but right now we have a problem." The Seal Team leader reported that one of the released hostages said that the commander that escaped into the woods with the five other jihadists arrived two days prior and spoke perfect English. She also said that they called him "the Imam."

Even Mountain couldn't help himself and replied, "Holy cow, you mean the man himself, Africa's most wanted warlord, the man with a seven-million-dollar bounty?"

Harry replied once again, "You got it."

Mountain unintentionally said out loud, "What would he be doing here?"

Harry answered, "My guess is that the Boko Haram leader saw a way to expand his presence outside of Nigeria. When he heard about this jihadist braggart on YouTube talking about a new califate starting in the Republic of the Congo, he coupled that information with the new uprisings next door in Chad to overthrow their long-time ruler and supporter of the West as not only a good idea, but one that is doable. He decides it was worth his time to pay a visit. A new caliphate with him as a leader has great potential to rejuvenate his cause if he can combine the resources of Nigeria, Chad, and the Republic of the Congo in the heart of Africa. He was probably looking to meet up with this new jihadist and recruit him after hearing of his work in a siege in which he proved himself worthy to the Imam by massacring dozens of women and children in a key Mozambique port city and sending thousands running for their lives through forests and mangrove swamps. This coupled with a raid on a prison that freed thirteen hundred militants showed an ability to plan and recruit."

Sam Mountain thought, "The Imam, a child beggar turned jihadist, kidnapped tens of thousands of children, forcing them into battle, suicide vests, or marriage. The longest-lasting terrorist in the world, he has survived inside remote forest hideouts while using the internet to marshal his brand of extreme violence. He has been described as possessing a photographic memory. And, here he is, no less, within our grasp."

He said to Harry, "Did the helicopter that pursued him have any news?"

Harry replied, "The helicopter was only doing a perimeter check to be sure the jihadists were not circling back behind the Seals to catch them unprepared. We don't have the necessary asset in place to find him at this point in this flora, but President Patience has a plan to welcome the Imam back to Nigeria, but right now I need you to return safely with the hostages."

Nigeria

In Nigeria, President Jonathan Patience was getting the good news that the Imam was spotted by the Americans in the Republic of the Congo. It was more good news that his friend Sam Mountain was there and would be heading his way in the not-to-distant future to help eliminate this plague upon his land. President Patience was excited. He spent what seemed a lifetime trying to find a way to stop this madman and had only been rewarded with car bombs in churches, grenades thrown in crowded bars, prison break-ins, bank robberies, consistent abductions of foreigners and the wives of government officials, and hundreds of school children taken and held for ransom. He now knew the Imam was out of the country and that this was his opportunity to pull his plan together to ensure the terrorist reign of this madman ended.

CIA Headquarters, April 2020

At Langley, Sam Mountain was finishing his double bourbon on the rocks and de-briefing Harry on his latest trip to the Congo Republic and finding the "Imam" there. When he finished, Harry said, "President Mokoco extends his deepest appreciation for your help." President Mokoco sent a message for you. It reads, "A clear message was sent to these jihadists that they are not welcome in my country. They now understand that any attempt to further establish an Islamic califate would be met with extreme prejudice. We could not be more thankful for the support that you and the United States military have provided. Thank you."

Harry said, "You sure landed in it down there, didn't you?"

Sam replied, "That snake scared the holy bejesus out of me. I was taken so unaware. That frightened me more. I must admit it shook me up."

Harry said with a smirk, "I got something coming up that would give that snake in your head at least some momentary pause. The Israelis are now formally requesting your assistance in stopping Iran's nuclear program."

Mountain replied sarcastically, "I thought I was a secret agent, and no one knew I existed?"

Harry rolled his eyes and didn't give him the satisfaction of an answer. Harry continued, "The Israelis are concerned that Iran is too far along in developing their nuclear bomb and we have agreed to help the Israelis impede their progress. The White House is concerned that we are getting blamed for Iran's success because we withdrew from the Iranian Nuclear Deal."

Sam said, "So, what's the plan?"

Harry said, "I'll let you know when I know.

CHAPTER TWENTY-TWO

HO LI CHUNG and ANTON LUPU,

THE WOLF (2017-2020)

By year's end of 2018, a very deadly disease was developed in the Wuhan lab and all expectations were for a cure by the following year. However, unexpectantly in mid-2019, the three Wuhan Center scientists all showed signs of infection. It appeared that one or more of the scientists underestimated the ability of the disease to spread and protocols were broken. An airborne disease was loosed and escaped the lab due to the scientists' travels outside the lab. The Wuhan marketplace became a petri dish for advancing the rapid spread of the disease and shortly, many Chinese were becoming sick and dying.

On 13 January 2020, WHO confirmed a case of what was now dubbed Covid-19 in Thailand, the first recorded case outside of China. President Li now had his pandemic, but no control of it. The USA President imposed a nationwide travel ban on China on January 31st, 2020, being the first to blame China for not being forthright about how, when, and where Covid-19 started. He received no support from the WHO and America's left condemned the travel ban by saying, "it typically supported the American President's record of hysteria, xenophobia, and fear-mongering."

The refusal of China to take responsibility for the disease coupled with the inability of the American President to receive the needed support of the American people, and especially the press and avowed left, killed many people in the following months and allowed the import of the disease within the communities of the world. The World Health Organization proclaimed the coronavirus a pandemic on March 11, 2020.

China's Fishing Fleet

From 2018 to 2020, President Li watched the growth of China's fishing fleet and could not be more pleased. By 2020, it was the world's largest and was having a much more effective impact on the world economy than President Li ever imagined. A growing distance water fishing fleet of seventeen thousand boats with fishing trawlers as large as two hundred feet, coupled with the building of a worldwide network of ports often defended by the Chinese navy, fuels a worldwide concern for China's aggressiveness and Taiwan as their low hanging fruit.

China's willingness to overfish, use illegally sized nets and other equipment, poach, deplete other nation's fisheries, break license permits, destroy others equipment and fishing nets, and send militia fishermen to set up settlements to help China act on territorial claims was bringing China to the forefront of the world's economy and building a well-fed Chinese middle-class that supported President Li's actions.

Additionally, China moved aggressively to establish dominance in the waters surrounding the Philippines, Vietnam, Malaysia, Indonesia, and Taiwan by building artificial islands in disputed waters from sand harvested from the ocean bottom to extend China's legal claims of fishing and mineral rights out another two hundred miles from the mainland as allowed by The Law of the Sea.

All indications were that the newer boats were armed and interchangeable between fishing and military use. The Philippines was the first to sound the alarm as over two hundred and twenty Chinese militia/fishing boats occupied the Whitsun reef west of the archipelago supposedly to fish. This was proven to be more of a trolling expedition for possible territorial claims.

Ho Li Chung's overall and clear message to the world was that "If you want to do business in China, it must be at the expense of American values."

∿∿∿∿∿

By 2020, Hong Kong was far along in being brought to its knees. President Li was ready to invade Taiwan. The Wolf, when asked by President Li, advised caution as China was being blamed for the pandemic, and coupled with an American president facing re-election, might force the United States into a full military response. The Wolf suggested that China's economy was presently vulnerable to American sanctions as being too closely tied to Wall Street and other capitalistic markets. There were also problems of corruption, control of public opinion on the internet, and a general lack of understanding of the party's' leadership role in values sought in both public and private matters. He suggested a tightening up at home by the party before an invasion was considered that would allow control of the narrative and the ability to survive American sanctions on the economy and in the financial market. President Li decided to take Wolf's advice to wait.

President Li was glad to have the Wolf as an advisor and knew that an invasion of Taiwan at this time would jeopardize China's economy and give rise to the voices of capitalism and democracy. He concluded that he needed to bring the people's expectations to align to party positions more closely. He knew he must prepare the country for war with his plan to take back Taiwan, and the people of China to speak as one voice with the CCP, China's communist party. President Li took immediate action to arrest and intimidate the independent and rich entrepreneurs of China's economy, disengage from Wall Street, the American financial market, and close the internet.

During these years of being a close advisor to President Li, Wolf worked the oil storage, mixing, and sales in coordination with Iran and Chinese officials and all is a go by the latter part of 2019.

CICIA Headquarters

Harry said, "I am seeing evidence that Wolf and maybe even the Russian have hooked up again to sell Iranian oil to North Korea and China in violation of United States sanctions. I have only speculation to date, but this reeks of Wolf's knowledge in the use of the black market for personal gain. We pulled an analysis of the oil business worldwide from the International Energy Agency for the first half of 2020. To quote IEA, "there was a global inventory increase of 1.39 billion barrels based upon an estimate of supply and demand. Out of this, it was observed that roughly a quarter had some spare storage in countries that are part of the

Organization for Economic Cooperation and Development, while 8% was in floating storage, 68% of the oil is considered missing."

Harry said, "There are a lot of reasons why this figure can be inaccurate, but what we do know is that a lot of oil is missing. Separate analysis revealed one other fact, that China's imports increased substantially in the first half of 2020 despite the substantially weakened economic activity and reduced refinery runs. I am going to assume that I think circumstantial evidence supports, and that is that oil was stockpiled by non-OECD countries like China and is being used or would be used to manipulate the financial markets. In the financial markets, this is truly a 'Black Swan. Although it appeared that China is the primary abuser, it was larger than a China problem. Since the OEPC is no longer able to set the standard price of a barrel of oil, non-OPEC countries like China are hiding or stocking oil waiting for a surge in demand to release their oil. These manipulated releases of oil, cause a sudden jump-rise in the price of a barrel of oil, resulting in millions of dollars of profits in the stock market to the speculators. The Wolf has the contacts, reputation, organization, and money to make this all happen. These actions, if known, could undermine the people's trust in the markets, and lead to a collapse of the entire financial market. Yes, it's only speculation right now, but yes, I do think he is the kingpin. He is a genius at this sort of thing."

Mountain said, "How are they avoiding the sanctions? I thought we had shut down the stolen oil business in Nigeria? And wouldn't we pick up on that vast amount of money being moved through the world's banking systems?"

Harry answered, "The Wolf didn't use Nigeria, a banking system, or stolen oil. He is transferring Iranian oil to Iraqi ships just miles offshore at the Iraqi port of Al-Faw in the Persian Gulf. The mixed Iranian and Iraqi oil is again mixed with oil cargoes from other countries to disguise its origins, and eventually ends up on sale in world markets as non-sanctioned Iraqi oil. Iraqi oil can be sold at a significant premium to oil of Iranian origin. China and North Korea appear to be the primary buyers at this time. The monies are exchanged on the internet as digital currency or cryptocurrencies that are not handled by the traditional banking systems that use bank money held on computers.

Mountain said, "Like bitcoin? "

Harry answered, "Exactly, but not bitcoin in this case, as bitcoin is too well known and is too public now, but the exchange used did meet the criteria for which we are looking. Any type of virtual currency that is unregulated digital money, which is issued and usually controlled by its developers, and used and accepted among the members of a specific virtual community. Bitcoin and its alternatives are based on cryptographic algorithms, so these kinds of virtual currencies are also called cryptocurrencies. Clear as mud?" Mountain just smiled.

Harry continued: "The Wolf may have his own cryptocurrency exchange, or it could be a test of China's new digital currency exchange run by their central bank or another exchange that is unknown to us at this point. They are doing a lot of experimenting with what is called neo-banking. The basic idea behind the term is that a digital wallet holding cash or cryptocurrency can be linked-to payments and other forms of commerce or financial services. These online systems, whatever they may be, are designed to allow possible avoidance of United States oversight and taxes or in China's case, it gave them oversight of Wolf's activities and accountability of their monies which gave them further reason to do business with him. So far, he has been able to evade our efforts to find him or under Chinese protection, but we may have to resort to a riskier assassination in Hong Kong if he is not traveling anymore. We obviously cannot let him go forward with his plans to manipulate the world energy market. With Russia now a major player in Europe, thanks to the completion of the Nord Stream II pipeline, and China's rise to the top player in the oil market in Asia, we need a more aggressive policy to eliminate the Wolf."

CHAPTER TWENTY-THREE

RIM-United States of America (2019-2020)

Harry Snead opened the first meeting of the CIA/FBI and Homeland Security meeting by stating the obvious, "If we can make General Nikolai Baskov disappear, we can save ourselves and our country a lot of heartaches. Fortunately, we are sworn to obey the law contrary to the actions of my favorite tv character Sergeant Hank Voight on Chicago PD. So, I would state clearly that what we must present to the President is a workable arrest plan to put him in jail. We need to have a focused consensus that American law means something and that we would fully support any better suggestions in handling this matter, but not if it entails an illegal act or cover-up. The President must be on the side of law and order in the way this is handled. There have been too many lies, or half-truths told to the American people over the years that have eroded overall confidence in government, but this would not be a lie told by us. We must trust the American people to see their way through all the noise and internal conflict this arrest may cause and believe in the old saying of 'what didn't kill you, only made you stronger, that we would land on our feet and somehow work together to find truth and justice for all people in our capitalistic society."

As such, the plan was finalized and agreed upon by all, but it was not perfect, and certainly not simple, but seemed the best solution available in addressing the need to immediately arrest Lev Petrov, Nikolai Baskov, while protecting his legal rights. As such, it was important that the plan mitigated where possible the impending media explosion, street demonstrations, and judicial costs when American citizens found out that Russia was planning and organizing a terrorist attack in the United States.

He said, "There would be also plenty of support for Nikolai Baskov and RIM. It must be emphasized to the President that a public trial of Nikolai Baskov would be necessary but could drag out for years causing inexhaustible internal debate, costs, and conflict. The trial would provide RIM with much-needed recruiting publicity and probably intensify conflict with Russia and China. It was bad enough that it just might prove RIM right that internal conflict would lead to the eventual demise of the American experiment in democracy. We are betting that it won't."

With all agreed, the plan was presented to the President with the Secretary of Defense in attendance. FBI Director Harold Thomas briefed the plan to the President with no staff otherwise involved. The Secretary of Defense had numerous questions, some of which had no immediate answers, but finally agreed to fall in line when the President placed his stamp of approval on it with two caveats. One was "that Congress was briefed before news of the arrest became public" and two, "that Nikolai Baskov's insurgency plan be addressed as viable, and as such, a plan was developed to negate it."

The President specifically noted, "that Nikolai Baskov's arrest would still leave his plan in place and gave additional publicity to the malcontents in understanding the need to better organize and join forces against our government despite their differences. He would become a martyr for the cause if it went to trial. This trial would truly challenge us as a nation."

The President wanted an immediate plan that addressed the protection of said prisons, considering the possibility of weapons used against them such as stinger missiles, drones, or simply rolling a heavy weapon like one of those old-World War II Sherman army tanks up to the main entrance and blasting their way in like Donald Sutherland did to that bank in Kelly's

Heroes. No one smiled at the President's suggestion of a tank as in yesterday's world it was fictional, but in today's world a reality.

He continued, "I further want a two-year plan of needed capital expenditures, repairs, extensions, equipment, manpower, and supplies for our current federal prisons. Include any contingencies and don't worry about the cost. I would combine this into a five-year plan for new prisons needed with consideration for mentally ill/drug felony facilities to include anything needed for their treatment separately.

"I want these plans available to present to Congress when notified of Nikolai Baskov's capture, and they are briefed on RIM and Russia's connection in all this. I will personally announce General Baskov's capture to the public, the exposure of his intended plan, and our plan to negate his plan. Maybe the public will demand that both political parties get on board with this. In any case, it would put the public on notice to report anything unusual."

The approved plan by the President required the immediate capture of Nikolai Baskov before he could further organize the neo-Nazis or leave the country as Natasha Ivanov had done, and after captured, he was to be moved out of the United States and onto Guantanamo Bay Naval Base and the Guantanamo Bay detention camp. "There he would be placed in an isolated cell without knowledge of where he was being held or that there were other prisoners in the facility until the 31 October threat is over. The other prisoners should not be told or know of his presence, if possible. If he is exposed earlier, we would read him his rights and go from there. I will take the responsibility of justifying him being held without legal counsel until 31 October due to the threat he presents to the nation."

The President continued, "A Seal Team will execute the capture with direction from the FBI in the planning. Homeland Security will coordinate with the Secretary of Defense on his extraction from the country and Southern Command, as responsible for GTMO or Gitmo, would take direction from the Secretary of Defense. All this action will be considered on a need-to-know, basis for only those involved until I have properly notified Congress and announced General Baskov's capture. He ended with, "If there are no other questions? No? Good luck gentlemen."

Guantanamo Bay naval base and the Guantanamo Bay detention camp located within the base, were both governed by the United States and still considered a legal American prison to hold Nikolai Baskov. The naval base, nicknamed GTMO or Gitmo, covered forty-five square miles on the western and eastern banks of the Bay. It was established in 1898 when the United States took control of Cuba from Spain following the Spanish American War. Joint Task Force Guantanamo fell under United States Southern Command located in Doral, Florida with responsibilities for Central America, South America, the Caribbean, and Panama, and is one of seven unified combatant commands in the Department of Defense.

The intent of the plan was to move him to a place that people could not congregate in rallying for or against his actions. It was the old thought "out of sight, out of mind." Secondly, control of the narrative allowed information to be presented in a way to help mitigate the situation."

The Arrest

Seal Team 4, normally assigned to South America but having urban experience, was assigned to FBI Director Harold Thomas for General Baskov's capture and arrest. Seal Team 4 could operate as a team of eight and Director Thomas intended to use every one of them.

The first necessity was to meet with the Navy Seals and brief them on RIM firstly and then on General Baskov's history, particularly his killing skills. He didn't take anything away from the professionalism and skills of Navy Seals but wanted to be clear to them about what they would be dealing with in General Baskov, especially since they were trying to take him alive.

The RIM briefing produced a few questions that were addressed quickly, and when everyone seemed satisfied, the briefing continued. "General Baskov is probably the most skilled professional killer you will probably encounter in your entire career. He is highly fit and a killing machine with no conscience. As a former Russian Spetsnaz and an assassin for President Ivanovitch, and now an assassin for RIM, he is almost daily on assignment. He can kill easily with his bare hands, explosives, or knives, or something as unexpected as an ink pen or broken bottle." He watched as they looked at each other, and one Navy Seal showed a scared face to another in jest with his right-hand fingers touching his lips.

Director Thomas continued his talk as if not noticing. "Planning and execution must be flawless." Director Thomas displayed on the overhead projector a blown-up picture of the Interpol poster of Baskov's Red Notice Listing and his killing of the three longshoremen in Japan and tells them the story. "He is also a billionaire and does this for the thrill of the action, not money." He showed an overhead projector display of the Ukraine newspaper claiming Adrien Balan as a hero. He told them the story of the train and the killing of at least four of his Russian comrades and one RIM soldier that he personally trained, just to maintain his cover as a RIM agent working for Russia. "As a result of his actions on the train, he was acknowledged as a Ukrainian hero and celebrated. He later killed his Ukrainian bodyguards and two more RIM soldiers he had personally trained who tried to kill him for what they perceived as him being a traitor to RIM. He faked his death to be extracted from Ukraine with Russian assistance. The last thing you need to know is that General Baskov traveled throughout the United States in promoting the supremacy of the white race on behalf of RIM, and when we locate him, you may have limited information and time as to what you may be used to. We have an undercover FBI man who may be involved in helping you and you will be informed of him before you go in if he is there." He opened the floor to questions and answered all that were presented. He felt better that they understood that they could not be too careful enough in dealing with General Baskov and that he had done everything he could to ensure their safety.

One month later, the call came in that the FBI had anxiously awaited. An FBI informant in Louisville, Kentucky said that "Lev Petrov is visiting his city to talk to

Neo-Nazi groups, including his, about an upcoming nationwide event to raise awareness of RIM and white supremacy issues. He promises it would be an event that would be history-making and no white supremacy group or individual would want to say they missed this opportunity. Petrov asked for a joint meeting of all the leaders of radical white groups in or near the city to include the Church of the Order of the National Knights of the Ku Klux Klan, The Dailey Stormer, National Socialist Movement, League of the South-Neo-Confederate and Nordic Knights of the Ku Klux Klan."

The cellphone call continued, "He will be here in two weeks for a Friday meeting at 4 pm with the Neo-Nazi group leaders and a rally speech for everybody at 6 pm. A converted former schoolhouse at the edge of the city has been provided by someone favorable to the cause that has the needed auditorium, bathrooms, and meeting space required." The informant relayed the address of the schoolhouse and disconnected. It was the break the FBI had been waiting for.

By the date of the Friday meeting, all eight Navy Seals knew their parts in the scenario that would hopefully play out as they had planned. They were now familiar with the school grounds and the inside of the school after visiting a similar school in another city and doing a walkthrough. They were also provided the school plans to study. It wasn't perfect, but it never would be.

The old schoolhouse was laid out in the same manner as most of them in the earlier years. Two large and rounded concrete steps with iron handrails on either side led up to the front doors. The large doubled wooden front doors opened to a medium-sized lobby that still had the old school trophy case now stood empty against the far wall with double wooden doors on either side of its opening to an auditorium with a curtained stage fronting it with a podium set up on the stage. Behind the stage was the music room and storage.

If you turned right in the lobby at the trophy case a hallway led straight down to classrooms, a teacher's lounge, bathrooms, and the lunchroom at the end. One of the classrooms would be used for the leader's meeting. If you turned left at the trophy case in the lobby it led to the gymnasium, bathrooms, walk-in storage, showers, offices, and weight rooms. A designated parking space in front of the school was marked on Thursday by the host organization for Lev Petrov's visit by pulling up in a pickup truck and unloading a sign that said, "Welcome Lev Petrov."

Four Navy Seals not in uniform had entered the school on Thursday night and stowed away in the chemistry classroom since it was not able to be set up to be used as a meeting room and would be a safe choice. This proved to be a good idea as the room across the hall was chosen on Friday morning to be set up for the meeting. It was noted that the setup consisted of eight chairs around a rectangular table with everything else pushed back against the walls. A notebook pad and pen were provided and two pitchers of ice water with two trays with four glasses each were centered on each end of the table.

The plan was to grab General Baskov as soon as he and all the leaders had arrived and sat down for their meeting. They were all expected to arrive around 3:45 pm and be seated at 4 pm. A larger crowd was not expected before 5:30 pm for the 6 pm rally. It appeared that there would be a maximum of eight leaders as observed in the setup of the meeting table and maybe some leaders with accompanying bodyguards or gofers. The extras in attendance would not be allowed in the meeting and would remain either outside to smoke or find themselves a seat somewhere in a classroom or in the auditorium, or in a worst-case scenario wandering the building.

At 4:05 pm precisely, all eight Navy Seals would act. Three would come from the outside and take care of anyone there and handcuff them to the handrails and place cloth sacks over their heads. Two would enter the school and contain anyone entering the lobby area, while the third would remain outside to contain any further arrivals. The fourth would drive the van from an unobserved space in an open lot across the street from the school to the front door of the school for their getaway with Lev Petrov in tow. The four Navy Seals in the chemistry room would come out, one covering the hallway to the left from anybody coming from the lunchroom area, and one covering to the right in case someone was missed. The other two would immediately breach the classroom and grab Lev Petrov and get him to the van. Again, it wasn't a perfect plan, but it would work. All of this was expected to be executed within five minutes.

At 3:40 pm, anxiety grew in the chemistry room as Navy Seals were informed of the leaders arriving. At 3:45 pm, the arrival of Lev Petrov. At 3:50 pm, their earphones exploded with, "Lev Petrov is down! He has been shot. Get out of there and I'll have the van pick you up behind the school!"

As they left the chemistry room, moving fast toward the cafeteria and rear of the school, the faint sounds of an ambulance could be heard in the distance. The three Navy Seals on the outside sprinted toward the van that was now out of the parking lot across the street and coming to pick them up. One of the Navy Seals was doing a play-by-play of what he was seeing. "The leaders are all running around the front of the school trying to locate the shooter and are now pointing at us. One just took a shot at us." As the three Navy Seals got into their van, the ambulance arrived, and more shots were fired at the van as the Navy Seals drove away. He continued his play-by-play, "The paramedics have placed Lev Petrov into the back of the ambulance and are now pulling out of the parking lot. I can hear police sirens in the distance."

The FBI van was now at the back of the school picking up the other four Navy Seals without any further problems. It left from the rear of the parking lot and turned down the street to the left and away from the main drag. Police sirens were now being heard as they approached the school from the main street.

At FBI Headquarters in Virginia, there was confusion as to what happened, and Director Thomas was trying to decipher the information as it arrived. The Secretary of Defense was on another phone wanting to know where his prisoner was, and the President wanted an update. Director Thomas was filling them in as best he could. There was no report of an ambulance picking up a body anywhere in the city, nor a morgue currently receiving a body from the school or any place else. The ambulance and body had just disappeared.

Meanwhile, the shooter had packed his scoped sniper rifle carefully away and was satisfied with the results as he drove the speed limit out of the city to a farm and an awaiting crop duster airplane to get him further on to safety and towards his return destination. The eight Navy Seals arrived at the US Naval and Marine Corps Reservation on what is now Louisville Muhammad Ali International Airport for a helicopter ride to Fort Knox where they would be housed for several days to be debriefed on their failed assignment. Fort Knox is a United States Army installation in Kentucky, south of Louisville sitting on 109,000 acres of land.

Months later and with all reports filed and evaluated, FBI Director Harold Thomas was no closer to understanding what happened at the school and who the shooter was. The President was still demanding his pound of flesh from everyone concerned privately, while silently happy that this bullet was dodged by the country. He knew that sooner or later in one of those tell-all books or death bed confessions, someone would confess to the true facts of the story and the conspiracy theorists would be alive and well. Harry Snead thought but did not express the thought to his colleagues, "There is only one person who has the resources and a clear motive to pull off what happened at the school. I guess the President thought that General Baskov's disappearance was imperative in protecting the country despite our legal system."

Several months later, there was one moment that did give Harry pause in having drawn the conclusion that the President was responsible. Shortly following General Baskov's reported death, there was an attempt on the life of President Ivanovitch's newest opposition leader to his presidency in August of 2020. The critic was poisoned on an airline flight from Tomsk in Siberia, Russia to Moscow. Doctors say he was exposed to Novichok, a soviet-era nerve agent developed at the Gosniiokht state chemical research institute by the Soviet Union between 1971 and 1993, a classic signature poison used by Nikolai Baskov.

Harry thought, "There was a second person that had the resources and a possible motive for what happened at the schoolhouse, and that was President Ivanovitch. It was possible that President Ivanovitch concluded that he still needed Baskov's special skills as his personal assassin and that General Baskov was doing such an exceptional job for RIM that he needed to extract him before he got Russia into a war with the United States." In any case, without the organization and leadership provided by General Baskov, the events on 31 October 2021, as actually played out that day, were favorable to the candy seekers and there was no attack on the prisons or the country. There was no sign that the stinger missiles were ever delivered or used.

One right-wing group did see an opportunity on 6 January 2021 with the election of the new United States President and the uproar of the incumbent of a fixed election, to try a coup in attacking the United States Capitol Building in Washington, D.C. A mob of approximately 2500 penetrated the capital defenses and left five dead before being rebuffed. Multiple weapons were found stored at a nearby hotel, but never got to the site of the insurrection for use. Harry's immediate thoughts were, "Every morning police officers get up from their bed and go to work knowing that there is a chance that it will be the last time they would ever see their family again. But never will I ever believe that the officer on duty that day that died in the attack upon the nation's capital believed it would ever happen to him as the result of American citizens trying to overthrow their government in what he probably thought was the safest place in the world to work."

CHAPTER TWENTY-FOUR

SAM MOUNTAIN, Iran (2020)

September 2020

After eight months of surveillance, the Israelis received notice from one of their spies within Tehran's government that Iran's preeminent nuclear scientist, Mormon Farrokh, would be traveling in a bulletproof car with his wife to an event on the eastern side of Tehran. Details of the itinerary of the trip were provided. The Israelis and Mountain had two months to prepare for his assassination.

When Mountain was briefed on the plan, he was rendered speechless. Harry said, "I can read your mind, you are hesitant. Remember, this is the Israeli Intelligent Service Mossad, and they are famous in his world for their covert operations. Mountain said, "You sort of say that with some kind of awe?"

Harry replied, "We haven't deployed a single nonofficial-cover officer inside Iran to sustain either intelligence collection or covert action since the failed Operation Eagle Claw hostage rescue in 1980. Israel has been penetrating Iran's Islamic Republic for at least the last ten years. They have stationary surveillance, hit teams, agents in Iran's Armed Forces, and Iranian assets like the Kurds mixed in with their employees. In June, they probably blew up the Natanz uranium enrichment site, and in 2018 they broke into the regime's main warehouse and stole the clerical regime's nuclear archive right out from under their noses."

Mountain replied," If you are impressed, then that is good enough for me. But you won't mind if I get out of here early enough to go to the Judge Advocate's office to update my will?" He faked a smile with no teeth showing.

November 2020

Sam Mountain arrived at Nasiriyah Airport; Iraq, in a C-5 Galaxy assigned exclusively in support of his mission. The C-5 Galaxy is the largest plane in the U.S. military's arsenal. Operated by the U.S. Air Force, the monstrous airplane is 247 feet long. The jet's cavernous fuel tanks allow it to fly up to 5,500 miles unfueled and this one has arrived after one stop in Israel, from Dover AFB, Delaware. Nasiriyah, Iraq is both a military and public airport. It was also known as Tallil Air Base, Imam Ali Air Base, Camp Adder by the U.S.

Army, and Ali Air Base by the Air Force. The ancient Babylonian city of Ur, known as the birthplace of Abraham, is located within its security perimeter.

The C-5 transports a specially built 4-door Nissan pickup with an elevator lift for a remote-controlled machine gun out of the roof of the back two doors cab portion of the vehicle. The vehicle is particularly heavy as it also houses a built-in bomb below the truck bed to destroy the vehicle after use. There is a separate Nissan car loaded with explosives aboard the C-5. It is to be parked near the pickup truck to explode and ensure the destruction of all evidence that could determine responsibility for the forthcoming assassination. The vehicles did not present themselves as anything other than normal older vehicles.

Both vehicles were designed and built by the Israelis and waited for further transport to Absard, Iran outside of Tehran, four hundred plus miles to the north. Absard is a typical small-town of approximately 12,000-15,000 people, to the east of Tehran wherein everyone knew everyone and a visit by the scientist would be a big deal if they knew he was coming, but they didn't. . It was also a town surrounded by vacation villas for the Iranian elite.

Iranians sympathetic to the Israelis would drive the vehicles with all their paperwork in order. The vehicles would be parked together on the side of the road off the main highway on an entry street to Absard.

Absard Road, the entry street to the city, is perpendicular to and a right turn off Highway 79, the main highway coming east from Tehran. The caravan of three cars with eleven bodyguards, plus the bulletproof car with the scientist and his wife, would be a one-hundred-and-sixty-five-yard shot for the remote-controlled machine gun over mostly level ground to the on-coming approaching caravan. A satellite dedicated to operating the remote-controlled machine gun provided Mountain the best entry and exit locations into and out of Iran while it tracked the approaching scientist's caravan.

The normal life of people living in Iran was comparable to a European country like Britain. People moved about and vacationed mostly within their own country and shops, parks, and restaurants were all open. There were not many tourists who visited Iran, except those that had family there, so overcrowding was not a problem. The two big noticeable differences other than Iran being ninety-nine percent Shia Muslim, were the beautiful mosques that existed everywhere, and it was not unusual for people to run off the streets at given times to pray, and secondly, at rock concerts, everyone must sit down as dancing was not permitted.

The dark side of life in Tehran was for those who didn't accept the religious police state. For them, it was a country of censorship, repression, and violence. Schools taught the children hate, bigotry, and terrorism. Roaming morality police beat women for not wearing the hijab and broke into parties where there was alcohol or co-eds mingling to beat and arrest young people. People were imprisoned for any perceived action against the government or their version of the Muslim religion. Some were brutally beaten or raped. There was no room for dissent.

Traffic in Tehran was usually bumper to bumper and backed up, so four days was allotted to the drivers for their trip to Tehran in case of delays that could happen for many reasons. The last two days would be used to reassemble and install the machine gun into the built-in hidden lift for the Nissan pickup. The back window of the pickup sat on top of the back panel of the truck bed as a one-piece lift-up opening that would allow the machine gun to be loaded onto the truck bed and pushed straight down the truck bed and onto the gun lift and the panel quickly lowered back in place to hide the gun.

The Bespoke-machine gun with the installed hidden lift weighed approximately a ton, and the built-in hidden explosives contributed another two thousand pounds to the overall weight of the pickup. The machine gun parts were smuggled into Iran by twenty separate Iranian and Israeli nationals carrying one piece of the gun each. The parts were dropped off at a central location for assembly, and the completed gun would be transported to the Nissan pickup when delivered and in place. Mountain would not travel with the cars but would be inserted into Iran separately. It was felt that he would stand out, even as a tourist, and probably be pulled aside to be questioned, if in a car or passed off as a tourist.

In Absard Iran, it was 27 November and winter snow covered the mountains overlooking the town. The roads were clear, and the scientist's caravan was fast approaching the turnoff to the city. Mormon Farrokh, a brigadier general in the Islamic Revolutionary Guard Corps, an academic physicist, and a senior official in the nuclear program of Iran, and his wife, were in the third vehicle of the four-vehicle caravan. Mountain was in place with his sniper rifle on a mountainside location to the left of the approaching caravan and patiently waiting for the caravan to hit the marker on the roadside that began the attack.

Mountain's insert into Iran and his journey began with a helicopter ride to the Ashgabat International Airport which is in the capital of Turkmenistan. This was the closest point of entry into Iran for his mission. There were five entry points into Iran in the immediate area, however, all of them did not allow private vehicles to cross the border, and all walkers, once across the border, must use Iranian transportation to their destinations. There was a lot of graft and corruption and time spent in meeting necessary entry paperwork, even if you had applied for entry in advance.

The Ashgabat International Airport and the close-by Mary-2 airfield served as subsidiary support bases for the Americans in refueling operations and processing of supplies in transit to Afghanistan via the Turkman Road and rail network. Mountain's only thought at arriving at Ashgabat was that "everything here is alien to the world as he knew it and very surreal, as in weird, strange, bizarre, freakish and unearthly, to his understanding of what should be here."

Ashgabat International Airport was as beautiful as the city. The many buildings were all constructed of white marble and elaborate fountains, statues, and clean streets adorn the manicured grounds. Most of the buildings were vacant and there were very few people anywhere. The state strictly regulated pretty much everything, and information was extremely restricted. Poverty was hidden, but since gas and electricity were free in Turkmenistan, some citizens opted to have their stoves burning 24/7 just to avoid the cost of using matches. Mountain would mentally compare and rank this country with North

Korean leadership, with the noted exception that the country was not impoverished, only its people.

Mountain was facing the unknown in entering Iran. He was using the latest experimental invention of the United States Air Force, a flying car. Even saying the words, Mountain felt suddenly old, and that soon technology would make his skills unnecessary. He slowly shook his head as if in denial. The Air Force Research Lab's AFWERX innovation program at Wright Patterson AFB announced in December 2020 the service's Agility Prime, the code name given its flying car, or "organic resupply bus," or ORB, had cleared several regulations that moved the program forward.

Prior to leaving for Iran, Mountain was flown to the Ohio Springfield-Beckley Municipal Airport, the new simulation and experimentation facility the Air Force was using for Agility Prime. Previously, the flying car, the S4, had passed a Technical Airworthiness Authority evaluation, the initial step that enabled the unusual aircraft to fly under Air Force contract. The airport housed the electric vehicles' charging station. The United States Air Force was planning to put its futuristic flying car through a series of tests that would help determine how the service could use the vehicle, at home or deployed, and this opportunity to use it to penetrate Iran's defenses would provide ample justification for further funding of the ORB.

Mountain spent two weeks at the Ohio Springfield-Beckley Municipal Airport, using the ORB and becoming familiar with its capabilities. The ORB was then transported to the Mary-2 airfield in Turkmenistan by another C-5 flying straight from Ohio with a Seal team escort. It was unloaded from the C-5 after midnight and towed to an American leased hanger where it was closely guarded by the Seal Team until morning. With the morning light, the flying car was readied for flight, towed from the hanger under a covered tarp to the isolated end of the Mary-2 airfield, where Mountain boarded the ORB, and took off.

The S4eVTOL aircraft took off and transitioned to winged flight. It was only as loud as a babbling brook and took about three minutes to transform from a car to an aircraft and vice versa. This flying car sat two, and a remotely armed bomb was installed in the passenger seat if things went wrong in Iran. It was comparable to a large drone with more capability. A takeoff and GPS coordinated landing spot had been identified in Iran providing the best chance of success.

Mountain made a low altitude transition into Iran from the isolated border location and experienced no problems in landing vertically at the designated location in Iran using the GPS coordinates provided. There was no indication that he was spotted at any point in his flight. He left the car and made his way five miles southwest to a mountainous dirt road where he was met by an Israeli asset. Leaving the car was necessary as it stood out as futuristic and would draw immediate attention if seen. The Israeli asset drove him within a mile of his destination, and he hoofed in the rest of the way and prepared his hiding and shooting location overlooking Highway 79.

When the Israeli satellite observed the fast-approaching caravan hitting the first highway marker of the pending attack, the remotely operated machine gun was activated and lifted through the opening roof of the Nissan pickup and into place. When the caravan hit the second marker, the attack began and would last a total of six minutes. With the opening three-minute burst of the machine gun, bullets hit the first two vehicles, then bounced off the scientist's bullet-proof windshield of the third car, bringing all four cars to a halt. The eleven bodyguards scrambled out of their three vehicles and took cover behind the vehicles with the mountains behind them. Three bodyguards were wounded by the machine-gun fire while exiting their cars during the initial machine gun burst.

Mormon Farrokh, the nuclear scientist, exited the rear-side driver door in a tucked position and turned to motion to his wife to stay inside the car and stay down. At that moment and after a five second delay the second three-minute machine gun burst started, and Mountain took this as his signal and put the first of three bullets into Farrokh, the latter ending his life.

Two bodyguards that suspected a second shooter turned towards the mountains and were quickly killed in succession by Mountain. The others were unaware and only sought to bury themselves in further cover. The second round of firing ended and was shortly followed with the Nissan pickup, housing the machine gun, exploding. This was followed in turn by the car parked behind the Nissan exploding. It took a few more minutes for everyone to finally determine that the attack was over, and movement started returning to normal.

At the time of the first explosion, Mountain started backtracking to his pick-up point to meet his Israeli contact for return to his flying car. His exit procedure followed exactly his entrance procedure. Three hours later, he was landing at the end of Mary-2 airfield and the ORB was quickly taken to and secured in the American hanger. Later that night, it would be reloaded into the C-5 for its return to Ohio.

Iran marked the death of Mormon Farrokh with a country-wide funeral. Supreme Leader Ali Khatami vowed to avenge the killings of his top Iranian nuclear scientist and his second in command who died in a U.S. drone strike in January.

Initial reports only reflected Israel, a satellite, and its remote machine gun as being involved in Farrokh's death. There was one mention of a second shooter by a noted journalist, but no mention of an alien aircraft. The fact was that there was no hard evidence to prove who did it or how it was done. The embarrassment to Iran was in failing to secure its borders and protect its leaders.

CHAPTER TWENTY-FIVE

IVAN IVANOVITCH,

PRESIDENT OF RUSSIA-UKRAINE

President Ivanovitch was preparing for an immediate invasion of Ukraine. In April 2021, he moved another thirty-eight thousand troops to join the eighty-seven thousand troops already stationed in the Crimea or on the Ukraine border. However, and unexpectantly, he received the good news that changed his mind in mid-course. Nord Stream Two, the eleven-billion-dollar undersea Baltic Sea oil pipeline extending from Russia to Germany was once again under construction with the election of the newest American president on January 9, 2021. The pipeline was within a hundred miles of completion. It would all but replace the Ukrainian transit system that had handled the bulk of Russian gas deliveries to Europe for decades. Nord Stream II, together with the existing Nord Stream I pipeline, would double annual export capacity to approximately half of Russia's total gas exports to Europe a year. German certification was expected to take only four months when completed.

President Ivanovitch thought, "When completed and approved, it would strengthen my grip on the European energy market, eliminate any geopolitical leverage Ukraine has with me and influence our leverage on the continent. When that pipeline is completed, I can take back Ukraine without the worry of loss of oil revenue, a NATO response, or providing the Americans a reason to bog themselves down in another war they cannot win, especially since a large portion of the Ukraine population favor being part of Russia again."

With that in mind, he modified his orders for Operation Restore to only threaten the invasion. Ivanovitch's plan now was to mask this movement of troops as a training exercise, threaten invasion, then withdraw most of the troops leaving weapons and supplies in place, and correct any problems until the Nord Stream Two pipeline was completed. He thought, "Once Nord Stream Two is completed and approved, I can then move troops rapidly into position and justify the invasion of Ukraine as necessary to protect Russian interests and citizens requesting protection."

Two other immediate concerns were driving President Ivanovitch's recent movement of troops to the Ukraine border. The first was the water crisis in Crimea. The situation was difficult — people currently received water for only a few hours per day — and it had the potential to get worse. The second factor was the new American President calling President Ivan Ivanovitch a "killer." President Ivanovitch believed that the United States wanted to take a tougher role with him but was not prepared for a new conflict in Ukraine.

Everyone knew that the new American President wished to shift the focus of U.S. foreign policy away from the Middle East towards China "as the only power that can stymie U.S. interests around the world." President Ivanovitch thought, "I am about to show the American President that disrespecting Russia has consequences."

Satisfied that he had done all he could to prepare for the invasion of Ukraine, he turned his thoughts to the Arctic. President Ivanovitch thought, "The progress of my plans for the Arctic have proceeded accordingly, and I have assumed the chairmanship of the Arctic Council from 2021-2023. I will soon announce and then implement a fee system to start in 2025 for use of the northern ocean route to the West. That would give all users the necessary time to moan and groan and then make the necessary adjustments needed to pay. They know that we are prepared for any dissent, and they would capitulate. They have no choice." President

Ivanovitch allowed himself a moment to enjoy his excitement over the Arctic.

CIA Headquarters

At CIA Headquarters, Mountain and Harry met on several areas of concern. Harry was following the Russian troop buildup on the Ukraine border that was the largest since just before Russia invaded Crimea in 2014-2015. The European Union estimated one hundred and fifty thousand troops with field hospitals, supply depots, and airpower needed to establish superiority over the battlefield. Harry said, "I guess this situation is going to be a Pentagon problem, but in every way, we are at a disadvantage to intervene if an invasion took place. We have brought this upon ourselves, but at least this president is publicly calling President Ivanovitch what he is, a killer. Maybe, we can at least deal with him honestly from here on out in the public's eyes."

Mountain replied, "Didn't the previous president deal with him?"

Harry replied, "Publicly, our president demeaned America by effectively saying we are no better than the Russians." The President said, "There are a lot of killers, we've got a lot of killers, you think our country's so innocent." In truth, he was probably letting President Ivanovitch know that if he made a move in Ukraine, he was not going to let it happen without a fight. But, when he made the situation one of who has the strongest military, instead of who acts with morals and principles, he undermined public trust and resolve. If Ukraine is lost to Russia by military means, the public will not support the president's lead on after actions, sanctions, support of insurgents, and publicly noting that a democratic country was invaded and dissolved covertly that was authorized and approved in writing by Russia much in the same manner that China is taking back Hong Kong. By letting the public know President Ivanovitch is a killer, and that there is morality and principle attached to why we fight, we at least have a chance to convince our citizens of a rogue Russia as a valid public concern for the next military action they may attempt after Ukraine. And don't get me wrong, every president up to now, gave President Ivanovitch permission to reach this point by patting the Russian President on the back and saying he is a fine fellow. In October 1993, when Russian tanks attacked their parliament, we congratulated their president; in 2001 our president said he "had looked the man in the eye" and "was able to get a sense of his soul." And in 2009 our president described Ivanovitch as "sincere, just, and deeply interested in the interests of the Russian people." America's presidents, for whatever reasons, have been afraid of what they may find if there is a serious effort to take the initiative to learn the truth about Russian exploits that impact our world. Now there was at least a chance to look on the other side of the wall and take real measures to hold the Russians accountable."

Harry continued in a more reflective mood. "Russia supplies much of the world with oil and gas and controls much of the world's oil and gas pipeline infrastructure and is the world's largest supplier of grain, sophisticated weaponry, high tech communication equipment, and nuclear power plants. But the completion of the Nord Stream Two oil pipelines from Russia to Germany are the key achievements necessary for Russia's future security and growth in Europe. It cannot be allowed to be completed." With some concern in his voice, Harry added, "We have got to quit underestimating Russia. To quote Winston Churchill, "Russia was never so strong as it wants to be and never so weak as it was thought to be."

Mountain said light-heartedly, "Do you have any good news?" and laughed.

Harry said, "Yes. My daughter graduated college this year and is getting married next Fall."

Mountain said, "Congratulations, I'll expect my invite." They both smiled as both knew that having time off, even for a family wedding, would require an extremely fortunate alignment of the stars.

Harry, continuing the charade that normalcy existed in their lives, said, "Is anybody new in your life?"

Both laughed again. Mountain said, laughing, "My life is a chosen burden as is yours. It says a lot about my life when you are my best friend."

Harry said, "Have you had any contact with your nieces since your twin brother died?"

Mountain said, "My nieces don't know me, only of me, but I try to send them an occasional letter and gifts on holidays and special occasions while keeping my whereabouts untraceable." Mountain said reflectingly, "Now that I thoroughly understand my situation, make my next drink a double."

CHAPTER TWENTY-SIX

SAM MOUNTAIN,

NIGERIA-THE KILLING OF A MONSTER (2021)

In the latter part of 2016, President Patience had noticed a distinct change in the Nigerian people in that they had grown ever increasingly weary of the brutal violence imposed by Abukarba Shesau, called the Imam. After taking the reins of Boko Haram after its founder died in police custody in 2009, Abukarba Shesau led its transformation from an underground sect to a deadly insurgency that had swept northeast Nigeria.

Under Shesau, Boko Haram staged bombings, kidnappings, and prison breaks across the region. And from 2014, the movement began overrunning towns in a bid to create an Islamic State under Sharia law. Since Shesau took charge, more than 30,000 people were killed and over two million displaced from their homes. Shesau's agenda was so radical that he was rejected by the Islamic State. As such, it gave rise to a breakaway group of former Imam followers from the Islamic State West Africa Province or ISWAP. ISWAP also focused on military targets and attempted to win the support of the local civilians, unlike Shesau whose forces were notorious for massacring and kidnapping non-combatants. The Islamic State employed a "hearts and minds" policy toward the local communities, gradually winning substantial grassroots support, and implemented its own government, including collecting taxes.

In 2018, President Patience saw ISWAP as an opportunity to broker a deal to capture or kill Shesau in return for the seven-million-dollar reward on his head. With the reward money as an incentive, President Patience turned two of the Imam's senior lieutenants against him in return for an opportunity to capture or kill the Imam.

When President Patience was informed the Imam was spotted in the Congo by Sam Mountain, it provided the perfect opportunity for the President and the two senior ISWAP lieutenants to meet and agree to set a trap for the Imam's return to Nigeria. ISWAP agreed to work with President Patience's representative Sam Mountain in springing the trap and verifying payment for the Imam's capture or death. When the President was notified that the

Imam was back in the Timbuktu region of the Sambisa Forest, President Patience notified the CIA, and Sam Mountain was requested by name as the President's representative to accompany the raid.

Sam Mountain landed at Abuja Airport, officially Nandi Azikiwe International Airport, the second largest airport in Nigeria after the Murtala Muhammed Airport in Lagos and was met by newly promoted Major David Uzeki. They hugged and laughed together like old friends that they had become. Sam was offered and once again accepted accommodations and meals in the Presidential Villa he had enjoyed in 2013.

Sam noted that the other two bodyguards accompanying Major Uzeki accepted his presence in the limousine as an equal, and Sam guessed that Major Uzeki had made that possible. It was here at the Presidential Villa in 2013 where he first met the President, and the following day took part in an attack on the Boko Haram forces in Northern Nigeria with then-Captain David Uzeki. Elton John might refer to this moment as a 'circle of life.'

Sam was met by the President and his wife at the door. The President seemed genuinely glad to see him, as did Areta, his wife. Sam was once again impressed by the simple effort of class shown by the President and his wife in greeting him upon arrival at the door. Sam was given a short tour of the house by the President as Areta begged off to complete what she laughingly called "one of her personally cooked and served great meals." Sam noted two new art additions in the foyer that the President pointed out with pride as Areta's. Mountain said, "She really is quite good." Following the brief tour, Sam was offered his opportunity to freshen up and joined the President fifteen minutes later for dinner.

After another great meal and continuing small talk with Areta and the President, Sam once again privately acknowledged their exceptional kindness and class. The President rose from the dining table and came around behind his wife and bent down giving her shoulders a hug while gently kissing her on her right-side cheek and thanking her for the great meal. He said to Sam, "Please join me for a cigar and nightcap in the sitting room before I retire."

Sam thanked Areta again for her hospitality and the meal. She took his hand and stepped in close so her husband could not hear, and said, "Sam, get this man, his deeds are tearing this country apart and my husband." She squeezed his hand and said, "You know you are welcome here anytime. We expect you safely back for dinner tomorrow night, whatever the outcome."

In the sitting room, the President said, "I asked Harry your favorite bourbon while I was requesting your help, and had a bottle flown in on your plane unbeknownst to you. So, my question is, single or double?"

Sam laughed, "Mr. President, I'll make a deal with you. Tonight, I'll have a single, and tomorrow you can pour me a double if everything goes right. I'll even call you by your first name, as you have asked me to do so many times, and I have consistently embarrassed myself by failing to remember. Is it a deal?"

The President said, "A deal?" and handed him a single pour on the rocks and smiled.

Sam thought, "Somehow, I believe that is the first time he has smiled in a long while."

After a moment, the President said, "This man is truly a monster, and this is the first opportunity in all these years that I have a real opportunity to kill him." He shook his head slowly as if the moment was surreal and took a slow sip of his bourbon and seemed to lose himself in his thoughts. He said, "I'm glad you are here, Sam."

Mountain noted the authenticity of hope in his comment that he could make a difference by being here.

The following morning, Major David Uzeki promptly woke him at sunrise and waited downstairs where the staff had prepared breakfast. From the Presidential Villa, he and Major Uzeki and the two bodyguards proceeded by limousine back to Abuja Airport and a hangar location where a helicopter and Sam's gear were waiting. Major Uzeki and Sam were greeted by Lieutenant Sani Faloya, a Nigerian Air Force pilot who would fly the mission, ISWAP Lieutenant Abubakar Kuti, a jihadist who on another day and at a different time and place, would be in the crosshairs of Sam's sniper rifle, and Major General Tukur Yahaya, the President's representative. The crew chief and side door gunner remained on board.

The Major General walked over to a nearby table and unrolled a map depicting the village and area where the Imam was expected to be this afternoon. He used two staplers, an empty jelly-jar half full of pencils, and his cell phone to pin down the four corners of the map to prevent it from rolling back up. Lieutenant Kuti stepped forward to point out on the map where his one hundred men were located and awaiting orders for the attack. The General acted as a translator when necessary.

There were twenty-five ISWAP jihadists assigned to each side of the village to prevent an escape. Each of the four groups was approximately a half-mile out and would attack when ordered by Lieutenant Kuti. The four group leaders were provided radios to coordinate their attack with Lieutenant Kuti. The attack would begin when the second of the two 'turned' lieutenants used the sixth radio to tell Lieutenant Kuti that the Imam was in camp.

The groups were to move hurriedly, but with as little noise as possible until contact was made. At that point, each group must get to the village as quickly as possible while ensuring escape routes were closed to the Imam. Sam would be with Lieutenant Kuti's group and would verify the kill for payment. The General said, "Expect anything. We do not know how many will fight on behalf of the Imam."

The helicopter was rolled out of the hanger and the blades quickly came to full throttle as Sam, Lieutenant Kuti, and Major Uzeki watched and then boarded for takeoff. Major Uzeki would remain on board during the expected battle to coordinate the helicopter actions with the crew chief on board and Sam on the ground.

The Imam had anywhere from one thousand to two thousand followers at any one time, but the meeting today was in a small village, and a large opposing force was not expected. Sam thought, "Surely, the 'turned' Lieutenant in the village would warn us if an opposing force were being gathered!"

By early afternoon, Sam's helicopter was far enough Northwest in Nigeria to be considered in position for battle if needed, and far enough away from the village that it would never be seen or heard. The only thing Sam and Lieutenant Kuti could do at this point was to be patient and hope that they would be soon informed that the Imam had arrived as expected in the village. Sam considered the mission fortunate that the ISWAP jihadists had held positions for hours now and had not been discovered. It was Sam's intention to join the advance with Lieutenant Kuti if any of the groups were discovered.

In the latter portion of the afternoon, and just when Sam thought that the Imam may not show, the radio call came, "The Imam has arrived and is on-site in the village." Lieutenant Kuti quickly notified all the group commanders to begin their advance. Sam anxiously waited for the first bullet of their small army to be fired and it took very little time before that happened.

The Imam had stayed alive for a very long time by never being taken by surprise. He had successfully lived through a major Nigerian army attack in 2015 that should have taken his life, but diligent precautions allowed just enough notification for him to get away. But today was not yesterday, and the Imam had been betrayed by his own commanders who knew his precautions and responses.

With the first shots, Sam's helicopter rose from its position and raced toward Lieutenant Kuti's group deep in the jungle area. When the group was located, the helicopter came in low to the ground and hovered and the thick rope went out the side door. The radio portrayed the sounds of all the groups engaging the jihadists and advancing rapidly towards the camp. Sam pointed to the rope, and with his hand motioned to Lieutenant Kuti to follow him down the rope to the ground.

Lieutenant Kuti looked confused about what was being asked of him, as he was not trained or knowledgeable in such matters. Sam handed him a pair of military gloves, and he watched closely as Sam put on his gloves and grabbed the thick rope and climbed down hand-over-hand until he found the ground beneath him. Lieutenant Kuti followed Sam's example and soon joined him. He radioed his group that they were on the ground and coming towards them. Sam followed him. The helicopter left and stayed out of the fight, an agreement arranged in advance and insisted on by Lieutenant Kuti as the combatants below would all look alike, and their allegiance could not be identified in advance.

Sam felt a little guilty that he had not informed Lieutenant Kuti that extraction from the helicopter would be in all probability by fast roping, a procedure first used by the British in the Falkland Islands. It was used there due to the terrain not having open areas on which to land. It was quicker than rappelling, although more dangerous because the rope was not attached to them with a descender that had a safety catch and release. In fast roping, the person held onto the rope with gloved hands and feet and slid down it. Several people could slide down the same rope simultaneously if there was a gap of approximately ten feet between them so that each one had time to get out of the way when they reached the ground. In any case, he had judged correctly that Lieutenant Kuti was athletic and brave enough to complete the necessary action.

The forest was dense, and the pace of the group was slow. Sam could hear both real-time gunfire and the radios bristling from reactions to the gunfire. Sam stopped Lieutenant Kuti and pointed to his radio to be turned off. He complied. Sam loosened his rifle and readied himself as they again advanced following the gunfire to find their group. When the gunfire showed itself to be just straight ahead and near the camp, Sam tapped Lieutenant Kuti to turn his radio on and announce their presence. They then proceeded to join the main body of Lieutenant Kuti's group.

Sam was very careful about this procedure as friendly fire often killed as many as enemy fire. Sam only had to remember enough history to remind himself of the danger. Thirty-five Americans and nine British troops were killed by friendly fire in the Gulf War. On April 22, 2004, Pat Tillman was tragically killed, according to the military, by friendly fire during an ambush on a road not far from the Pakistan border. Patrick Daniel Tillman Jr. was an American professional football player in the National Football League who left his sports career and enlisted in the United States Army in May 2002 in the aftermath of the September 11 attacks. The great Confederate commander Stonewall Jackson was fatally wounded at Chancellorsville on May 2nd, 1863, while trying to re-enter his camp after assessing his lines and the enemy positions.

Some of Lieutenant Kuti's group were already farther ahead and almost at the camp's edge. The group passed a body as they moved forward. Sam did not know if it was one of Lieutenant Kuti's men or not, as he showed no reaction and moved on without stopping. Sam turned on his radio and quickly updated Major Uzeki on their progress.

Two more bodies lay dead on the ground as they entered the West side of the village campgrounds. In front of them, four jihadists were dead and three more were running backward and firing as they ran. Sam found the farthest one seeking cover and now turned to fire and killed him before he could fire. The other two threw down their weapons and surrendered.

Sam noted that the groups on the East and South had entered the camp, and gunfire was heavy at times, but most jihadists were now dropping their weapons and being allowed to surrender. Sam was glad there was no massacre, and some commanders seemed aware that this was more about a change in leadership. Sam guessed that the two Lieutenants that betrayed the Imam trusted some of their commanders with the truth which could have been a recipe for disaster, but as luck would have it, had said nothing. Sam thought, "There's that word luck in my thoughts!" and dismissed it immediately with prejudice.

Sam saw the loyal jihadists continuing the fight and circling the Imam on the Northside. It was clear to Sam that most of the jihadists were escaping East as that was the closest border, and Lake Chad provided additional avenues of escape. He chastised himself again that he had not considered that and wondered how long this thing called luck would keep him and people dependent upon him safe. It was also clear to him why the North team had not entered the camp as they were engaging people leaving it trying to escape.

The Imam suddenly turned and threw up his hands in what appeared to be an attempt at surrendering. He dropped his weapon on the ground. His followers stopped shooting but did not immediately lay down their weapons. They looked to their Imam for guidance. They seem confused he would give up and not fight to the death. The shooting slowly ceased everywhere as all militants had either surrendered, died, or were facing off with the traitors in front of them and the Imam. Everything was now focused on the Imam, and everyone thought the same thought. "Was he surrendering?"

The Imam slowly reached down with his left hand and unbuttoned his shirt exposing the explosives attached to his body. The explosives were attached to a detonator now seen and held in his right hand. Lieutenant Kuti's men backed up hurriedly and far enough away from the explosion area, but with their guns still trained on the Imam. Many of the jihadists moved away also and surrendered their weapons to Lieutenant Kuti's men. Still, the Imam did not trigger the explosion as he seemed to contemplate his options.

Only three jihadists were left with the Imam, and one ISIS commander from Syria that would be identified later. Lieutenant Kuti tried to negotiate with the Imam, and for a while it seemed promising. Sam moved to a shooter's position and believed he could kill him if there was any relaxation of his finger on the detonator but was not given permission by Lieutenant Kuti. He decided that he would kill the Imam without permission if he made any attempt to run towards Lieutenant Kuti's men.

Sam could only guess as to why the Imam had not moved. There were only two good reasons. Either he had a force on the way to the village and was waiting for them, or he was hesitant to die. Sam tapped the button for Major Uzeki and asked him to take the helicopter on a swing around the camp perimeter to see if there was an approaching force of any kind. Meanwhile, his rifle remained squarely centered on the Imam's chest. Shortly thereafter, Major Uzeki reported no jihadist movement seen, and at this moment the Imam bolted forward, but was killed instantly by Mountain at his first movement. The explosion triggered as he fell.

It was guessed that the Imam decided he had no other choice but to become a martyr and would take as many of the traitors with him as he could. The four men that stayed with him and one of Lieutenant Kuti's men that were too close to the explosion all instantly died with him. Lieutenant Kuti approached Mountain and loudly said, "I told you that you were here for observation only and you disobeyed my order to not fire your weapon. You are responsible for the loss of one of my men." He turned and walked away. One of the jihadists standing close to the conversation and leaving to follow his lieutenant nodded his thanks to Mountain as he passed by him for saving his life.

On the return helicopter ride, Mountain thought about the events of the day and suddenly remembered what a history professor at Georgia said one day in class. "I am going to give you a number to remember, and that number is twenty. Most of you would never think about this number again until an event happens in your life that would bring it home to you in such an impactful manner that it would jolt your memory back to this day in my classroom and me. It is my gift to you."

He continued "The Italian polymath, economist, philosopher, and engineer Vilfredo Pareto showed that eighty percent of the land in Italy was owned by twenty percent of Italians. Soon the 80/20 ratio was being used here and there and the number twenty became a catchy, historical catchphrase known as the Pareto principle. Twenty percent of patients use eighty percent of health care resources, twenty percent of criminals commit eighty percent of crimes, twenty percent of customers make eighty percent of the complaints made." Mountain added one more to the list: twenty percent of bourbon drinkers drink eighty percent of the bourbon. The Pareto principle simply stated that for many outcomes, roughly eighty percent of consequences came from twenty percent of the causes.

Sam really didn't know whether the observation he made about bourbon was a fact, but it did bring a smile to his face that he may be a part of an elite group. What brought the Pareto principle to mind was a comment made earlier by one of the Nigerian soldiers. "Well, that ends the life of a twenty-year terrorist." The soldier may have been off in the exact years. Shesau was a terrorist and only Shesau knew the exact time when his mind decided to become a jihadist. Mountain said out loud and to no one, "In any case, the number twenty is certainly germane to what happened here today, so thank you, professor."

Outside the hanger area, Lieutenant Kuti and Sam were met by Major General Tukur Yahaya and his two bodyguards. The suitcase with seven million dollars was attached to a chain from his wrist to the suitcase handle. The helicopter was waiting for the boarding of the passengers. Lieutenant Kuti asked for the suitcase and was denied. The major general said, "I will travel with you to the village to ensure delivery and that all of the jihadists are aware of receipt." The anger and humiliation were evident on Lieutenant Kuti's face.

The general walked back to Sam and shook his hand and said thanks to him for all he had done. Sam said, "I am glad you have planned to accompany him."

The general replied, "As if I would trust a terrorist with seven million dollars not to parachute out somewhere with the money and end up spending it on some island in the South Pacific." He laughed at his own joke. "At least in this way, I can at least guarantee they can fight over the money. Goodbye Sam."

"So long, General," Mountain said.

That evening, Sam enjoyed his double shot of Maker's Mark and laughed with the President and Areta and was content that for this one moment in time the world was as it should be. The meal was great as always and both he and the President enjoyed a cigar before bedtime. Mountain took great comfort in how relaxed the President looked. The following morning, Mountain said his goodbyes and accepted the thanks of a grateful nation. At the airport, he shook hands and hugged Major Uzeki as both were emotional as he boarded the plane for his departure.

The local Nigerian newspaper reported:

"On May 19, 2021, Abubakar Shekau, the longtime leader of Boko Haram (also known as Jamā'at Ahl as-Sunnah lid-Da'wah wa'l-Jihād or JAS) was killed during a clash with the Islamic State West Africa Province (ISWAP). During the attack, Shekau reportedly detonated his suicide vest, killing himself instantly.

"Shekau's death is a symbolic win for the Nigerian government, even if it had no role in the extremist's death, and it potentially signifies the beginning of the end of JAS's decade-long reign of terror. For many Nigerians, Shekau —

more so than ISWAP—was the force behind the region's plight and misery. Given his preference for attacking civilians, as opposed to ISWAP's focus on government and foreign targets, his death would be a relief to many northeastern residents."

"The death of Mr. Shekau, if true, marks the end of a brutal era for northeast Nigeria and its neighboring countries in the Lake Chad region."

"But it could also signify the beginning of a new era, in which ISWAP took new territory after getting rid of its chief rival, and amps up confrontations with the Nigerian state and its military. ISWAP splintered from Boko Haram, reportedly in part because of Mr. Shekau's violence against Muslim civilians."

"ISWAP has lately posed a greater threat to the Nigerian military, which is stretched because it was deployed to fight various crises in almost every one of Nigeria's states. ISWAP has pledged allegiance to ISIS, the Islamic State in Iraq and Syria, which has been decimated in the Middle East, but is shifting its energies to insurgencies in Africa."

CHAPTER TWENTY-SEVEN

THE AXIS OF THREE

IRAN

"It was time for the Americans to pay," Supreme Leader Ali Khatami said in addressing the inter-circle of leadership counsel of Iran. "We have the Americans with few choices and our Russian and Chinese friends would complete our effort in eliminating their efforts as policemen of the world. The pact of three would regionalize the world and control access to the world waterways and the economies. Now is our time."

Supreme Leader Ali Khatami estimated that it would take six to nine months to have the uranium necessary to build a nuclear explosive, prepare a test site and carry out a nuclear test. He had vowed once again to avenge the killings of his top Iranian nuclear scientist Brigadier General Mormon Farrokh in November and his second in command who died in a U.S. drone strike last January, Major General Sayat Mansouri.

Iran was paid $100,000 and released the South Korean flagged oil tanker impounded in 2019. It was confiscated as Tehran's attempt to force Seoul, an American ally, to release the estimated seven billion that banked in South Korea froze in 2019 to comply with United States sanctions restricting financial transactions with Iran.

In response, Israel exploded a limpet mine on an Iranian ship used as a base for the paramilitary Revolutionary Guard off Yemen. No one was killed, but the ship required major repairs. At Natanz, Iran, power was cut off across the facility, which was made up of above-ground workshops and underground enrichment halls. This followed a mysterious explosion at the Natanz advanced centrifuge assembly plant, now being rebuilt deep inside a nearby mountain.

Yemen

Armik Soruri saw that the newest American president was pulling away from his support of the Saudis and their allies in Yemen. He thought, "Mansouri was right all along, I just needed to not give in to the American bluff." The new American president was halting support for Saudi-led military offensive operations in Yemen and had removed the

Houthis from the United States list of terrorist organizations. He was trying to return to the Iranian Nuclear Deal that was vacated earlier by America's previous president.

The Saudi foreign Minister proposed an immediate cease-fire in the war. But the moves by the American president had emboldened Armik Soruri and the Houthis fighters as they felt victory was now within their grasp. The new Iranian commander in Yemen brought a new level of battlefield sophistication to the Houthis in the use of advanced weapons. In the month following the announcement, they launched more drone and missile strikes than in any other preceding month. Armik Soruri thought, "Now is our time."

China
The newest American president was showing no interest in policing China and ensuring American oil sanctions were not being violated. The mixing and sale of oils was happening as quickly as the Iranian oil could be brought to market. Oil was over one hundred dollars a barrel and the American president's shutdown of America's oil fields was proving disastrous in rising inflation because of the cost of gas and moving goods around the globe. The oil the Wolf stored in China was worth millions over what was paid. Russia was flush with cash.

President Li, "My nation is prepared for the sacrifices of a war with the United States in the invasion of Taiwan. We have control of our economy, the pandemic, and the dissidents; most importantly we have the needed oil in reserve, the largest and most modern navy in the world and the military is now properly trained and well equipped. The Wolf has served me well. What I need now is the right timing for the invasion. The American presidency is weaker now than it's ever been. Their pullout of Afghanistan would have been the right time, but Wolf and I had agreed that our country was not prepared for the war then as it was now. If Russia decides to invade the Ukraine that would seem a perfect time to both invade Taiwan and seize control of the territories in dispute with other nations in the Pacific Rim. At a minimum, the threat of us attacking other nations in the Pacific Rim, in view of American overall responsibilities to its allies, provides the Americans an excuse not to engage their submarines in the Taiwan invasion. After the winter Olympics are concluded would be a perfect time for the Russians and us. I cannot wait too much longer and sustain the restraints on the people, the economy, and China's military readiness."

In that regard, he thought, "The effort to contain China's expansion efforts in the Far East has led to U.S. treaties with Palau, located in the

Philippine Sea and closely aligned with Taiwan diplomatically, and the Marshal Islands and Micronesia. Palau wants American bases, port facilities, airfields, and troops. Additionally, the United States Coast Guard traditionally focused on protecting United States maritime borders, is now deployed to the South China Sea to help counter our growing naval power there. It reflects their lack of ships and desperation for regaining control of the region."

Chairman Li's evaluation of it all was best expressed in two thoughts; one of those thoughts by Lenin, "You probe with bayonets; if you find mush, you push. If you find steel, you withdraw." The other by himself, "Containment as an American policy has worked well in the past but is too expensive and physically too far away in today's world to stop our advantage of location. This "over the horizon" military strategy as expressed by the American president was a wish and a prayer in today's world. Now is our time."

Russia

President Ivanovitch was kicking himself. He had again made a mistake. He had learned early in life on the rough streets of Leningrad that "If you are going to fight, throw the first punch." He had forgotten this axiom regarding Ukraine. He had hesitated in 2004 when a popular uprising known as the "Orange

Revolution" rejected Russian meddling in Ukrainian politics. The first punch was inadequate, and he was dealt a defeat from which he had never recovered.

A second opportunity was provided in 2014. Russian political interference inspired another spontaneous street revolution to replace the pro-Russian government, which became known in Ukraine as the "Revolution of Dignity." Because he did not handle it decisively with an invasion army, it set the country on a path of integration with the West and away from Russia. Crimea was won with decisiveness, but releasing pro-Russian supporters for violence in Ukraine's northeast President Ivanovitch only provoked more anti-Russian sentiment and inspired Ukrainian nationalism.

The President had rallied again in April 2021 to invade Ukraine when the Nord Stream II pipeline to Germany was shut down. With an election of a new American president in January 2021, the invasion was postponed as the new American president supported finishing the Nord Stream II pipeline. Not recalling the troops that were ordered to the border for the invasion proved another misstep as Germany and the European nations rallied against approval to open the pipeline due to Russia's aggressiveness. Coupled with Russia's unwillingness to provide natural gas to Europe during the winter shortage, it clearly demonstrated to European governments that Russia would use the pipeline as a political weapon against them in meeting their expansion demands.

Again, President Ivanovitch knew he should have invaded Ukraine when the United States pulled out of Afghanistan in August 2021 showing their inability to organize. It was a true opportunity and he had not accepted that the newest United States president and administration could be as incompetent as they were shown to be in leaving Afghanistan. His building impatience with his continued bad decisions had reached an uncontrollable rage when he felt he had made another misstep by offering a negotiated settlement with the United States and Europe. He thought that what he offered had no acceptability and would be immediately dismissed giving him justification for an invasion, but instead found the United States willing to negotiate. However, for President Ivanovitch this quickly proved a ploy for time and a continued frustration for him and his military.

He thought, "This is a nightmare of my own making. I cannot get to where I want to be without an invading force, and I have boxed myself in by my indecisiveness. Now I have forced the United States President to take a stand he didn't want to take. Even if I switched focus to South America and Cuba, war is the only way Ukraine would be a Russian territory again and I must have the Ukraine to have back the rest of the old U.S.S.R. The Russians and Ukrainians are one people and I have failed clearly to make my case to the world community. Instead, I have given support to Lenin's disastrous decision in 1922 in establishing the U.S.S.R as a federation of equal republics, to have the right to secede."

He continued, "My legacy is centered on Ukraine being a part of Russia and now I would have to make it ugly for the world to accept our reconciliation rather than the celebration it would have been otherwise." He made his decision. The ice would be solid in three weeks, the military would be in place by the time the winter Olympics were over, and he gave the orders he should have given years earlier.

As the weight of the world comes off his shoulders in having made the decision to invade Ukraine, he sat back in his chair mentally exhausted, his brain exploding with the howling of the tzar's approvals and final acceptance of him as one of them.

President Ivanovitch shook his head back and forth and thought, "I don't understand this idea of democracy. People would always vote for what is best for them individually or at best for their immediate family members, not for what is best for a country. People are too ignorant to understand there is always a wolf outside their door and the wolves are countries like my Russia that would soon have a tzar that would always take away their individual greed and replace it with a tzar's greed." He laughed to himself at his simple observation. "I can assure them that the HOWL would get increasingly louder outside America's door. Their politicians don't believe in anything except money and power. The politicians and their ignorant live for today. These political hacks and corporate heads and their herds of followers are the greediest people I knew, and they will kill you in a second if they think they might lose a dime. And, even when caught and have to payout millions or billions of dollars to settle rightful claims they must demonstrate their power by forcing the innocents to wait many years for payment just for having their implied authority challenged. The rich, the educated, the well-spoken, the minds of the criminal greedy would always define America: power means money and money means more power. Equality in America is a pipedream. The vanishing educated understand that processes and ethics would never be allowed a voice in their schools and therefore the government. They can't even agree on a process to enter their country. A system like capitalism requires educated believers, sacrifice, and time. My Russia learned that lesson in Afghanistan. We thought the Taliban was just another terrorist organization and we were wrong. Our approach should have been that they are a religion, a very bad one in my eyes, but a religion, nevertheless. Every Taliban is taught basic understanding of the Koran, and they were willing to die for it. They didn't care whether you were a Russian or another terrorist, if you didn't believe in exactly what they believed, you were the enemy. To them, history was not complicated and, in their world, boiled down to a few simple rules that every Taliban knew and that any differences to those rules were scams and needed to be silenced. We couldn't win. There was no negotiation to be had or partnership to be obtained. You can't defeat a people that can't be scammed by false promises and dangling carrots, so we were right to pull out. The Americans learned the same thing that we did and paid dearly for that knowledge."

He laughed to himself and thought, "I do not have the time to wait for the United States to decline and fall under their own weight of ignorance. I have an empire to rebuild and little time to do it. I must discipline myself to act quickly and decisively. Now is our time."

Switzerland

Near Geneva in Switzerland at the Large Hadron Collider at CERN laboratories, scientists reproduced the conditions that existed after the Big Bang within a billionth of a second by colliding beams of high-energy protons or ions at colossal speeds, close to the speed of light. This was the moment, around 13.7 billion years ago, when the Universe was believed to have started with an explosion of energy and matter. During these first moments, all the particles and forces that shape our Universe came into existence, defining what we now see. The collider is seven times faster than the most powerful particle accelerator built to date, weighs close to 100,000 pounds, and runs in a sixteen-and-a-half-mile circular tunnel underground. The laboratory is dedicated to the pursuit of fundamental science.

Katina Turgenev, a former Russian particle physicist and the second woman to be Director-General at CERN in Switzerland, heard of the assassination death of the nuclear scientist in Iran and turned to the clock on her wall and said, "It was down to minutes." Since childhood, she has been obsessed with the thought that life as we knew it depended on lesser minds not making a mistake or overreacting to a threat or a world event such as the one in Iran precipitating a launch of nuclear weapons in response.

Her hero growing up was Soviet military officer Stanislav Petrov who made a split-second decision to deem an apparent attack by the United States a computer error and refused to trigger a counterattack, thus averting a potential nuclear war.

The clock on her wall was her own personal demon. It was a replica of the Atomic Scientists Doomsday clock, a symbol that represented the likelihood of a man-made global catastrophe. Maintained since 1947 by the members of the Bulletin of the Atomic Scientists, the clock was a metaphor for threats to humanity from unchecked scientific and technical advances. It was currently set at two minutes to midnight, the closest it's ever been to nuclear apocalypse.

CHAPTER TWENTY-EIGHT

ANTON LUPU, THE WOLF (2022)

The Wolf could not be happier in the way events have evolved over his years in China. Chairman Li was happy with his work with the mixed oils and resultant sales. The country was now prepared for an invasion of Taiwan and a resultant war with the United States if it came to that. Money was now rolling in and America's sanctions had become nothing but words. Chairman Li listened with respect to his advice and China had become a world leader in all aspects of world events. The Wolf had relaxed his guard somewhat and now felt entitled to race his boat on the ocean. He had once again joined the Hong Kong Yacht Club and participated in weekly racing events with his new sailboat.

The American president had decided to take CIA Director Elizabeth Downing's advice as recommended by Harry Snead to assassinate Anton Lupu, the Wolf, as a show of America's commitment to the protection of Taiwan and the world's financial markets. It was hoped that this and the containment efforts demonstrated by the United States in the Asia Pacific Rim would be enough to convince Chairman Li that unlike Great Britain and its failure to protect Hong Kong from China, the United States would keep its commitments.

It was a serious policy change for the United States in lieu of their disastrous exit from Afghanistan, but a recognition that if Taiwan was invaded with no consequences from America, then the world might as well be handed to the 'axis of three' for their leadership and direction, and this president's legacy cemented in 'the downfall of America.' Henry Kissinger's words rang out in the President's ear as he made that decision, "To be an enemy of the United States is dangerous, but to be a friend is fatal."

Ma Chen, as the manager of the Macau China safe house was contacted by his CIA handler for a meeting. At this meeting, he was informed of the impending assassination of the Wolf in his next boat run to the Macau safe house. He was told that when the assassination happened, he was to immediately head to the Philippine Consulate in Macau where arrangements have been made for his leaving China and eventually join America's witness protection program.

Ma Chen's only job now was to notify his handler of when the Wolf was expected or if the Wolf had arrived unannounced. He was to stay in place until the assassination was done and continue to act as if everything was normal until the assassination happened. He was told, "Do not for any reason prepare for leaving. The Wolf would immediately take notice of a packed suitcase. If the assassination did not occur due to unforeseen circumstances, then plan on it happening on the next visit or the next until it did happen. It would be done as quickly as possible."

Ma Chen was notified two weeks later, and the night before the Wolf was leaving Hong Kong for a gambling weekend stay at the safe house. He asked for dinner at 6 pm to allow time for a shower and appropriate dress for the casinos and early shows. When the CIA was notified of Wolf's impending trip to the safe house by Ma Chen's handler and given an approximate arrival time of 4:30 pm to 5 pm, the timing seemed to fit perfectly in the CIA's scenario for the assassination.

The diver carefully placed the improvised explosive device at the head of Wolf's boat slip, and he was back in the water by 2:30 pm. The device was built by the CIA and placed within a gasoline can designed for ethanol-free gas common to small boats so as to not draw attention. The device was five pounds and was lethal up to fifty feet. The diver then moved up from the safe house via an ocean swim approximately one hundred yards to a small boat pulled behind a mound with a large area of cordgrass. Since its introduction four decades ago, salt-water cordgrass had been spreading along China's shores much in the same manner as kudzu has spread uncontrolled in the United States southeast. Over forty-eight percent of China's salt marshes were overrun with cordgrass. From there he watched anxiously with binoculars for the approaching speedboat.

At approximately 3:45 pm, the boat approached with speed and rapidly decelerated the closer it got to the boat slip until it finally stopped in the slip provided. When the Wolf had turned off the motor and had gathered his things, he stepped out of the boat onto the dock. That was when he fully noticed the out-of-place gas can at the bow of his boat, but it was too late. The explosion took out most of the dock, broke most of the back windows of the house with some damage to the interior, and caused Ma Chen to hit the floor with his hands covering his head.

Hearing no further explosions, Ma Chen rose and desperately tried to calm himself. He left by the front door. The number of debris did not allow sight of the dock, but Ma Chen assumed the assassination had occurred successfully and left everything in the house and departed in his car. He had thought about this moment every day for the last two weeks and settled into his plan. He needed nothing with him to start a new life except his personal papers, money, and passports that he now retrieved from his lockbox at the local bank. He couldn't help but think, "If the assassination had happened ten minutes later, the bank would have been closed, and then what would I have done?"

He parked the car two blocks from the Philippine consulate, wiped down the interior, and left the car unlocked with the keys in it. He had previously filed off the car registration number and wiped down the motor for prints. He now took off the license plate and replaced it with an old out-of-date plate previously found in a junkyard. He carried all his car registration, plate, and ownership papers with him into the consulate and had it all destroyed by the attendant

He again couldn't help but think aloud, "The Philippine Consulate closed at five o'clock, and everybody was gone by five-thirty, except one person who was prepared to leave when I arrived. It was clear the CIA had not notified the consulate that I was coming. What would I have done if I had arrived after the consulate had closed? There were no procedures in place." There was no one there to answer his concerns, and he wondered how far the CIA would value him in their promise of a new life in America.

When Natasha heard of Anton Lupu's death, there was a scream of agonizing grief as she collapsed to the floor. She pounded her fists and yelled a resounding promise of "They will pay!"

THE END

AUTHOR

I hope you have enjoyed the second book of this series. The third book, "Natasha Ivanov" will be out soon. I hope, in some small measure, my efforts have brought a smile to your face, or the satisfaction of time well spent.

"The world is a book and those who do not travel read only one page."
Saint Augustine

Author's notes:

RIM: There is no purely domestic terrorism statute in the United States, but in April 2020, the first time in history, the State Department designated the Russian Imperial Movement (RIM) and members of its leadership as Specially Designated Global Terrorists. The American President said, "In one voice, our nation must condemn racism, bigotry, and white supremacy. With today's action, we are adding the powerful authority held by the State Department to counter terrorists to that voice."

RIM and its leaders, Johann Wolfgang Bayer, founder, and overall leader, Stanislav Gariyev, head of RIM's paramilitary arm, the Imperial Legion, and Denis Crutchlow, RIM's Coordinator for External Relations were all designated terrorists pursuant to Executive Order 13224, as amended by Executive Order

13886, for providing training for acts of terrorism that threaten the national security and foreign policy of the United States and being leaders of such a group.

President Putin: There is no logical justification for President Putin to invade Ukraine, but the sense of power it affords him. Power made small-minded people rationalize their entitlement. We certainly can't hold President Putin up as an exception. America's leaders at all levels have distinguished themselves with small-mindedness, ignorance, and the rationalization of entitlements afforded by power. Formal problem solving, ethics, and the development of processes at all levels of society are the most valued tools a society can learn, and yet they are not taught in our schools and therefore are least understood in their importance in group dynamics. If might made right continued as the only group dynamic learned then soon there would be no right or wrong, only survival.

CERN (European Organization for Nuclear Research) in Switzerland: Fabiola Giannotti is a much-acclaimed experimental particle physicist, and the first woman to be Director-General at CERN. She has been the Director-General at CERN since January 2016. She is not

Russian, but Italian, and the stories told of the character are not a part of her history.

Characters and stories: The characters of the book are fictional, as are the events. Some stories may follow actual historical timelines. The book is meant to entertain, though my strong background in education finds me preaching at times. Blame it on my parents. My father was a superintendent of schools, and my beautiful mother was a third-grade teacher.

BOOK SUMMARY

Anton Lupu, the Wolf, and his partner Nikolai Baskov, the Russian, gather themselves after facing almost certain death in the 2013-2014 Asian Pacific Rim War to use their criminal minds and abilities in support of the Presidents of Russia and China against the interests of the United States of America and their allies. The Wolf is especially brilliant in finances and strategic planning at the highest levels and the Russian is a stone-cold killer and President Ivanovitch's personal assassin. Natasha Ivanov is President Ivanovitch's personal bodyguard and confidant, and lover of Nikolai Baskov. Harry Sneed, CIA Director of Clandestine Operations, FBI Deputy Director Harold Thomas, and Sam Mountain, CIA Field Operator match wits with them as their adversaries.

The world is changing fast and particularly for the United States. Russia and China's advancing technology in cybercrime, use of online currency, communication, and the upgrading of their militaries, coupled with Russia and China's open aggression presents a daunting challenge to the Americans and their allies. Follow the characters in the story as they provide a sounding board for current events and the difficulties of problems presented.

China, Russia, and Iran have similar goals as the axis of three and align against, the Philippines, Australia, Japan, Vietnam, and the United States in the Far East.

This is the author's second book that follows the fictional thriller "The Russian."
"The Russian"
Great read. This is one of my favorite books of all time.

April Rozzelle
Great read. What a great story. The author has a keen insight into world events and how to weave them into a great story. A real page-turner. I loved the character, Sam Mountain. Hope that we see another novel with this character.

Craig Hutto
Lots of interesting facts and a great storyline. Enjoyed the writing style very much.

Mary Arterburn